C

PART C

Zirconia Cristata Riddle, the vampire mother of Zara Riddle, could have woken up anywhere in the world, and yet she woke up on a low-quality sofabed in a messy, overcrowded hotel room of equally low quality.

A single aggressive mattress spring was attempting to bore its way through her heart from behind.

The slender, black-haired vampire sat up quickly, causing the wretched bed to squeak and groan.

"And I thought my joints were creaky," said the pregnant redheaded witch who was already up and making tea in the suite's tiny kitchenette.

"It was the bed," Zirconia said, and bit her tongue before the rest could come out.

Why did her own family members take such pleasure in antagonizing her? She had been conscious for mere seconds, and already the first insult had been lobbed by none other than her own sister, a woman who was not without her own flaws—not that Zirconia would comment on those flaws within seconds of her sister awakening.

Never.

Zirconia had class. She had standards. She always took the high road.

The redheaded woman was Zirconia's slightly younger sister, Zinnia Riddle. She was heavily pregnant, and for the past month had been using the pregnancy—a geriatric one, no less—as an excuse to be exceedingly rude.

"You should take the cot," Zinnia said as she sprinkled magic herbs in her tea. "It's just foam, no squeaky springs. I can barely sleep with this baby pressing on my bladder anyway. I'll trade you for the sofabed."

Zirconia Riddle knew a trap when she heard one. She replied indignantly, “And have to hear you complain to everyone that *your sister* stole the only good bed in this cursed hotel suite? I should think not. I won't give you the satisfaction.”

“You need a therapist.” Zinnia frowned over the pot of tea she was brewing. “No. An exorcist.”

The tea was perched on the narrow bit of counter that wasn't covered in the Riddle family's personal items, ranging from dead-smelling books to clothes to pets and all their offal-scented pet detritus.

Zirconia fluffed her pillow. “The sofabed is adequate for my needs,” she said with her usual stoicism. “It just makes unpleasant noises, like everything else around here.”

Zinnia raised an eyebrow knowingly. “Someone woke up on the wrong side of the coffin.”

Shots fired!

Zirconia was ready for it, and replied with a volley of wit.

“Oh, right,” Zirconia said in her I'm-taking-the-high-road-now voice. “I sleep in a coffin because I'm a vampire. How terribly clever, Zinnia. You must be so pleased with yourself and all that you've achieved in your life. Just look at you. Homeless *and* pregnant at fifty. It's a wonder no man has made you their wife.”

Zinnia pursed her lips. “Forty-nine.”

“Forty-nine what? Forty-nine lovers, and not one of them has gotten down on one knee and produced a ring?”

“I'm forty-nine. Not fifty.”

“If you say so.”

“I'm not fifty.” Confusion crossed Zinnia's freckled face. “Am I?”

Poor old geriatrically-pregnant Zinnia had been suffering brain fog due to the pregnancy hormones. The year had been challenging for the unmarried witch so far. Having her house torn apart by a tornado back in January certainly hadn't helped. Now it was June, six months later, and Zinnia's belly was enormous. She looked ready to give birth, even though she still had weeks left.

Zinnia went on, talking more to herself than anyone. "I was forty-seven when I moved back to Wisteria. That was the year Zara moved here... which makes me..."

"If you're going to lie, make it worthwhile," Zirconia said. "Make yourself forty-two. Then I'll be forty-three."

Zinnia scoffed. "You? Forty-three? Nobody would believe that."

"You're right. I barely look thirty. It's time for us to start telling people I'm your younger sister. Your *much younger* sister."

Both of Zinnia's eyebrows shot up. She clutched her belly and shook like she might give birth on the spot.

The cat jumped onto the counter, knocking down a stack of paperbacks. They let out the musky scent of dead words as they fell.

The cat was a needy white hairball that didn't know when to leave well enough alone. If the foolish feline lived to see its next birthday from the outside of the belly of another carnivore, it would be a miracle. Zirconia had considered eating the cat a few times herself. Live prey was always tastier than synthetic blood.

"Not on the counter," Zinnia said, half-heartedly shooing the cat away.

"Ham," said the cat. Ham was all the cursed creature thought about, and therefore all it talked about.

Then the other potential midnight snack—the feathered pet—joined in the chaos.

"Find me," screeched the green budgie from its cage. "Find me! Find me!"

Zinnia smiled. She found the irritating antics of the pets amusing.

Zirconia did not.

The vampire kept her gaze and voice restrained, so that the weakling wouldn't shed any more feathers, and said, "Marshmallow, you have to hide before you say that."

The bird cocked its head and gave her its usual blank look. Was there even a brain inside that tiny skull? Nothing a stiff breeze couldn't blow straight out its little head.

The bird said, defiantly, "Find me."

"I know you heard me," Zirconia said. "You're a stupid bird, Marshmallow."

"His name isn't Marshmallow," Zinnia said. "Are you sure you're feeling okay? You look tired."

"You should talk. I'm in excellent health. And I know the bird's name. I choose not to say it, because he screeches when he hears his name."

"What's his name?"

"It's too early. I'll get a headache from his screeching. It's bad enough I have to talk to you."

Zinnia narrowed her hazel eyes in a combination of suspicion and delight. "Fine. Don't say the bird's name. What's the cat's name?"

"I know the cat's name."

"What is it?"

Zirconia swept her memory banks as she lifted her chin and hazarded a guess. "Snake."

Zinnia could scarcely hold back her delight. "Wrong," she said with a too-eager lick of her lips. "The cat's name is Boa."

Zirconia kept her chin up in spite of the abuse. "That's what I said. Boa."

Zinnia blinked rapidly. "No. You said Snake."

The vampire doubled down. "I said Boa. You need to get your ears checked. Stop trying to pick a fight with me. Our parents are dead. There's nothing to be gained from sibling rivalry. The prizes are in their graves."

Zinnia's mouth dropped open.

Zirconia slid into some clothes and shoes, grabbed her purse, and headed for the door. It was a small hotel suite, so she was at the door in no time, even with the cat—Snake would have been a much better name for the cursed feline—running interference.

"Don't go far," Zinnia called after her. "Zara said she wants to talk to you about something." Zara was Zirconia's daughter, Zinnia's niece, and their roommate at the hotel suite.

Zirconia muttered under her breath, "Would you consider Venice too far?"

She escaped to the hotel hallway, and had the door closed behind her before Zinnia could answer.

Much better. The hallway was about as attractive as a prison latrine, but at least it was free of absurdly-named pets and demanding relatives. A better location would be the dark recesses of the lounge downstairs.

On the other side of the door, there was a POP. It was a magical sound, like a soap bubble popping, if that soap bubble were a hundred feet in circumference.

A puff of multi-colored smoke seeped out underneath the door and dissipated around Zirconia's shoes.

Whatever the spell was, it was a new one to her. She felt mild curiosity but little more.

She was not curious enough to go back into the suite, with the irritating pets and irritating pregnant sister.

She did not investigate. That was something her trouble-seeking daughter Zara would have done.

Zirconia Cristata Riddle was *not* her daughter. She was infinitely more sensible.

She walked away from the mysterious POP and the smoke, and headed downstairs.

Today would probably be as long as a regular day, as far as she knew, but it was already feeling too long. Therefore, her top priority was to fortify herself with a morning beverage. She might even get some caffeine put in it.

CHAPTER 2

Zirconia perched at the hotel bar, about to take her first sip of bourbon, when she was rudely interrupted by a member of the hotel staff.

"You can't drink that," the young man said.

"Incorrect. I *can* drink it, though it does require some effort, given the low quality, but I suppose one cannot expect top-shelf liquor from a two-star hotel such as this."

He puffed his cheeks in frustration. "I mean you can't drink that because the bar is closed."

"Watch me." She lifted the heavy glass tumbler closer to her lips. Her mouth watered in anticipation.

To her absolute shock, the young man lunged forward and wrested the glass from her hand.

Without any forethought, she placed her invisible vampire hand—it wasn't a hand, but there was no word in the English language for what it actually was—around the insouciant boy's throat, and squeezed.

His face would redden and his eyes would bulge.

Any minute now.

To her surprise, there was no change in his expression.

He continued to breathe normally, as though an icy vampire death grip wasn't squeezing his neck. If anything, he appeared to be pleased with himself.

He leaned over the bar and discarded the unsipped bourbon down the bar sink.

Zirconia sniffed. "I'd say that was a waste, but it wasn't. The fumes of that airplane fuel were already burning the inside of my delicate nostrils. Thank you for gallantly protecting my equally refined taste buds."

He gave her a wary look as he set the glass aside. He bravely maintained eye contact while dusting his hands in the universal gesture for pious self-congratulations on a job well done.

She used her invisible hand to squeeze his neck hard enough for his head to pop off. Alas, it did not pop off.

He continued to exude smugness, with his head still attached.

“Well, well, well,” Zirconia said. “Look who grew some external reproductive organs. Enough with the games.” She twirled her invisible vampire hand in a last-ditch compulsion gesture. “Now be a dear and open a bottle of whatever atrocity you people consider the house red.”

“Not today, lady.” He put his hands on his hips. “Your tricks aren't going to work on me today. I know what you are.”

“You mean... a paying guest?” She blinked rapidly, covering for the sinking sensation in her body.

“You know what I mean.”

“Do I?” He probably knew, but it never hurt to play dumb. That was something Zirconia wished her daughter could do, rather than constantly opening her mouth to appear smarter than she was. Silly Zara. It wasn't smart to reveal your cards to your opponent.

Sweetly, Zirconia said, “What is it you think I am? Besides a paying guest who might not be leaving a tip for the bar staff this morning?”

“You're a va—.” He coughed.

Zirconia's sinking sensation reversed. Yes, it was disappointing that her powers weren't fully working on the minimum-wage lackey, but she was not utterly defenseless.

He tried again. “You're a v—.” More coughing.

“I'm a VIP guest who has been taken for granted lately. But I can be forgiving.” She scanned the back wall of liquor. “Forget the wine. I'll settle for a light beer.”

In a hoarse whisper, he said, “You're a creature of the grave.”

The words registered as an attack, a slap across the cheek, accompanied by a punch in the gut. *Creature of the grave.* People could be so cruel with their words.

Zirconia's hackles rose up. Like her vampire hand, her hackles were invisible to most.

Anger shot through her cold veins.

She clenched her flesh hands into protective fists—not to protect her, but other people. It had been decades since she'd thrown witchly fireballs, but those original powers had never fully extinguished. Times like this, she worried fireballs might fly out and catch the nearby upholstery on fire. *Wouldn't everyone love that! Burned-up draperies!* Then the dumpy hotel could make her foot the bill for a much-needed remodel.

The young fellow kept talking, as if he hadn't already made himself perfectly clear. It was just like an overly-confident man to prattle on long after his point had been made. "I know you're a creature of the grave."

She said flatly, "Oh. So you must think I'm less than you, just because I happen to be different."

Her words had a slap and a punch of their own, even without the vampire hand.

Time had taken so much from Zirconia Riddle, closing doors and dimming the light, diminishing her feminine gifts, yet it had given her something else—a gravitas that even the young and foolish could sense.

He was on his back heel immediately.

She kept her chin high, refusing to take his shame.

He stammered, "That's n-not what I—."

She cut him off before he could throw more hurtful jabs.

"Well, if you're so adamant about adhering to the bar hours, and it means so much to you to prevent a paying guest from having a few minutes of peace away from her responsibilities, then you win." She punctuated with a big, heavy sigh. "I'll go. I didn't want to sit here anyway. The lighting in here is all wrong." She hopped off the bar stool, loudly double-striking the fake-marble floor with her boots. Clack CLACK. "I'll go somewhere my business is appreciated."

He looked suitably admonished, head tilted down, posture softening as he took a step backward.

"Lady, you don't have to leave," he said guiltily. "The coffee counter is open, over in the cafe."

"If I'd wanted to drink brown water with coffee grounds floating in it, I'd have remained upstairs in my suite, thank you very much."

He looked surprised. "Is there something wrong with your unit's coffee maker?"

"Yes. She's lazy and doesn't get out of bed."

He laughed as though she'd told a joke, which she had not.

Still chuckling, he said, "You mean... your daughter? The librarian?"

She pointed a finger at him. "Do not laugh at me, and do not act as though you are familiar with my family. We are not friends."

"But I am familiar with your family. You ladies have been staying here for almost six months. You're practically—"

She lifted her upper lip to show one fang, and she moved in close, so her pointed finger was an inch from his face.

The smile fell off his face. He stared at her manicured fingernail as though it might be the poisoned tip of an arrow.

"Please," he said weakly. "I didn't mean anything I said. I'm an idiot. You can have anything you want."

"It's too little, too late. I've lost my appetite."

She turned on her heel and left the lounge at vampire speed.

She slowed to human speed in the lobby so that she didn't break the hotel's creaky old front doors on her way out.

The world blasted her with its ceaseless inferno.

Ah, summer. Even in Wisteria, it was too much. She nearly crumpled under the oppressive heat.

It would be a mild day by anyone else's account, but to her fair vampire skin and delicate eyes, it was yet another assault. First her sister, then the bartender, and now the sun itself. What other indignities must she suffer in one day?

A nondescript vehicle sat idling at the curb's edge. Good enough. She sought respite in the back seat.

Both the driver and his passenger turned around with surprised expressions.

The driver, a man, said, "Ma'am, this isn't a taxi."

"I know, but it will have to do," she said, and then gave the driver an address, along with a low-effort wave of her vampire powers of persuasion.

The woman said nothing as her eyes went blank.

"I guess we could give you a lift," the man said slowly as the magic shuffled his thoughts. "We're passing by there anyway."

He put the car in gear, and they drove away from the hotel.

The passenger, a woman who was most likely the man's wife, said cheerily, "I checked the weather, and it's going to be a perfect day. Just perfect."

Zirconia slid down in her seat.

A perfect day? Not likely. Not with a start like this.

CHAPTER 3

Zirconia handed the driver a tip. It was exceedingly generous, considering he'd made several wrong turns. Being a tourist and not a taxi driver was no excuse.

She stepped out of the not-a-taxi into the withering glare of the sun. Moments like these, she was glad to be aging. Someday she would be free of the whole world's cruelty.

Staying within the protective shadow of the street's awnings, she dashed up the sidewalk, to the door of Dreamland Coffee, and entered.

The welcoming scent of adequate quality, witch-roasted coffee beans filled her senses. Living was hard, but at least there was coffee.

She hopped onto a bar stool at the long counter.

The man standing at the cash register tilted his head and stared at her with a curious, befuddled expression, like how pets looked at their owners.

The man was handsome by anyone's standards. In a generic way. Like a catalog model who would never get booked for a fashion runway show by anyone of note.

He said, "Hey, Toots." That was his usual greeting for all women.

His name was Humphrey. They had met several times, yet he regarded her now with the wonderment of someone with a skull full of brainweevils. Hungry brainweevils.

Humphrey said, "I can take your order over here, pretty lady." He was six feet away, and made no move to close the distance between them.

"Humphrey, you have my express permission to take my order over here."

"Huh?"

"A gentleman doesn't say *huh*. Come over here to take my order." She tapped the counter in front of herself.

What was it with customer service people who didn't understand the basic premise of their job? She was the customer, and their job was to service her.

She tapped the counter a second time.

He swayed from the hips up, like a palm tree in the wind, but his feet remained planted.

She was tempted to use the vampire hand, but Humphrey was as weak in the mind as he was strong in the body. He wasn't even human.

Humphrey was a komodo dragon who had been spending more and more time in human form, so as better to meet the many varied needs of his caretaker, a witch named Magenta, or Mitsi, or something ridiculous like that.

"I'm already seated," Zirconia said. "Hasn't your mistress taught you manners? Or the basics of customer service? Rule number one, the customer is always right."

Humphrey glanced around as though seeking permission from a higher power, but they were the only two in the coffee shop.

She tapped the counter a third time. The third time was always the charm—or the curse, when everything good and evil broke loose.

It was the charm this time.

With the heavy feet of a reluctant underling, he shuffled over.

"I can take your order now," he said neutrally. "We have met. My name is Humphrey. You are the mean lady who does not like jam on her scone."

"Wrong, Humphrey. I don't like your big, dirty *thumbs* all over my scone. Jam is fine."

He grinned his big, simple grin. "You might be very pretty if you smile."

"You're a man of simple needs, Humphrey."

"I like pickled herring. I do not eat household pets." He leaned forward to add in a soft tone, "Unless it is a special request."

"Not yet, but I'll keep you in mind." Zirconia scanned the menu on the wall. There were more types of coffee than she remembered from her last visit. "What would you recommend?"

"The restaurant up the street." Humphrey laughed hard. "That was a joke. I am learning about humor from a book. It is called *All About Humor, A Guide for the Atypical*." He spoke in a hushed tone again, "I am atypical."

"I would never have guessed. I'll take a triple-shot bourbon misto, with ice, heavy on the bourbon, hold the coffee or toss it down your own gullet, along with the frothed milk. Oh, and I'll have it in a glass tumbler, not a mug."

Humphrey got to work.

He poured three shots of coffee, and quaffed them with his catalog-handsome mouth, followed by the frothed milk. He poured a brown liquid over a glass of ice—the bourbon—and set it in front of Zirconia.

She paused to savor the moment.

At last, she would get to feel human.

She took a sip.

It tasted like burnt sugar mixed with fluids from the bottom of a dripping garbage bag.

She spat the foul liquid directly into Humphrey's face.

The shifter didn't even blink.

"That's not bourbon," she said.

"It's a flavor," he said.

"It sure is. It's the flavor of you not getting a tip."

He explained earnestly, "It's a flavor, like vanilla, or huckleberry. It's not real bourbon."

Just then a tall, whip-thin, enviably beautiful, black-haired witch appeared behind Humphrey.

The woman, who was the owner of both Humphrey and the coffee shop, said, "Is there a problem?" She did a double-take when she met Zirconia's eyes. "Oh. It's you."

She made a show of looking around her empty, unpopular cafe. “Traveling without your entourage today?”

“Taking a personal day,” Zirconia said. “They'll have to manage without me.”

The dark-haired witch picked up a white bar towel, and mopped the bourbon-scented effluence from her pet's face.

He leaned forward and closed his eyes.

The younger woman's arms were so long, as were her fingers. Zirconia felt the burn of desire. If only she could possess such long, elegant hands. Hers were small, and had become knobby at every knuckle. No spell or cream could help camouflage knobby knuckles. The indignities of aging never stopped.

The owner finished mopping Humphrey's face. “All better.” She gave Zirconia an expectant look.

“I'm sorry,” Zirconia said. “Sorry that your pet failed to warn me that the bourbon in the bourbon misto is a blend of high-fructose corn syrup and brackish waste water.”

The witch dismissed the heartfelt apology with a shrug. “You're not still holed up at the Cerulean Lagoon, are you?”

“Sadly, we are. This town has nothing available in the way of adequate accommodations. The local real estate agents have a sick sense of humor when it comes to listing descriptions.”

“It shouldn't be that hard to find a three-bedroom.”

“We need four. At minimum. For when the baby comes.”

The woman with the long, perfect, not-at-all-knobby fingers said, “Zinnia should just marry the Chief and move in with him.”

“Zinnia wouldn't know the right decision if it jumped out of a teacup and performed a two-hour musical with a ten-minute encore.”

The other woman laughed as though Zirconia had made a joke, which she had not. Zirconia had simply stated the truth. Why did most people find the truth so laughable?

Humphrey, whose face shone brightly from the cleaning, said, "I know how to find a place with four bedrooms." He pointed to a publicly-accessible corkboard. "You have to look there. When I wanted a saxophone, I looked there every day until I found a flute."

"A flute is not a saxophone," Zirconia said.

"It is not," he said. "They are both wind instruments but the carrying case for the flute is much smaller."

Zirconia jumped off the stool and went to the corkboard.

"There's nothing on here but junk," she said before she'd even read a single word. "People trying to pass off their garbage as..."

A square of paper caught her eye.

The paper read: *House for Sale or Rent. Four bedrooms Plus Den.*

Zirconia didn't read the rest. She tore it off the corkboard and left Dreamland Coffee without paying or even saying goodbye.

She heard Humphrey call after her, "Hey, toots! I need money!"

She yelled back over her shoulder, "Don't we all!"

CHAPTER 4

The house was all corners.

It was boxy and modern, with tall windows, razor-sharp lines, and an exterior finish of raw concrete. It didn't fit in with the other houses on the street. It looked more like a sculpture than a comfortable home.

In other words, it was perfect.

Zirconia walked up the tastefully gray, elegantly unadorned steps, and pressed the sleek sliver of a doorbell.

On the other side of the door, a harsh, electric buzz echoed through the boxy spaces.

Now *that* was a doorbell. Not the garish ding-dong that most people settled for. Not the low-class clatter that caused the less sophisticated members of her family to run about a place yelling "doorbell!" at the tops of their lungs as though they had no brains at all.

The door opened to reveal a stick-thin blonde in a white suit and high heels.

The woman looked Zirconia over with pursed lips and said, "You don't have an appointment."

Zirconia slapped some sense into the blonde with her invisible hand.

"I don't need one," the vampire said, more for the benefit of anyone passing by than for the blonde. The slap of her vampire hand would do the trick—assuming this stranger wasn't up to the same magical-defense trickery as the rude young man at the hotel.

The blonde's head bobbled like an oversized head on a toy, then righted itself. A faint smile crossed her thin lips as a better attitude set in.

"Thank you for coming by on such short notice," the blonde said, taking a step back. "Please, come in."

Please, come in. In other words, *you may enter freely, vampire.*

Zirconia stepped inside. She could enter houses without an invitation, but there were side effects. As with all parties, it was much better to be invited.

The woman said, "I must apologize for the state of the floors. The new cleaners leave a lot to be desired."

"It's so hard to find good help," Zirconia agreed.

The house was immaculate. Then again, compared to where Zirconia had been staying, there could have been live chickens and donkeys running around and it still would have been better than the hotel suite.

"I'm Sylvia Dabrowski," the woman said. "My great-uncle bought this property as an investment. Nobody's ever lived in it."

"Why not?" Zirconia gazed up at the chandelier. It sparkled with crystals that resembled daggers dangling next to what appeared to be actual daggers. Standing underneath it, her life was in danger.

This house could kill her.

She felt so alive.

Sylvia said, "My great-uncle didn't want to devalue the property by having anyone live inside it."

"I'm sorry for your loss."

"Oh, he's not dead," Sylvia said. "Some of his other investments have failed during this current crisis, and he's looking to invigorate his portfolio with some cash flow."

"Invigorate his cash flow," Zirconia said with a knowing air. Thanks to her social circles, which included the nauseatingly wealthy, she understood the euphemistic language perfectly. "So, he's broke and pawning his good stuff to cover his butt," Zirconia said.

Sylvia chuckled in a low tone. "Uncle Dorian doesn't have to pawn everything, as long as he gets some cash coming in. If we can find a suitable renter, he'll become a slumlord." She quickly corrected herself. "I mean a landlord. No offense."

"None taken. Renting is such a loathsome activity. My family is only seeking rental accommodation short term, until some expected funds become available."

Apropos of nothing, Sylvia said, "Uncle Dorian invested heavily in an apparatus for hunting ghosts. He's lost millions."

"Why would anyone hunt for ghosts? He should have invested in an apparatus to banish them. The world would be a better place."

Sylvia laughed as though Zirconia had made a joke.

The two started their tour around the house.

"Heated seats," Sylvia said of the toilets. "Genuine marble," she said of the tubs. "The architect got a little carried away," she said of the room with fourteen separate windows arranged like a puzzle.

"The baby can go in here," Zirconia said of a small room.

"This is a broom closet," Sylvia said.

"Babies don't need a lot of space," Zirconia said.

Sylvia nodded in agreement.

At the end of the tour, Zirconia said, "It may take me a day or two to locate a reputable moving company."

Sylvia fished a vibrating phone from her suit pocket, and excused herself to take the call.

Zirconia returned to the kitchen, which didn't even look like a kitchen. All the appliances—fridge, dishwasher, even the stove—were hidden behind sleek panels and clever folding doors.

She imagined her family making a mess all over everything. They would also complain about the layout. The other Riddle women didn't understand that great style required sacrifices.

Sylvia returned to the kitchen. "I see you're frowning," she said. "You must be psychic."

"Only a little, and it's more of a nuisance than a gift. Now, if you could refer me to a moving company that—"

"I'm so sorry," Sylvia said with the sharp edge of someone who wasn't sorry at all. "The house is off the market as a rental."

"Are you certain?"

"Quite." Sylvia wrinkled her nose. "Uncle Dorian won't be a slumlord after all." Another nose wrinkle, this time big enough to offer a view up the blonde's nostrils. "Sorry," her mouth said. *Not sorry*, her face said.

"Perhaps if this other offer falls through—"

Sylvia cut her off with an arrogant lift of the chin. "I'm *so* sorry to have wasted your time. There has been an offer to purchase the property outright, and my office is receiving the paperwork right now."

"No, they aren't," Zirconia said with a power-infused hand wave.

Sylvia's head bobbled in reaction, like slow-motion whiplash, before settling upright. "My mistake," she said in a meek tone—her real voice. "I don't know what I was saying. My office must be lying. You can move in immediately."

Zirconia realized the error she'd made in her eagerness. House lust was as intoxicating as any lust, and she'd succumbed.

She waved her invisible hand again. "Never mind. Rewind, and never mind."

Sylvia blinked in confusion. "Huh?"

Zirconia had no one else to complain to, so she growled at the blonde, "I can't exactly vamp away physical paperwork as well as cleanly erase multiple people's memories, now, can I?"

Sylvia took a few ungainly steps backward. She'd been steady-footed before, but now she wobbled on her white high heels like a newborn goat.

"Do I know you?" Sylvia asked as she patted her suit pockets self-consciously. "I was supposed to be finished showings an hour ago. What's happening?"

Zirconia twirled her invisible pinkie. “You took a nap, Sylvia Dabrowski. You're feeling much more refreshed.”

Sylvia brightened. “I did. I am.”

“How much was the offer?”

“I really can't say.”

In response, Zirconia did what she had to do. She placed her invisible vampire hand on the blonde's throat. She took barely any personal pleasure in doing so. A matriarch had to do what was necessary to provide for one's family.

Sylvia's eyes bugged out. “F-f-full price offer,” she finally choked out. “Conditional only on inspection.”

Zirconia released the pressure as she pulled the corkboard flier from her pocket. She took a closer look at the paper. It was the tattered kind, with removable tabs at the bottom. One tab had been removed.

There was a sale price on the listing, which she'd previously ignored. The number had been absurdly high, seemingly a typo, but now that Zirconia had seen the house with her own eyes, she knew better.

The house was worth every penny and more. And now there was an offer that wasn't hers. How could that be?

Heat blossomed in her core and made its way to her skin in a flash.

She burned.

She burned with resentment that someone else had beaten her. How dare they? The house wanted to be hers. It *was* hers. She just hadn't known it was hers until today.

Sylvia awkwardly edged toward the front door, regarding the vampire with wide, frightened eyes. She looked like a newborn goat that's been cornered by a predator, and is too young to know what a predator is, yet has enough ancestral wisdom deep in its bones to know when it's about to be eaten.

Sylvie tripped over her own feet and fell messily to the floor.

"I'm okay," she said quickly. "I'm okay. It's just these stupid shoes."

People without magic could be so clumsy, always blaming their shoes.

Zirconia sighed and finished what she'd started. She swirled her pinkie once more to fully wipe the blonde's memory.

"Sleep now," the vampire said. "Awake refreshed."

She stepped over Sylvia's splayed legs and left.

Once outside, Zirconia didn't dare look back at the house, lest she be overcome with rage over the loss.

Even so, she felt the house watching her, longing for her right back.

She slid into the back seat of a waiting car.

The driver and front passenger were the same couple who'd been driving her around all day.

The man said, "Where to, ma'am?" He had moved past his denial of being a taxi driver.

The woman said cheerily, "Perfect weather today. What a perfect day."

Zirconia snuck one glance back at the boxy modern house.

As it stood, framed by the car window which blocked out the garishly colorful neighboring houses, the house looked better than ever.

Her blood went from hot to boiling.

The man said again, "Where to, ma'am?"

"Nowhere," she said, then, "Anywhere. Put your foot on the gas and drive. Don't you dare touch the brakes until we're in a town with a different name."

He said, "What about stop signs?"

Zirconia let him know how she felt about stop signs by using a swear word. She was usually above coarse language, but the day had used up all of her goodwill.

The woman in the passenger seat clapped her hands. "I do love a road trip. How fun!"

The man at the wheel hit the gas.

Disappointment was sour in Zirconia's mouth. Just like the passage of time, disappointment was also sneaky. Each time it crept up on you, it felt like some novel emotion, some depth never before experienced. Yet it was always that same, old feeling that deserved more than a single fourteen-letter word. Other languages were better than English, for they had more variants that described the terrible pain of longing for what was not fated to be.

Zirconia leaned her head back on the seat, and closed her eyes. She would keep her eyes closed until she could only see Wisteria through the rear view mirror.

The universe had sent her a sign. It was time to go.

CHAPTER 5

Zirconia and her attendants didn't make it far, but they did reach the next town.

It was inland from Wisteria, and was, like most towns, unremarkable.

"Pull over here," Zirconia said.

The driver did as she commanded, as he was well under her spell.

The woman said, "Ooh! This does look like a nice place to stop for lunch. And look at the sign over there. They have Bloody Marys on special. Yum yum."

The man said, "A little hair of the dog sounds about right."

The woman said, "I didn't realize how dry my mouth was until I read that sign and it started watering!"

Same here, Zirconia thought but didn't say.

Everyone got out of the vehicle, and entered the roadside restaurant as though nothing was out of the ordinary, and the three of them always went on road trips together.

The waitress was quick to bring them a starter round of adult beverages.

To Zirconia's surprise, the couple finished their Bloody Marys before she was even halfway through hers.

She said, "I see I've found some travel companions who are capable of keeping up with me."

The two laughed, and the woman said, "We really tied one on last night at the hotel."

"Did we? I'll have to take your word for it," the man said. "I don't remember much."

She said to him, "Me neither, but I do remember you being a naughty boy. You didn't believe me that the black and white swans in the lagoon were real. You went right into the water, fully clothed."

"I did?"

"You're lucky there was an off-duty lifeguard nearby. A big firefighter named Bon."

"You and your firefighters," he said. "Did you ask this one to give you mouth-to-mouth?"

"Of course not." Her cheeks flushed. "You were the one who nearly drowned when the swans wouldn't let you out of the lagoon."

"I don't remember any of that, but it does explain why the front desk clerk was so hasty to get us on our way."

The man signaled the waitress to bring another round.

He sighed and said to Zirconia, "We may not be welcome back at the Cerulean Lagoon, which is a shame, because rumor has it there's a coven of witches holed up in one of the suites."

Zirconia leaned forward. "Tell me more about the witches."

"I'm Darren, by the way," he said. "I don't know much about the witches, but we did hear they're all part of a family."

"I'm Darren's wife," the woman said. "I'd love to meet a real live witch."

"They're not that remarkable," Zirconia said.

The wife continued to gush. "I bet they're just like the Adams Family, but in real life. We kept looking for them, but we were only staying for a few days, and it wasn't long enough to get lucky." The waitress arrived, and she grabbed her second Bloody Mary directly from the woman's tray. "Darren and I are both members of a ghost hunting club. We went to that town specifically to visit the haunted library."

"We sat in the haunted chair," Darren said proudly, chest puffed up. "I didn't feel anything, but she did."

The woman smiled. "I'm very sensitive to energy. It's a family gift."

Darren opened and closed his mouth like he'd been about to say something but changed his mind.

Zirconia flat-out asked, "Do either of you have magical powers?"

They both laughed, and the man said, "Only the power to eat more than my weight in loose-meat sandwiches." He patted his stomach.

"So, no powers," Zirconia said. "Not even mage level."

They both laughed uproariously.

Zirconia shrugged. "I'm a vampire," she said. "You never can tell unless you ask."

They both nearly fell off their chairs laughing.

The woman wiped tears from the corners of her eyes. "It truly is a perfect day. Honestly, it started a bit rough, but that's the best sort of day, because things can only get better."

"And tomorrow's another day," Darren said, raising his glass in a toast. "A toast to tomorrow."

"To to-to-to." The woman giggled. The vodka was affecting her systems. "You can't say *to tomorrow*."

"You just did," her husband said.

This time, Zirconia joined them in their laughter. They were a charming couple, and she felt charmed.

The day was looking up after all.

They drank, they laughed, they ordered appetizers.

They drank, they laughed some more, they ordered lobster.

The waitress informed them the restaurant didn't serve lobster.

They laughed themselves nearly to incontinence, and they ordered prime rib, rare.

Eventually, the restaurant tried to close for the day. It took the waitress three tries to get the trio to leave their table.

Zirconia kept saying, "Third time's the charm or the curse," which everyone but the waitress found delightful.

The trio stumbled into a motel room across the street.

None of them noticed that they hadn't booked or paid for the motel room at the office. Zirconia had simply grabbed Suite Thirteen's door handle and given it a vampire twist, letting them in.

Suite Thirteen was always a good bet, as most people were too superstitious to take it when given their choice of numbers.

The two ladies flopped on the pair of queen-sized beds while Darren raided the mini-bar to make nightcaps for everyone.

Zirconia noticed that her head didn't feel right.

Was she sobering up already? What a disappointment.

She wasted no time tossing back Darren's concoction, but it didn't help at all.

"Something's not right," she said to the couple.

Her vision went dark. She nearly slipped away.

She fought to get her eyelids open again.

She found herself lying on the bed again, staring up at the wife's face.

"Darren, something's wrong," the woman said to her husband.

Zirconia croaked and gestured for them to fetch her purse.

She would be fine. She just needed a sip from the vial of liquid she carried with her. It was a special serum for vampires. With all the excitement of the day, she'd forgotten all about it. She hadn't taken any serum in... how long had it been?

Oh, floopy doops. That wasn't a good sign.

If it had been *too* long, she might be dangerously close to...

The innocent woman's neck throbbed invitingly over Zirconia's parched lips. The vampire's mouth watered. Her fangs began to emerge.

"My purse," Zirconia said hoarsely.

"She needs her bag," the tasty-necked woman said. "Check to see if there are any medications." Her words were slurred, but adrenaline was keeping her lucid.

"Ooh. Medications," Darren said. "Sure, why not."

His wife snapped her fingers. "Not for us, for her. For... our friend." At least she had a good grasp on the seriousness of the situation.

Darren wasn't doing quite as well. He had the Good Time Clumsies.

He managed to fetch Zirconia's purse, only to toss the contents on the carpet between the beds.

"Whoopsie daisies," he said. "Wow. That's a lot of stuff. How did all that stuff fit inside this tiny bag?"

Zirconia moaned, "It's a spell."

This caused Darren to laugh so hard he began to cough. After several coughs, he covered his mouth and ran to the bathroom.

Zirconia was having problems moving.

Oh, she *could* move. She had been compromised by too much alcohol and too little serum, but she could move if she had to.

However, she didn't dare move.

Not with her travel companion's tasty neck right there, mere feet away, in a dimly-lit motel suite where nobody had any record of any of them being there.

Zirconia held her body very still and pointed to the vial that sat at the edge of the mess from her purse.

"You want something," the woman said. "Is it this?"

She held up a tube of lipstick.

Zirconia shook her head, no.

"Is it this?" A mirrored compact.

Zirconia growled. Why would she want lipstick or a travel mirror at a time like this?

The woman was an idiot.

She deserved to be bitten.

"Is it this?"

The woman held up a miniature book of relaxation poetry. It had been a gag gift from Zirconia's daughter. It had worked as intended, for Zirconia gagged every time she saw the ghastly thing. She hated books of all kinds. So many dead words written by dead people. Books were worse than ghosts.

The room swam around her.

The darkness folded in, encircling her.

Meanwhile, the woman's jugular pulsed strongly, sped up by adrenaline.

Ah, the sweet taste of blood spiked by adrenaline.

There was nothing else in the world like it.

Darren emerged from the bathroom with a bang of the door.

“Tada! I'm ready for the next round,” Darren announced proudly. He staggered away from the door, waving his hands through the air. “Don't go in there for a few minutes.”

The woman said to her husband, “I think something's wrong with... with... with...” She leaned over Zirconia and looked down, which made her face look fat and swollen. *Not an attractive angle*, Zirconia noted to diminish her appetite.

“She's just resting,” he said. “We'll switch her over to seltzer for a round.”

“I think she's beyond seltzer.”

“She'll rally. Come on, uh, Maggie? Doris? Betty?”

Zirconia was so offended by his use of names that obviously belonged to women a full generation older than her that she nearly levitated off the bed and flew fang-first at the man.

“She's not rallying,” his wife said.

Darren finally grasped that the party might be wrapping up. “Do you think we should take her somewhere?”

The woman said, “Like a hospital?”

Zirconia managed to say, “No.”

In unison, the two asked her, "Where?"

Zirconia tilted her head to the side and scanned the contents of her purse. She saw the vial she needed. It was empty.

Of course it was empty.

She'd used it up, and had forgotten to restock her purse.

It was all her sister's fault for chasing her out of the hotel room that morning. Zinnia didn't understand how much time it took a vampire to prepare for her day. That wicked witch.

The woman held Zirconia's hand by the wrist, and asked her husband, "What if she dies? Her pulse is really weak."

"We have to take her back," Darren said.

"Back where?" The woman was really panicking now. Zirconia could hear the whoosh of blood, and the fear making her blood even more tasty and full of antioxidants.

Zirconia licked her lips in sweet anticipation.

"Back to the hotel with the swans," he said with a certainty that had come out of nowhere.

"Don't joke about swans at a time like this."

"I'm not joking. I don't know how to explain it, but I have this very strong, very specific feeling right now. It's like the feeling I get when I pick the winning scratch and win tickets at the gas station. Or when I know everyone at the poker game is bluffing."

The wife replied softly, "Okay. I believe you."

"We'll take her back. And I can revisit my friends, the swans."

The wife remained serious. "Yes. We'll take her back to the hotel." She looked around. "Speaking of hotels, I don't think we registered for this room."

"Then how did we get in here?"

"I don't know, but I'm getting a spooky feeling. Like when I sat in the chair at the library."

"Give our friend some space. They always say that in the movies. A person needs air to breathe, not a big crowd sucking up all the oxygen."

The wife moved away from the vampire, retreating to the other bed.

Zirconia felt a wave of hot disappointment mixed with a cool wash of relief. The lady's tasty neck was no longer within easy striking distance.

Darren said, "I should be good to drive soon enough." He poked noisily at Suite Thirteen's complementary coffee maker and supplies. "I'll make a pot of coffee to go, then we'll hit the road."

"You're so good in a crisis, baby," the woman said. "You're my rock."

"I'm nothing without you, Debbie. You're *my* rock."

"I love you so much."

"I love you, too. How's our friend doing?"

Zirconia's eyes closed. She felt sleepy.

The woman—Debbie—said, "I think she's going to be okay." To Zirconia, she said sweetly, "Hang in there, hon. We'll have you back home in no time."

CHAPTER 6

Zirconia Cristata Riddle woke up on a sofabed with a mattress spring poking into her shoulder blade.

She was back in the hotel suite at the Cerulean Lagoon.

She had no memory of returning.

Apparently her new friends had been successful in getting her back... not *home*, really—a hotel suite was not a home, not like that beautiful modern house she'd lost out on—but back to her temporary place of residence.

She sat up. The bed made a squeaky, rusty sound.

"And I thought my joints were creaky," said the redheaded woman who was already up and making tea in the suite's tiny kitchenette.

"It was the bed," Zirconia said. "Again. Get some new material."

Zirconia's geriatrically-pregnant witch sister, Zinnia, made a hurt face. "I was going to offer to trade you for my cot, but forget it."

"I don't want your cot. We covered this yesterday. I know a trap when I hear it. If I traded you beds, you would only complain to everyone that your sister stole the only good bed in this cursed hotel suite."

Zinnia frowned over the pot of tea she was brewing.

With a cranky voice, she said, "Someone woke up on the wrong side of the coffin."

"Says the homeless single woman who's knocked up at fifty."

Zinnia frowned. "Forty-nine."

"If you say so."

"I'm not fifty." Confusion crossed Zinnia's freckled face. "Am I? Let's see. I was forty-seven when I moved back here. That was the same year Zara showed up..."

"You've lost your mind, Zinnia. You're repeating yourself more than usual. Forget blaming it on pregnancy hormones. We need to get you treated for brainweevils."

Zinnia found this amusing. She clutched her belly and shook as though she might give birth on the spot.

The cat jumped onto the counter, knocking over tattered paperbacks full of dead words.

"Ham," said the cat. "Ham, ham, ham."

The green budgie screeched, "Find me! Find me! Find me!"

Zirconia resisted the urge to gobble both pets as morning snacks. "That's enough out of both of you, Snake and Marshmallow. Compose yourselves and show some restraint, or I'll make you into a two-meat sandwich."

Zinnia said, "You need a therapist. No. An exorcist."

Zirconia stuck out her tongue at her sister. It was childish, but her sister brought it out in her.

Zinnia said, "Your tongue is pale. You look closer to death than usual."

"I had a few adult beverages last night with some new friends."

"Were you with those ding-dongs who were chasing the swans around the lagoon? I met them briefly at the coffee shop. Darren and Debbie Darnell."

Zirconia snorted with indignation. "Those don't sound like my sort of people." She followed up by asking, "Was he back in the pond again?"

"Darren? Yes, he was. Why? Did you make him do that?"

"Never mind. Stop trying to pick a fight with me. Our parents are still dead. There's nothing left to be won or lost."

Zinnia's mouth dropped open.

Zirconia dressed quickly, and headed for the door. The cat tried to kill her by weaving around her ankles in a tripping spell. Zirconia plucked three hairs from the tip of the cat's tail, sending the spoiled thing running off in a tizzy.

"Don't go far," Zinnia said. "Zara wants to talk to you about something."

"Then she should have gotten up earlier," Zirconia said as she closed the door behind her.

The empty, quiet hallway was a welcome sight. Even with the garish carpet straight out of a horror movie.

She would have preferred to have successfully left town the day before, but today was just as good a day as any to make an exit.

Yesterday could be considered the dress rehearsal. Today would go better. She just had to go easy on the mixed vodka drinks and make sure she had a full supply of—

Her vial.

The one in her purse was empty. She hadn't restocked.

She reached for the suite's door handle and paused.

Considering she'd passed out the night before without fortifying herself, she wasn't feeling too bad. She could make it a few more hours. Maybe a full day, if she didn't expend her powers much.

There was a POP from inside the room.

A puff of colored smoke seeped out underneath the door. It slowly dissipated around Zirconia's shoes.

She pulled her hand away from the handle. Whatever spell Zinnia was getting up to inside the suite, her vampire sister wanted no part of it.

Zirconia would get another vial elsewhere. She could call Dr. Ankh and arrange a quick meeting. Maybe a full medical checkup, since it wasn't like her to black out the way she had the night before.

Since there was nothing she truly needed from the hotel suite, she walked away.

She took the stairs, as she had the day before, quietly slipped into the hotel bar—still closed, as usual—and jumped over the bar to get a bottle. She chose bourbon, all the better to wash away the lingering memory of the previous day's fake bourbon coffee flavor.

CHAPTER 7

Zirconia lifted the bottle of bourbon to her lips. She was too thirsty for a glass. She was, once again, rudely interrupted by a member of the staff.

"Hey! You can't do that," the young man said. His body vibrated with nervous energy, even though he should have been more confident thanks to his win the day before.

"Watch me." Her mouth watered in anticipation of the first delicious sip.

The young man lunged forward and grabbed at the bottle.

But, as the cowboys Zirconia socialized with in Texas would have said, this wasn't her first rodeo.

She dodged the young man's lunge, twirled around at vampire speed, and victoriously... dropped the bottle by accident. It smashed to pieces.

"Look what you made me do," she said to the young man.

He held his hand to his mouth, like he might throw up. So much for his bravado.

The scent of the spilled booze wafted up in a cloud, offending her nostrils. The cheap alcohol at the hotel bar really did smell like airplane fuel. She tried to wave the scent away, to no avail.

They both stood there, looking at the mess for what felt like an eternity.

For some reason, she thought of something her daughter Zara would have said. It was ridiculous and flip, like so many things Zara said, but Zirconia said it aloud anyway. "Cleanup on aisle three."

"Aisle three?" He narrowed his eyes at her. "Nope. Your tricks aren't going to work on me today. I know what you are."

"Of course you do. I'm a paying guest until such time as I check out, which will be any minute now. Right after my wake-up drink."

She scanned the row of bottles for the second-most appealing liquor. Vodka? No. Not after last night's Bloody Mary blackout. Tequila? Maybe.

The young man skirted around, and placed his youthful, blood-filled body between Zirconia and the mirrored wall of alcohol. He stretched out his arms to emphasize his message.

Zirconia exhaled loudly. "Not again."

"I know what you are," the young man said. "You're a va—." He coughed, choking on the word. Just like he had the day before.

"This routine of yours is getting stale," she said.

He tried again. "You're a v—." More coughing.

"I'm a *vampire*," she said. "If you can't even say the word, maybe you shouldn't stand in front of one, with your arms up and your weak points exposed. I can smell your brachial and basilic veins uniting to form your axillary vein." She licked her lips. "Such a tasty spot to nibble."

In response, he sweated visibly, drips running down the sides of his forehead.

"Look at all that sweat," she said. "That's a sign you have healthy blood."

He said, "I know you're a creature of the grave."

"Yes, yes. We covered that, darling. Do you have anything new to say?"

He did not.

She said, "Any more pulsing flesh you'd like to show me? Would you like to lift up your shirt and expose your navel?" She grabbed the bottle of tequila. "It's been a few years since I've done body shots, but I'm willing to try if you are." She leaned forward and sniffed the side of his face. "How old are you, anyway?"

"Lady, you, uh, you, uh, you don't have to leave the hotel. The coffee counter is open, and the cafe."

He put his hand on the tequila bottle.

She didn't let go.

His hands were slippery from sweat, and one of his moist pinkies slipped over her thumb. With her sensitive skin, it felt to her the way a regular person might feel if a stranger pressed their entire moist, sweating body against them. Her pulse skipped ahead to match his.

He said, "How about a nice cafe latte?"

"I told you yesterday. I don't want coffee."

He puffed up his chest bravely and tugged on the tequila bottle. She didn't let go. He was strong, but compared to her, he was hardly an adversary.

"Ma'am, you don't have to enjoy our tasty selection of in-house coffees, but you can't... you can't be here in the bar." He glanced around, and then talked to her in a friendly voice, as though they were friends. "And you can't just help yourself to the alcohol. I let you get away with it a few times because it was cute, but enough is enough."

Cute? Did he say cute? She was so surprised, she let go of the bottle.

He staggered backward, also surprised.

"Thank you," he said, hugging the tequila bottle. "Thanks for seeing it from my perspective. You're kinda-sorta okay, you know?"

She didn't like his tone or his familiarity. She was not "cute" and she was not "kinda-sorta okay."

Zirconia wanted so badly to place her vampire hands upon him, but there would be no point in trying. He wore a protective spell or enchanted amulet. She felt it around him, like a magnetic force field.

He said casually, "Any plans for the day?"

She replied tersely, "How dare you speak to me as though we are equals. As though you and I are acquainted. We are not friends."

"But I know your family. You ladies have been staying here for almost six months. You're practically—"

"Stop," she said. "We are not having this conversation again."

With more boldness, he said, "If you don't like the songs, don't come see the band." He cracked a smile at himself, then added, "The bar and lounge will be open after five. We'll be happy to serve you then."

She stood at full height—vampires had the ability to make themselves two inches taller—and made a solemn pronouncement. "I will see this cursed two-star hotel razed to the ground before I will see the inside of this bar again."

"Uh, what? Razed? You mean like... is that a threat?"

She turned away. They were done.

She left the lounge and then the cursed two-star hotel.

Outside, she recoiled from the blast of heat. The sun was blazing hot again. Was there no relief? Why was there never a single well-placed cloud when you needed it?

A car was waiting at the curb.

It was not a taxi, but that didn't matter. To someone with vampire powers, no door was ever locked and no vehicle was not a taxi.

She slid into the back seat.

The driver and his passenger turned around.

Zirconia's mood, which had been very sour thanks to the oppressive policies of the uptight hotel staff, abruptly turned sweet.

What a pleasant surprise. They were her friends from the day before, the couple who'd been able to keep up with her.

"You're still here in town," she said to the couple. "You stayed another night!"

"We probably shouldn't be here at all," the man said, rubbing the sleep from his eyes. "I understand we got up to a bit of trouble last night."

"We certainly did," Zirconia said.

He said with uncertainty, "Because you were... partying with us?"

"I suppose you could call it partying," she said. "You're both a lot more fun than my stodgy family."

The woman, Debbie, gave Zirconia a blank look, as though she'd forgotten the previous night's events. She probably had, being a nonmagical regular human. To her, it would all be a blur.

Zirconia patted the woman on the shoulder and warmly said, "Debbie, thank you so much for taking care of me after I blacked out."

"Oh," Debbie said, recovering quickly. "You're welcome." She chewed her lower lip. Zirconia could practically see the slow human-speed cogs turning inside the woman's brain.

Zirconia said to Darren, "Don't tell me you were swimming with the swans again last night."

Darren grinned. "I'll never tell."

"He was!" Debbie exclaimed. "We had to get an off-duty firefighter to drag him out."

"You must mean Bon," Zirconia said. "Did he give you mouth-to-mouth, Debbie?"

Debbie's eyes and mouth twitched.

"Maybe next time," Zirconia said with girlish glee. She liked Debbie. Debbie was fun.

Darren drummed on his steering wheel and said, "Where to, ma'am? Since you're in the car already, I might as well give you a lift anywhere you want to go."

Zirconia wasn't sure. She had been caught off guard by finding a willing driver who didn't need magical convincing. Sometimes it paid to make new friends, even if they weren't wealthy or famous.

Where did she want to go? Besides directly out of town, as soon as possible?

"Ooh, I have a request," Debbie said. "I don't know about you two, but I'd murder someone for a cup of decent coffee."

"I know just the place," Zirconia said. "And we don't even need to murder anyone."

She gave the address of Dreamland Coffee—the downtown location—to Darren, and off they went.

As they drove, Debbie said cheerily, "I checked the weather, and it's going to be a perfect day. Just perfect!"

"It can certainly try," Zirconia said. "It started off rough, which is the best kind of day, because it can only get better."

Debbie gasped. "That's what I always say!"

"I know," Zirconia said. "You told me last night. Several times."

Debbie covered her mouth with her hand. "I may have had too much to drink last night."

Her husband said, "You think?"

And then all three of them laughed and laughed.

CHAPTER 8

Zirconia led her new friends into the coffee shop.

The air smelled pleasant, though she could now detect the brackish odor of the artificial bourbon flavor. At least she wouldn't have to taste it again.

The place was empty again—the owner really needed some tips on how to draw a clientele—and the catalog-handsome komodo dragon shifter, Humphrey, was working again.

"Hey, Toots," he said to Zirconia, then, "Hello, people I have not met," to the other two.

The three customers took a comfortable seat near the window.

Humphrey stubbornly called over, "I can take your order at the counter."

Zirconia said, "Humphrey, you have my express permission to take our order over here."

"Huh?"

"A gentleman doesn't say *huh*. Come over here to take our order." She tapped the table and said to her companions, "What is it with customer service people who don't understand the basic premise of their job?

Debbie and Darren exchanged a look the way only long-married couples and psychics could. It was the red flag look. Both pushed their chairs back and began to rise.

"Sit," Zirconia said with a pinkie-finger-swish of vampire glamour.

They sat, exchanging a longer, wary look to follow up their red flag look.

Everything would be fine. Zirconia would win back her new friends.

She gave Humphrey no glamour at all—it wouldn't be needed with someone so weak—as she tapped the table a second time, and then a third.

With the heavy feet of a scolded child, Humphrey shuffled over.

He came with glasses of water, which he placed in a perfect triangle on the table, using a precision that wasn't human.

"I can take your order at this table," he said. "My name is Humphrey." He said to Zirconia, "You are the mean lady who doesn't like jam on her scone." To the visitors, he said, "You are from out of town. Your clothes are not the same as the clothes people typically wear."

Darren said, "You got it, my man," and offered Humphrey his hand.

They did a complicated fist bump followed by a handshake.

Darren whipped out a business card and gave it to Humphrey.

He said, "I'm Darren Darnell, and this is my wife, Debbie Darnell. We run a real estate office back home. I'm only in town visiting, but if you've got an eye on a property, let me know and I'll help you write up an offer. My clients always get their dream homes, guaranteed."

Zirconia's ears, which had an increased range of motion thanks to her powers, perked up and swiveled toward Darren. His clients always got their dream homes?

Interesting.

Perhaps it wasn't too late for her to get the house she'd seemingly lost out on the day before.

The real estate agent's wife patted him on the chest. "Honey, we're on vacation. I'm sure the handsome man has a local agent."

Humphrey said, "I have a local barber. For the hairs on my head."

Good ol' Humphrey. Almost human.

Debbie asked Humphrey, "What have you got for hangovers?"

Zirconia lifted a glass of water and took a sip.

"The bourbon misto is popular," Humphrey said.

As Zirconia recalled the foul bourbon syrup, her mouth expelled the water she'd been sipping. She used her vampire reflexes to rapidly turn her head away from the Darnells.

She sprayed Humphrey from his waist to his knees.

He didn't seem particularly shocked.

The Darnells giggled. They were a fun couple.

"I am wet," Humphrey said.

"At least it's only water this time," Zirconia said.

"I am thirty percent wet," he said.

She waved him off. "Go get your mistress to dry you off, and come back with three big mugs of that special brew she keeps for her book club. The good stuff."

Humphrey nodded obediently, and left to make their drinks.

Darren said, "You must be a regular here." He looked around. "It's a nice place, but I have to ask. Why is it called Dreamland? Coffee keeps people awake."

Zirconia had no answer. She'd never given it a second thought.

Debbie said, "I bet it's because all the other names were taken. If you're setting up a place like this, you want to have franchise potential. You want to sell mugs and T-shirts and refrigerator magnets. There's a high profit margin on branded items." She smiled. "I worked in corporate marketing before I joined Darren's real estate team."

Just then, a tall, whip-thin, enviably beautiful, black-haired witch appeared behind the Darnells. It was the owner of the coffee shop. She might have used magic to sneak up on them.

"Hello, you," Zirconia said, omitting the witch's name when it didn't come to her. "As you can see, I've traded my usual entourage for a new one. This is Darren and Debbie Darnell."

The witch shook their hands. "I'm Maisy Nix. Poor old Zirconia can never remember my name."

Zirconia snorted.

Maisy said, "We all love to tease each other. We're a tight little bunch." She winked at the vampire.

"Sometimes too tight," Zirconia said.

Maisy ignored the comment and said to Darren, "Did I overhear that you're a real estate agent? Perhaps you can help Zirconia find a house that suits her *particular* needs."

Darren said, "Is Zirconia a friend of yours?"

He said it in such a way that clearly revealed he did not understand that Zirconia was sitting at the table with them.

Maisy gave Zirconia a look of malevolent glee. *Busted*, her look said. *You call these people your friends, and they don't even know your name.*

Maisy's look was surprisingly specific. He was using a twist of her witch tongue magic to enhance nonverbal communication between herself and the former witch.

Zirconia gave Maisy an equally specific look. *Names are the least important thing to remember about a person, far below, for example, whether they can be trusted or not.*

Maisy shot back. *Oh, we are all going to talk about this at the next coven meeting, especially if you are not in attendance as a guest.*

Zirconia stretched one inch taller. *Less psychic chatter and more getting our coffee.*

Maisy arched an elegant eyebrow, and left the conversation.

"Brrr," said Debbie after the witch was gone. "Did you feel that draft? How unusual. It's such a sunny day." She showed her forearm to her husband. "Look. I've got goosebumps."

More secret looks were exchanged between the couple.

Darren explained to Zirconia, "My wife is sensitive to energies, and... well, I've got something of a special power myself."

"You're probably a card mage," Zirconia said. "That's why you win at poker, and why you pick out the winning scratch-off tickets."

"A *card mage*," he said slowly, moving his jaw as though chewing on the idea. "That does sound familiar. Come to think of it, I heard that phrase a lot when I was growing up. The grownups in my family talked about it on camping trips when they thought us kids were asleep."

Zirconia grew bored. She didn't want to hear about young Darren on camping trips.

She looked down at her fingers. They looked particularly knobby that morning. It had to be the terrible lighting in the coffee shop. Dreamland would never become a franchise until they fixed their lighting.

Darren was still talking about the grownups in his family. "My uncle tried to tell me something once, but my dad wouldn't let him."

Zirconia looked out the window and said wearily, "Parents try to protect their offspring from family curses, but you know what they say about magic. It has a mind of its own, and its power will not be denied."

When she turned back to the couple, both had stunned expressions.

Debbie leaned forward and whispered, "So, you're a believer?"

"We covered this all last night," Zirconia said. "Didn't I show you my fangs? It was right about the time we got our prime rib."

"Your fangs," Darren said with a smirk. "Wouldn't that be something?"

"Last night is a bit of a blur," Debbie said.

Darren slapped the table. "And if we're lucky, tonight will be, too!"

Humphrey arrived with their very special mugs of brew. The java was a special blend that included Seed of Purpureus. It enhanced cognitive powers even more than regular coffee beans. It was purple instead of brown, because the beans were a variegated red and blue.

Darren sniffed the purple coffee and said, “This smells so darn good, I don't know if I should drink it or dump it over my head.”

Humphrey said, “Drinking it will be more hygienic. Why would you dump it over your head?”

“Just a figure of speech,” Darren said with a big laugh. “That's a compliment where I'm from.”

The Darnells took their first sips.

“Mmm,” Debbie said. “Mmm, mmm, mmm.”

Darren pointed at Humphrey. “Get the next round started, my man, because this one tastes like another.”

Humphrey shuffled off to make more of the purple brew.

Zirconia and her new friends chatted about the good coffee.

It made them all very loquacious.

They chatted about franchise ideas for Dreamland Coffee, then about the shortcomings of the Cerulean Lagoon Hotel, particularly their zero-fun policies regarding lounge hours and swimming with the swans.

As they were leaving, a piece of paper on the corkboard caught Zirconia's eye.

A single one of the pull tabs had been removed.

It was an exact copy of the paper she'd seen the day before, listing the modern house for sale or rent.

An idea emerged in her head. She'd been mulling it over subconsciously for a while, but now it was fully formed.

She grabbed the listing from the board and held it to her chest.

She said to her new friends, “Did you mean what you said about your real estate clients always getting their dream homes, no matter what?”

“Absolutely,” Darren said. “We do whatever it takes.”

"The Darnells Get it Done," Debbie said. "There's a capital letter on every word because we've trademarked it as a slogan."

"If it's your slogan, it must be true," Zirconia said.

CHAPTER 9

Zirconia and her new real estate team walked up to the house, the one that almost got away.

"It really is all corners," Darren said. "And such sharp ones. I like it for you."

"Raw concrete is low maintenance," Debbie said, as though she were the seller's agent, not the buyer's. "No painting, staining, or spackling. It will look the same in a hundred years."

"Those tall windows are great for resale," Darren said.

"I don't plan to *ever* sell it," Zirconia said. "Not as long as I reside on this planet."

She rang the doorbell, which made an electric buzz that she liked even better the second time.

The door opened to reveal a stick-thin blonde in a white suit and high heels.

The woman looked Zirconia over with pursed lips and said, "You don't have an appointment."

There was no recognition on the blonde's face—but of course there wouldn't be, since Zirconia had wiped the woman's memory the day before, replacing their interaction with the memory of a nap.

"I'm here to purchase this house," the vampire said. "I know you have another—"

The blonde cut her off with a hasty, "Come in! Come in! I was about to leave for the day, but I always have time for a buyer. Qualified, I assume?"

Darren Darnell handed the woman his business card. They did introductions all around—regular ones, not supernatural ones—as they stood in the entry underneath the breathtaking, deadly-looking chandelier.

Darren said, "I assure you, Ms. Dabrowski—"

"Call me Sylvia."

"I assure you, Sylvia, my client is highly qualified. Thank you for seeing us in this unorthodox manner. I would have called first, but my client tells me time is of the essence, as you have another offer."

A funny look crossed over Sylvia's features. Zirconia recognized it as the expression a person makes when given the opportunity to lie about something for their own benefit.

"Y-y-yes," Sylvia said. "Yes? Yes. We do have several parties who are quite interested, and a deal *may* be at hand."

Zirconia said to Darren, "She told me yesterday that her office had a deal coming in. A full-price offer, subject only to inspection."

Sylvia looked perplexed. "I did?"

Of course she looked perplexed. People did that when you referred to events that you'd wiped from their memory.

Zirconia said, "What I meant to say was that I heard a rumor there was another offer." She put on a smile. "A little birdie told me." She looked around. The house was exactly as she remembered.

No.

It was better.

Darren said, "We should have a quick peek around before we sign the paperwork, of course. Do I have your verbal acknowledgement that an offer from my client is incoming, or shall I call your office to formally register?"

"You have my word," Sylvia said. "Please, look around. I must apologize that the new cleaners leave a lot to be desired."

They walked around, the sound of their footfalls echoing through each empty room and hallway.

Debbie whispered to Zirconia, "They should have staged it with furniture. Rooms look smaller without furnishings. But that's okay. Their mistake is our win."

Darren tested the lock on a sliding wall of glass. "I see a speck of rust here and there. Sylvia, how old is the home?"

"My great-uncle bought this property a few years ago as an investment," she said, avoiding the question. "Nobody's ever lived in it. He didn't want to devalue the property by having anyone dwell inside it."

They walked through the whole house. Twice.

Debbie and Darren provided their running commentary —tough but fair—throughout. Debbie pointed out the positive features, such as the private views and luxurious finishes. Darren pointed out the flaws, such as the room with fourteen windows, not a single one of which opened for fresh air from the garden.

Sylvia fished a vibrating phone from her suit pocket, and excused herself to take the call.

She rejoined them in the sleek kitchen with the hidden appliances and said solemnly, "We have received another offer. We have a multiple offer situation on our hands." She made a sad face that did not hide her excitement. "Which is a shame, since it will be a lot more paperwork for everyone."

Zirconia asked, "How many people are bidding?"

Sylvia scrunched her lips. "I can't say."

Zirconia could make her say. But she didn't. She could get this house the regular way.

Darren asked, "Sylvia, we need something to work on. How close is the offer to the asking price? Ballpark?" He winked.

Zirconia already knew that the one from the previous day had been at full asking price. She'd mention that fact to Darren. Either he'd forgotten or, more likely, he was fishing.

"I can't say," Sylvia said again. "But it's a very attractive offer." More winks. "Why don't the three of you crunch some numbers, and put together your best offer? Your best-best offer. I'll present all the offers to my uncle at five o'clock sharp." She wrinkled her nose. "When he returns from his latest adventure. Long story. You don't want to know."

Zirconia took a shot in the not-so-dark. "Ghost hunting?"

Sylvia's head jerked back in surprise, but she recovered quickly.

"I really can't say," Sylvia said. "Now, if you'll excuse me, I should lock up."

She and the Darnells exchanged details about how to get the offer to her office, and they parted ways.

As Darren, Debbie, and Zirconia climbed back into Darnells' rental car, Debbie said, "This is shaping up to be a perfect day. There's nothing like buying a house."

"Easy now," her husband said. "The battle has just begun." He turned to Zirconia and asked, "Is there a place in this town with an office space we can rent?"

"We could go to my daughter's bookstore," Zirconia said. "They have all sorts of computers and tables."

"I love bookstores," Debbie said. "Especially the biographies. So many lives, well lived. So much wisdom."

Zirconia shuddered at the idea of reading biographies—the deadest of all dead words—as she gave Darren the address.

They drove to the building where Zirconia's witch daughter worked, which was not a bookstore at all, but the Wisteria Public Library.

CHAPTER 10

Zirconia usually avoided the dusty old Wisteria Public Library because all the zombie pages gave her a headache.

Today, however, would be different. She had important business to attend to, plus the powerful purple coffee from Dreamland was preemptively chasing away brain fog and other cognitive maladies. The delicate vasculature in her brain was wide open and ready for business, every light switched on, dimmer switches all the way up.

Her two companions headed to the computer terminals.

Zirconia approached what the librarians called the circulation counter, or what she called the customer service desk.

She tapped the silver customer service bell, which rang out loudly enough to disturb the dust on the top shelves.

A well-dressed man with snowy white hair appeared as though summoned by magic.

His name was Francis, or Foster, or something like that. He was good friends with Zara, and he had powers. He could turn into a duck, or a platypus, or some other bizarre creature. What mattered most—more than his name—was that he could be trusted.

"Hello, gorgeous," the snowy-haired man said to Zirconia. "You're looking lovelier than ever. What have we done to deserve your company today?"

"Hello, darling." She leaned over the service desk and air-kissed his cheeks. "I've popped in to do some paperwork. A mere formality. But since I'm here, I should say hello to my daughter."

The stylish shifter frowned. "Zara's not here. She called in sick again."

"Why would she do that? She's not ill."

His expression turned sad, which made him look older —poor thing was past his prime—and he shrugged.

"She's not ill," Zirconia said again. "I'm her mother. I would know if she were ill."

He shrugged again. "We can't force her to come to work."

"Well, that's ridiculous. She loves selling books, or buying books, or whatever it is you do here. It's her favorite thing. Books, books, books. That and collecting vagabond animals that nobody else wants, but mostly books."

The man flashed a dazzling array of crowded but very white teeth. "You are an absolute delight, Zirconia. Your sense of humor is razor sharp. We should socialize more."

"We should."

He handed her a card.

It was an old-fashioned calling card with his name written in calligraphy. Frank Wonder.

Yes, that was his name. It had been on the tip of her tongue.

She tucked the card into her purse. She didn't have one to give him in return. And why was that? Why didn't she have her own calling cards with her name written in calligraphy? She would have to ask Frank for the name of his printer.

Yes.

As soon as she moved into her new house, she would print up calling cards, some with her new address and some without.

"You are needed," Frank said.

"Pardon me?"

She jerked her head up and took better notice of Frank Wonder. His jaw was crooked, which gave him a regal, kingly elegance. Some of the best people had crooked features. And he had a delightful duality, a vague placelessness that would allow him to fit in anywhere. He was both worldly and small-town charming, in an old-fashioned yet also contemporary way.

They *should* socialize more. They *would* socialize more.

"You are needed," he repeated.

A buttery warmth spread through her, from the tip of her nose, past her ears, and down to the heels of her feet.

She was needed.

It was the nicest thing anyone had said to her in a very long time. Hot tears welled up in her eyelids.

"Over there," Frank said, pointing behind her. "You're needed over there. Your friends at the computer stations are waving to get your attention."

She blinked back the tears. The buttery warmth turned to a slick, oily fever. She'd nearly stepped right into a trap of her own making by misinterpretation.

What a silly old fool she was. Getting weepy over absolutely nothing, and in front of her daughter's coworker at the used book emporium, no less.

She should know better than to let her heart soar like a kite in the wind. There was nothing to be gained by getting emotionally invested in being of value to other mere humans. People were mercurial and cruel. They forgot about you so easily.

"Thank you, darling," she said, covering with an impeccable smile.

She signaled to the Darnells that she would be with them in a moment.

To Frank, she said, "Lovely suit, by the way. I know the designer personally, which is why I recognize it. That cut is perfect for you."

"Flattery will get you everywhere," he said with a flirty smile. "Let me know if your friends need any help with your paperwork. I have a wonderful way with forms and envelopes."

"And you're certain my daughter called in sick?"

His smile dropped away. In a grave tone, he said, "I'm concerned about her. We all are."

She felt the sting of his implied insult: that she hadn't been taking care of her daughter.

How dare he.

She hadn't put her life on hold and stuck around this dump of a town for months on end to enjoy the local nightlife, which made barn dances look like royal balls in comparison.

"Thank you for your concern," she said matter-of-factly. "I'll see that she's back at her post tomorrow."

"Only if she's ready," Frank said. "She keeps saying she's ready, and occasionally she seems like the Zara we know and love, but then we find her weeping in an alcove. It's heartbreaking."

Zirconia didn't like the sound of that. Weeping in an alcove? It was undignified.

"Enough said." There was a steely edge in her tone that wasn't there by accident. This conversation was over.

The white-haired man nodded and backed away.

She couldn't resist a few more words to set him straight.

"Riddle women are tougher than we look," she said.

He disappeared behind a door.

She left to join her real estate agents. One thing at a time. Get the house today. Get her daughter back on track tomorrow.

As she walked past the tomb-like rows of dead words, she decided things were about to fall into place, starting today.

Zara's outlook would be vastly improved by waking up in a new bedroom, in a bed of her own.

Once Zirconia acquired the dream house, everything else would come together. How could it not?

That was, after all, the whole point of a dream house.

CHAPTER 11

Hours Later

Darren Darnell raised his glass in a toast.

Zirconia's head felt as bubbly as the champagne in their glasses.

He said, “Here's to the best client we've ever worked with. Congratulations on getting your dream house. I can hardly wait for the invitation to your housewarming.”

Debbie chimed in, “We'll come to town a few days early to help you get ready for the party. Or just to chill out with our new friend.”

“With our new friend,” Darren said.

Zirconia didn't mind hearing the flattery, but she didn't believe it. People were mercurial and cruel. The Darnells would move on as soon as their commission fee landed in their account.

No matter.

They could still be pretend-friends today.

“Here's to the new house,” Zirconia said. “And better times ahead for all of us.”

They clinked their glasses, then drank.

A young man who'd snuck up on them in the darkness cleared his throat.

They were back at the Cerulean Lagoon, in the lounge, which was awfully quiet. And dark. The lights were all off for some reason.

“You again,” the young man said to Zirconia, holding up both hands in exasperation. “The lounge isn't open yet.”

The trio exchanged looks of mock horror. None of them showed any signs of getting up from their seats.

Darren said, “We're only a bit early.”

Debbie said, “We're paying guests. Can't you make an exception.”

The hotel employee looked right at Zirconia. “You,” he said accusingly. “You swore you would see this hotel razed to the ground before you would see the inside of this bar again.”

“Did I say that?” Zirconia batted her eyelashes.

Darren took control of the situation.

He pushed his chair back and stood up.

“Come on,” Darren said in a friendly tone, lolling his head to one side. “Let us have one little drink.”

The young man scrunched his face. “The lounge will be open in half an hour. Can't you wait?”

Darren held out both hands. “Come on,” he said again.

“It won't be much longer.”

“Come on,” Darren said for the third time.

That was it.

The young man took in a deep breath and exhaled, “Okay. Fine.”

He shook his head like he couldn't believe what he was doing.

Debbie grabbed Zirconia's hand under the table, and squeezed it like they were successful pledges at a new sorority. She gazed up at her husband with adoration.

“But keep it quiet in here,” the young man said. “At least until we officially open the lounge.”

Darren checked his watch, a fancy digital device that performed all manner of functions.

“Quiet time for half an hour,” Darren said. “Then Happy Hour.”

“We don't have a Happy Hour,” the young man said.

Zirconia muttered, “Sounds about right for this place.”

The young man gave her a dirty look as he touched something on his chest, below his collarbone. When he dropped his hand away, a lump was visible through his shirt.

He probably hadn't wanted to give away his secret, but Zirconia had seen it.

There was one mystery solved. He wore an anti-vampire amulet.

Unfortunately for him, he'd forgotten the first rule of wearing an anti-vampire amulet. Don't let the vampire see it.

If the two were to ever tangled again, he would live to regret his mistake—assuming she allowed him to remember their interaction.

He left, and they finished their toast.

As they started their second bottle, which Darren had liberated from the cooler himself, Darren turned to Zirconia and grew serious. "I hate to do this to you, but the deal isn't final yet. I'm afraid I must broach the topic of..." He winced.

"Money," she said, also wincing. It was so distasteful to discuss money, yet here they were. "I understand. Let me put your mind at ease. Money will not be a problem. I have access to unlimited funds."

He coughed on his champagne. After regaining control, he said, "Unlimited funds?"

He and his wife exchanged a look.

Zirconia knew that look. It was the uh-oh look. She had inadvertently raised more red flags with her careless wording. The mistake needed correcting.

She reluctantly flexed her invisible vampire energy.

She hated to have to use it on her new friends. They'd been having such a lovely time. But she didn't want to waste another minute discussing such a vulgar thing as money, and how she was going to pay for the house that she'd acquired by offering twenty percent above the asking price.

Mind-control magic rippled over the Darnells.

It didn't take much, as the champagne was doing two-thirds of the job.

"I have *sufficient* funds," she said carefully. "Not *unlimited*. That would be preposterous. But I do have *sufficient* funds."

Darren continued to give her a skeptical look. The glamour was affecting him, but not as strongly as it might have if he hadn't built up a tolerance due to having spent the day in close proximity to Zirconia.

He asked cagily, "And where might these *sufficient funds* be?"

"In a treasure chest at the bottom of the ocean," she said flippantly, reminding herself of her daughter.

Her daughter.

She interrupted her own thoughts.

Zara.

Where was she?

Zirconia had asked the front desk to send someone to the room to fetch Zara and the others so they could all be together to celebrate the acquisition of their new home.

Why wasn't Zara there?

Was she truly feeling ill, as her coworker at the used bookstore believed?

Should Zirconia have known that her daughter was ill?

Was Zirconia a bad mother?

Of course she was. She was a terrible mother. A selfish, dreadful, cold-blooded monster.

She pushed the thought away.

Zirconia tried to be a good mother.

She tried so hard.

And yet she always managed to get it wrong.

When she got it wrong, it made her sad.

And when she got sad, she felt empty.

And when she felt empty, she tried to fill that hole inside herself, but nothing ever filled the void.

Someone touched her arm.

As quickly as it had begun, she was yanked out of her downward spiral by the touch of a human.

It was Debbie. Sweet, naive, moist-handed Debbie. Debbie who believed she had psychic powers just because she occasionally noticed the coolness of a spectral cloud. Who couldn't? Half the human population could feel a sufficiently strong astral field.

Debbie said, "We should get the name of your bank for the paperwork. I'm assuming you were joking about the treasure chest at the bottom of the ocean."

"It wasn't a joke, but gold isn't very liquid, so let's forget about that." Zirconia named a reputable bank, part of a chain, and said, "I'll have the funds in your office's trust account by the end of the business day tomorrow."

The Darnells looked relieved.

"So, you'll be cashing some investments," Debbie said.

"In a manner of speaking," Zirconia said.

She scanned the dark lounge for her family.

Where were they? Had the front desk ignored her perfectly reasonable request? Did she have to climb the stairs and drag the other Riddles out of the squalid one-bedroom suite all by herself?

Debbie said, "I'm sure your family is okay. They'll be along any minute."

Maybe Debbie did have some psychic abilities after all.

"I shall not worry about it," Zirconia said.

Darren refilled their champagne glasses. "Someone will let us know if there's anything to worry about."

Debbie gave her husband an appreciative look. "You're probably right."

He chuckled. "There are no sweeter words to a husband's ears."

She rolled her eyes.

The lounge was quiet. Too quiet.

"Happy Hour can't start soon enough," Darren said. "Is anyone else hungry?"

"I could eat," Debbie said.

Zirconia picked up the menu for appetizers, which were on special for the first hour the lounge would be open. If that wasn't a Happy Hour, she didn't know what was.

Zirconia perused the menu, then said, “They have six kinds of chicken wings. How is that possible? I didn't know there were six kinds of chickens.”

The other two didn't laugh.

She looked over her menu to find them both staring at her blankly.

“That was a joke,” she said.

They both said “ah” and fake-laughed.

“I learned that joke from a famous comedian,” she said. “He's dead now, so he doesn't perform anymore, but he likes to get new jokes out there.”

Debbie said, “I don't understand.”

“It's a play on the phrase *six kinds of chicken wings*,” Zirconia said wearily. The most wasted words in communication were those used to explain humor to people who didn't get it.

Debbie said, “Maybe I need to cut back on my adult beverages, but did you imply your friend is supplying jokes from beyond the grave?”

“He only faked his death,” Zirconia said. “Didn't we have this discussion already over prime rib and Bloody Marys? I'm getting a strong déjà vu.”

The Darnells tilted their heads to indicate they had not yet had that discussion, and would like for it to happen now.

So, she told them.

Zirconia explained the whole undead thing to them, and how magic was real, but hidden from most people.

Also, that the unluckiest people in the world were the Nothing People who knew about magic but couldn't perform it, but that, on the bright side, Zirconia had a feeling that one or both of the Darnells had mage powers.

The couple took it well, though they did use the shock as an excuse to have another round.

And another.

Then six kinds of chicken wings, and more drinks.

The Darnells used the shock of learning about magic to get absolutely obliterated on adult beverages.

"This is so silly," Zirconia said, slurring her words. "You've had too much to drink, and I'll have to explain it all to you again tomorrow night, just like last night!"

"Last night," Darren groaned as he smacked his palm on his forehead.

The room got darker. Zirconia's view was contracting, as it had the night before.

It was almost midnight.

She got to her feet and said, "I need to get something from my room. A little vial of... of..." She couldn't think of the right word.

"More drinks," Darren said cheerfully.

"Order for me," Zirconia said, one finger in the air. "I'll be right back."

She made it up the stairs and into the suite.

The sofabed was unfolded, but in a different spot than it had been that morning.

There were other things wrong in the room, but she only cared about sleep.

She fell forward like a tree in a storm.

The sofabed squeaked in protest under her.

She promptly forgot about getting her vial of synthetic blood, and about getting back to the party in the lounge.

All she wanted to do was close her eyes and let the day become history.

The bed springs poked at her without mercy.

Unfamiliar shapes lurked in the shadows all around. Something was wrong with the hotel suite, and the springs urged her to investigate, but investigation wasn't her thing. That was for Zara, always playing detective, chasing ghosts and demons and who knew what else.

"Just another good night of rest," she said to the bed. "I've got a big day ahead of me."

And she did have a big day planned.

Her first order of business would be getting into Zinnia's stock trading account so the two of them could fill up a bank account.

They didn't need the full purchase price for the house right away—they could take it slow to avoid suspicion—but they did need enough cash for a deposit.

"Sleepy time," she moaned into her pillow, and soon she got her wish.

Everything went dark.

CHAPTER 12

Zirconia Cristata Riddle woke up on the sofabed with the usual spring poking into her.

Her eyes opened, and she oriented herself inside the hotel suite. She was staring at the usual water stain on the ceiling, which meant the sofabed was back in its usual position. Had it not been turned the other way the night before? And what about the room? It had been in disarray.

Had she been dreaming about a mess? In a hypnagogic state before her head hit the pillow?

There was another, more logical explanation. The other Riddle women who shared the suite must have tidied up overnight. And it was good they had, for today she had more important business to attend to than cleaning up their mess.

She had to convince Zinnia to help her raise the funds for the house purchase.

She sat up, ready to get started.

The sofabed let out its usual groan.

"And I thought my joints were creaky," said Zinnia, who was making tea in the kitchenette.

Again with the creaky joints? Had Zinnia given up on having new ideas? The strain of confinement to the small hotel suite was getting to the pregnant witch.

"Still the bed," Zirconia said neutrally. She would not take the bait. She would not fight with Zinnia. Not this time. It would seriously stand in the way of the stock market business they needed to take care of.

"You should take the cot," Zinnia said. "It's just foam, no squeaky springs. I can barely sleep with this baby pressing on my bladder anyway. I'll trade you for the sofabed."

And here they were in their cabin fever loop, having the same conversation yet again.

Zirconia stared at her sister. Was Zinnia wearing the same outfit she'd worn yesterday? It was hard to tell. All her clothes were similarly not-quite-nice.

Zinnia said impatiently, "Do you want to trade or not?"

"You *do* have brainweevils."

"I do not."

"Yes. You do. We had this exact conversation two days ago. The primary symptom of brainweevils is absolute denial that one has brainweevils."

Zinnia frowned over the pot of tea she was brewing.

"I don't *think* I have brainweevils," Zinnia said softly. "But it would explain my memory problems."

"We'll see Dr. Ankh after we finish our business," Zirconia said.

Then the vampire looked down to find, to her surprise, that she was wearing her silky pajamas. Her clothes were folded neatly next to the sofabed.

"Did you undress me last night?" Zirconia asked her sister. "When you were fixing the room?"

Zinnia raised an eyebrow knowingly. "Someone had too much to drink last night."

"Ha ha," Zirconia said. "And I suppose I also woke up on the wrong side of the coffin."

"You said it, not me."

"At least I'm not homeless, unwed, and pregnant at fifty."

Zinnia pursed her lips. "Forty-nine."

"If you say so." Zirconia waved away the inevitable age argument and moved on to the task at hand. "I'm glad you're here, because we have some important business to discuss."

Zinnia said nothing. She looked tired yet beautiful. She had that glow of pregnancy.

Zirconia couldn't remember having had that glow. She remembered being sweaty.

Finally, Zinnia said, "What business?"

"Resist your contrary urges to say no until you hear me out," Zirconia said, talking quickly as she pulled on her clothes, which were a freshly-washed version of the same clothes she wore every day—a perfectly tailored white blouse with impeccable tan slacks.

"You're the contrary one," Zinnia said. "You ought to see a therapist about that."

"Maybe I will," Zirconia said. "Or an exorcist."

Zinnia barked out a laugh. She hadn't been expecting that.

Zirconia ran her fingers through her hair and shook out her silky blackened locks.

"I found us the perfect house," she said. "It will fit all of us, and there are a few spots that would be perfect for Baby Bearclaw." Bearclaw was not the baby's name. The expectant mother was leaning toward Fyrsil, of all things.

Zinnia had a dazed look. "You said I'm fifty. I'm not fifty, am I?"

"You're not listening to me."

Zinnia shook her head. "And why would you think I undressed you?"

Zirconia snapped her fingers. "Focus."

"Something's not right." Zinnia glanced around. "The energy in here is stagnant, pooled up. We ought to check the perimeter wards."

"Check later," Zirconia said. "The thing about the house is, it's not a rental. I know we were planning to wait until all the insurance money came in from both Zara's house and yours, but I couldn't—"

Zinnia wasn't paying any attention at all. She stared into the distance, muttering to herself.

"I was forty-seven when I moved back to Wisteria. That was the year Zara moved here... which makes me..." She counted on her fingers.

Zirconia looked around the hotel suite like a person who suspects they are part of an unfunny hidden-camera prank show, which was redundant, because all hidden-camera prank shows were universally unfunny.

Just then, the cat jumped onto the counter, knocking down a stack of paperbacks.

"Not on the counter," Zinnia said, half-heartedly shooing the cat away.

"Ham," said the cat.

"Find me," screeched the green budgie from its cage. "Find me! Find me!"

Zirconia was sick of the bird. She leaned down, looked it straight in the beady little eyes and said, with her unbridled vampire snarl, "I have found you."

The bird shed a trio of feathers, slowly swung to the bottom side of its swing perch, and dropped to the floor of its cage.

Dead.

Zinnia gasped and ran to the cage. She checked the creature's vital signs, then stared at her vampire sister in horror.

"You killed him," the witch said. "You killed Marzipants."

"Did not."

"Did too."

"Old age killed him."

"An old vampire killed him."

"Stop trying to pick a fight with me," Zirconia said. "We have important business to take care of."

The cat said, "Ham?"

Zirconia turned her irritation on the furry monster. "The ham in the fridge is for people, you foul-mouthed freeloader. Not another word from you. Ever."

The cat looked up, twitched, and fell over.

Dead.

"Oh, no," Zinnia said. "Oh, no, no, no."

She checked the cat's vitals then hissed at her sister, "How could you? Zara is going to be crushed. This will set her back months."

Zirconia took a moment to consider her options. She wouldn't get very far with her money goals if everyone was in a tizzy planning pet funerals.

She did what any pet-owning vampire would do.

She used one fang to pierce a hole in the finger, and prepared to give some of her life to them.

"They're not dead," Zirconia said to reassure her sister, and any circulating bird and cat spirits. "They're not dead until they're dead and cold."

Zinnia muttered, "You're the one who's dead and cold."

Zirconia ignored the insults and used her blood—her precious life force—to revive both of the ungrateful pets.

As the bird and cat revived—with an extra spring in their step—none of them thanked their vampire caretaker.

Zinnia regarded her sister with squinty suspicion. "You look very practiced at reviving dead pets."

Zirconia could not deny that she may have performed that particular task a half dozen times over the past few months.

Zinnia's eyes narrowed to the point of almost being closed. "And Marzipants and Boa don't seem that surprised, either."

Indeed, the animals were now grooming themselves as if nothing had happened.

"There's no need to discuss the matter further," Zirconia said. "Now help me get the deposit for the house."

"What house?"

"The perfect house. For all of us. And Baby Bearclaw. I already signed a deal on it yesterday."

Zinnia's whole body shook. She looked like she might give birth right then and there, weeks early.

"You did not," she said with a loud exhale. "But of course you did. Without consulting any of us. Oh, this is so like you, Zirconia."

"Wait until you see this place. You'll eat your words."

Zirconia grabbed her purse and dug through it for the purchase papers. She also had the printed copy of the tour package, with plenty of glossy photos showcasing the crisp, never-used rooms.

Except she didn't.

"Someone must have cleaned out my purse," Zirconia said. "Were you digging through here last night? If you want some makeup to improve your coloring, just ask. You don't have to steal my lipstick. We're not children anymore."

"Never mind about your lipstick. We ought to—"

"I don't care about the lipstick. This house is not the sort of thing that comes up all the time. We have to seize the day. We—"

"We'll deal with that later," Zinnia said tiredly. "We ought to have a family meeting. Zara needs to talk to you about something."

There was a rustling sound on the other side of the bedroom door. Zara was getting out of bed.

"Hold that thought," Zirconia said, her mind reeling as she imagined losing the house over a few stupid errors. "I must have left the paperwork downstairs in the lounge. I'll run down, grab the papers, and come right back up. Give me a dirty look if you agree to my plan."

Zinnia gave her a dirty look.

Zirconia let out a snort of triumph and raced out of the room.

She was already whipping down the stairwell at vampire speed when a puff of smoke ebbed from the suite, into the hallway.

CHAPTER 13

Zirconia was searching the couch cushions in the hotel's lounge when she was approached by a member of the staff. It was the same young man who'd been preventing her from getting a drink the last two mornings.

He said, "Can I help you with something?"

"Obviously you can," she said in a friendly way, like she was talking to an old pal. They'd developed a bit of rapport the night before, and he'd even told her his name—not that she remembered it.

"Okay," he said with a light smile. "What are we doing here? Explain it to me like I'm an idiot."

"*We* are looking for some paperwork I left down here." She tossed cushions left and right, revealing only coins. "It has to be here."

"If you've lost something, we could check the hotel's Lost and Found."

Zirconia shuddered at the thought of her precious papers mingling with the assortment of debris left by strangers and other guests.

Other guests.

Like the Darnells.

"No need," she said, brushing the dust from her hands. "I just realized where my papers are. The Darnells must have them. That's the nice couple who extended their stay. What room are they in?"

"I can't give out the room numbers of other guests."

"Oh, but you can." She waved a little glamour his way, but the amulet he still wore under his shirt kept shielding his mind.

"I can't do that," he said.

"Then I'll simply knock on every door in the place."

The fellow looked for a moment like he might vomit.

"Or... you could give me their room number," she said. "You saw all of us socializing last night. You know they are friends."

She watched his expression as reason and logic overrode his strange zeal for the rules. "Did you say the Darnells? They're actually checking out right now. I saw them at the front desk a few minutes ago."

Checking out? But they couldn't leave yet.

As she left for the front desk, the young man called out behind her, "You're welcome."

The lobby was empty. There was nobody at the desk.

The scent of the lotions and styling products that the Darnells used lingered in the air like neon arrows. Tracking people by scent could be ridiculously easy for a vampire.

Their car was parked outside the front doors. Debbie was climbing in the passenger side.

Zirconia stepped out into a furnace blast of hot sunshine just as the car drove away.

She stared after the red tail lights, barely visible in the brightness of the day.

Had Darren and Debbie actually checked out of the hotel without saying goodbye, much less finalizing the paperwork on the real estate deal?

Her cheeks and chest burned with the sting of rejection.

She'd been used.

They had never been her friends. The Darnells had only been interested in her money—the commission on the real estate transaction.

She clenched both fists and shook a curse at the vehicle, but it was too late. The car was out of range. Even if she still retained her witch ability to hex people, that curse would only start a dime-sized patch of rust on the car somewhere it wouldn't be noticed for five years.

A taxi pulled up.

It was the old-fashioned style some of the companies in town used, with a yellow body, and black and white checkered accents.

Zirconia didn't like real taxis. Their back seats resonated with the energy of too many strangers' anxieties. And other things.

She slid into the back seat anyway, if only to escape the relentless onslaught from the sun.

The driver said, “Where to, ma'am?”

“Follow that car,” she said, pointing in the direction the Darnells had gone. “Hit the gas and spare the brakes. Don't you dare lose them.”

“Yes, ma'am.”

CHAPTER 14

The taxi driver doggedly tailed the Darnells all the way to Dreamland Coffee.

The couple got out of their car and approached the coffee shop at a leisurely pace, as though seeing it for the first time.

They lingered on the sidewalk, holding hands and reading the menu posted in the window before going in. Debbie leaned her head on Darren's shoulder, still holding her husband's hand.

In the back seat of the taxi, Zirconia shook out her own hands, which had been clenched in cool, dry fists.

She'd been furious at the Darnells for leaving town, but had she been too hasty?

A softness settled over her.

Maybe it was the ruthless efficiency of the taxi driver, or maybe she was losing her sharp edges in her old age. Whatever the cause, she experienced a change of heart.

She must have jumped to conclusions about the Darnells because of her past. She would always meet new people, and get excited about finding suitable companions, only to be dumped when they didn't feel the same way in return. It had happened far too many times.

Today, however, felt like a day for second chances.

She would give the Darnells a second chance. Or, at the very least, make sure they stuck around long enough to close up the deal on the house.

Zirconia paid the driver, and entered the coffee shop.

She was greeted by the komodo dragon shifter working at the front counter in human form. Did his mistress ever give him a day off?

"Hey, Toots," Humphrey said to Zirconia.

She walked past him to the community corkboard, where Debbie and Darren were browsing flyers for outdoor concerts and garage sales.

"Fancy meeting you two here," Zirconia said neutrally, testing the waters. "How is the traveling real estate dream team this morning?"

Darren turned to her with a big grin. "Hard at work, or hardly workin', pick one!"

He offered his hand to shake, but Zirconia didn't see it.

Her focus had gone to the corkboard, and a familiar-looking sheet of paper. The one listing a certain house for sale or rent.

How could that be?

Darren rambled about something else, but she didn't hear anything over her pulse rushing in her ears.

"This shouldn't be here," she said, yanking down the paper listing. "This is *my* house now. Mine. Fair and square."

She handed the paper to the couple so they could share in her outrage.

"It sure does look like a great house on paper," Darren said, still grinning.

"Congratulations," Debbie said, smiling hard enough to make her eyes small.

Despite her confusion over the paper, Zirconia was glad to see the couple.

Based on their friendliness, she concluded that they hadn't been ditching her. They'd just needed a coffee. They had only checked out of the Cerulean Lagoon to switch to a better hotel for the next night. Who would blame them?

Debbie looked up from the paper listing and asked, "Do you have a big family to fill up all four bedrooms?"

"Getting bigger every day," Zirconia said. "Did I tell you my sister is pregnant? At fifty?"

The two exchanged a confused look. As they ought to.

"I know," Zirconia said. "She thought it was the Change of Life. Her Second Spring. But no. She was just plain ol' knocked up."

"I've heard of such things happening," Debbie said with a shudder.

"We never had kids," Darren said. "Plenty of cats and dogs, but no kids. What's your sister's name?"

"Didn't I tell you? Her name is Zinnia. Like the flower." Zirconia wasn't too surprised they'd forgotten. People often got her family members mixed up because of the similar Z names.

In unison, Debbie and Darren said, "Lovely name."

"She's also a witch, like my daughter," Zirconia said dryly. "I'm sure the Cerulean Lagoon will be happy to get rid of all its resident witches soon."

"Oh," Debbie said eagerly, her eyes wide. "The witches who live in the hotel!" She elbowed her husband. "We *did* hear about that."

Darren said with a forced casual tone, "How many witches are in your, uh, family?"

"Depends on how you categorize. In the immediate family, somewhere between two and four."

Just then, the owner of the coffee shop strode up to them on her long, skinny legs. She looked down her nose at all three.

The owner said, "Zirconia, are you gossiping about everyone, or just your family?"

Zirconia pointed at the black-haired woman and said to the Darnells, "You must know this witch. She roasts the best beans in town, and she flies a mean broomstick."

"Not lately," the witch said. "No thanks to the devil himself, and the coven's foolishness."

Debbie clasped her hands together. "The coven!" She elbowed Darren again. "Did you hear that? This beautiful lady is in a coven." One of her hands fluttered, as though she was feeling a temptation to touch the other woman's long, silky hair.

The witch pointed to her chest. “I'm Maisy. Maisy Nix. Poor old Zirconia can never remember my name.” She gave them one of her carnivorous smiles. “And what manner of creatures are you?”

“Real estate agents,” Darren said.

“They're mages of some sort,” Zirconia cut in to explain. “I haven't figured out the specifics because these two are always plying me with alcohol. Things got out of hand again yet again last night at the hotel.”

Debbie giggled into her hand. “We may have overindulged. I don't remember much of last night after Darren jumped in the pool after the swans.”

Again with the swans? Zirconia had turned in too early, and missed out on the fun.

Maisy said, “Since you all overindulged last night, I won't keep you waiting for your brew.” She snapped her fingers for Humphrey, who came running.

The komodo shifter had an odd gait, like a child pretending to ride an invisible pony. The poor thing hadn't adapted to having two feet instead of four.

Maisy whispered something in her pet's ear, then left him with the others.

“I will bring your order to your table,” the cute-but-simple fellow said. “My name is Humphrey.”

“It's on your name tag,” Zirconia said. “You don't have to tell me every time we meet.”

He said to her, “You do not have a name tag. You are the lady who doesn't like jam, or complimentary garlic bread.”

To the visitors, he said, “You are from out of town. Your clothes are not the same as the clothes people typically wear.”

Darren said, “You got it, my man,” and offered Humphrey a fist bump.

Zirconia got a funny feeling, like when she picked up a decorating magazine and didn't realize right away that she'd already read it a month before. She would keep turning pages, wondering why the rooms didn't look surprising or innovative in any way.

Darren whipped out a business card for Humphrey.

"We're only in town visiting, but if you have an eye on a property, let me know and I'll help you write up an offer. My clients always get their dream homes, guaranteed."

Humphrey nodded like it was the first time he'd met the Darnells, even though they'd gone through the same routine the previous day. He was such a simple creature.

The three took a seat at the same table they'd used the day before, and Humphrey brought over three mugs of purple brew.

Darren sniffed the purple coffee and said, "This smells so darn good, I don't know if I should drink it or dump it over my head!"

Humphrey said, "Drinking it will be more hygienic."

"That's a compliment where I'm from," Darren said with a big laugh.

Zirconia stared at the two men making the now-eerily-familiar exchange. Had they not said those exact things, word for word, the day before? Humphrey was a simple creature, and Darren was a mage, but even so, it was odd.

Very odd.

The Darnells took their first sips.

Zirconia looked at Debbie, and predicted the woman was about to say *very nice*.

"Very nice," Debbie said.

Zirconia looked at Darren, and predicted he was about to order another round.

Darren pointed at Humphrey. "Get the next round started because this one tastes like another!"

Humphrey shuffled off to make more of the purple brew.

Zirconia looked down at her mug. Humphrey had poured her foamed milk in the shape of a crooked heart, the same as the day before. Exactly the same.

Zirconia stood abruptly. "I need to do something," she said.

"Aww," Debbie said, pouting. "Do you have to leave already? We just met."

"We did not," Zirconia said. "We met two days ago."

The two Darnells exchanged couples-only looks that said *our new friend may be exhibiting some red flags*.

"You two should be concerned," Zirconia said, and then she made her pronouncement: "Someone has been wiping your memory."

Yes. Someone had been wiping their memories. That was the most logical explanation for what was happening.

Darren laughed. "And that someone's name is Jack Daniels. Or was it Jose Cuervo?"

"This is more than the effects of alcohol," Zirconia said. "Keys." She held out her hand.

Darren jerked his head back. "You want to drive my car?"

"I'm not going to fly a broomstick," she snapped.

He looked at his wife, who gave him a little nod, and handed her the keys.

Zirconia took off at top vampire speed.

There was no time to waste. The Darnells weren't just friends, they were her real estate dream team.

If she didn't get to the bottom of who or what was erasing their memories, she would lose her dream house, and then the last three days would have been a complete waste of time.

CHAPTER 15

City Hall - Wisteria Permits Department

Zirconia strode past the menagerie of employees in the Wisteria Permits Department. Did every one of them have to be so quirky? She went straight into her sister's private office, decorated with a floral wallpaper that didn't suit a corporate environment.

Zinnia Riddle was typing away, facing a computer screen.

Without looking up, she said, "You don't have an appointment."

"It's me," Zirconia said.

"I know it's you."

"Do you?"

Zinnia reluctantly glanced up, quirking one eyebrow. "You think I don't know the sound of my own sister marching on the warpath? What's flown up your chimney now?"

"Someone's been erasing people's memories."

"And?"

"And they shouldn't be," Zirconia said.

Zinnia leaned over and called around her sister, "Xavier, could you bring me a Form 100CX?"

"This is important," Zirconia said.

"I gathered that," Zinnia said calmly. "The Form 100CX is for reporting the unauthorized use of memory alteration." She pursed her lips. "The funny thing is, most of the time the guilty party that people are reporting for memory alteration is the same guilty party I'm looking at right now."

"I don't have time to fill out forms," Zirconia said.

The young man ran up to the doorway of the office while his other quirky coworkers stared curiously.

Zirconia held her hand up in front of the face of the young man. He halted in his tracks, nervously twitching the paperwork in his hands.

He said, "Uh, Zinnia?"

"Never mind, Xavier," the witch said with a weary sigh. "We ought to assign one of our interns to follow my sister around town. It would result in a net savings of countless staff hours."

"I could do that," Xavier said eagerly. "Can I do that? Please?"

Zirconia turned and looked him up and down. Follow her? He wouldn't last half a day.

She said it. "You wouldn't last half a day."

"I wouldn't, huh?" He puffed up his chest. "Care to make it interesting?"

Zinnia, who remained seated at her computer, waved for her coworker to back down and return to his workstation.

"They're like a box of chocolates around here," Zirconia said. "Mostly nuts."

Zinnia didn't laugh at her sister's excellent joke. She said in a hushed tone, "He really ought to be promoted out of here. He's under-utilized."

"What are you talking about?"

"He's under-utilized," Zinnia repeated. "He has tons of potential, but nobody—"

Zirconia cut her sister off. "I heard you," she said. "I just don't understand why we're still talking about Zachary."

"Xavier."

Zirconia stamped her foot. "Somebody's been wiping memories."

"Somebody besides you?"

"Why would I wipe the memories of my own real estate agents?"

Zinnia shrugged. “I don't know why you do half of the things you do, but I suspect Pinot Grigio may be involved.”

“I don't have time for your little barbs. If I don't get to the bottom of this, we're going to lose our dream house.”

“*Our* dream house?”

“Yes. The one we're all going to move into, if I can get the deal to go through.”

Zinnia squeezed the bridge of her nose. “I remember now. This is what you were going on about this morning. Forgive me for not figuring it out sooner. I suppose I was distracted at the time by you murdering both of Zara's pets.”

“They'll be fine,” Zirconia said. “I've resurrected them both many times.”

Zinnia's hazel eyes widened.

“Ha ha,” Zirconia said. “Just kidding.” She was not.

“Did you talk to Zara?”

“Not yet. Are you going to help me figure out who's been wiping people's memories? It's important.”

“Sure.” Zinnia reached for a paper notebook with sloth-like speed, and opened it to a fresh page.

She wrote on the page: *New business: run tandem spell to audit for unauthorized memory wipes.*

“Can't you do it right now?”

“I need another witch. It's a tandem spell. You know that.”

Zirconia pointed her thumb over her shoulder at the collection of mixed nuts in the main part of the office. “What about your buddy Marzipants?”

Her sister tilted her head. “Do you mean Margaret? Margaret Mills? You ought to know, Marzipants is the name of the budgie. Have you been taking dirt naps in brainweevil territory?”

Zirconia didn't dignify the question with a response.

“Margaret doesn't do spells during office hours,” Zinnia said. Her eyes added, *except for when she does*.

"But you have to promise you'll figure it out," Zirconia said. "As soon as possible."

"If anyone is casting memory spells—anyone who isn't currently in this room—we will get to the bottom of it. I promise. My word is my bond."

"Good," Zirconia said.

"Is there anything else I can help you with?"

"As a matter of fact, there is one other thing."

Zirconia grabbed a visitor's chair, circled around the desk with it, and sat next to her sister. She poked at the computer screen. "How do you use this thing to get money?"

Stiffly, Zinnia said, "I don't know what you're talking about."

"The stocks and bonds. The trading stuff," Zirconia said. "Do the thing where you make a million dollars out of nothing by using all the... money computers."

Zinnia flicked her wrist, and used a spell to close the door to the office. The witches had suffered a loss of some powers, and were not able to do quick-and-easy levitation, but some specific spells for moving objects still worked.

Zirconia was all out of patience. "Well?"

Zinnia spoke solemnly as she stared down at her hands. "I don't do that anymore."

"You have to do it just one more time. It's important. Oh, Zinnia, you should see this house. It's everything I've ever dreamed of and more. Plus there's so much room for the baby. You need to get us the money. It's for the baby."

"No good can come from manipulating the stock market," she said.

"Tell that to everyone who got rich doing it," Zirconia replied.

Zinnia crossed her arms over her growing belly. "I won't do it. My decisions affect more than just me. You wouldn't know. You always put yourself first."

"I do not."

"You do." Zinnia made a show of fake-yawning. "Let's not go down this road again."

"Fine. If you won't get the money, show me how, so I can do it."

"It's not that simple."

"Are you saying I'm not as smart as you?"

Zinnia pursed her lips very tightly.

"Show me the basics," Zirconia said. "Show me how to set up an account, and make the first pile of money. Then I'll just repeat that until I have enough for the house."

The redheaded witch stared at her a long moment before saying, "Sure, why not? I could use a laugh."

She showed her vampire sister how to set up a trading account, log in, and make trades.

She even transferred some of her own cash into the account to get Zirconia started.

CHAPTER 16

Zirconia would never have admitted that her sister was a good teacher, but she was.

The vampire was actually getting the hang of how the stock market worked.

It was so obvious, once you saw it. The whole racket was just a big, giant gambling game. Especially the big players who claimed to be above such things, like banks. She'd always known the financial system was one third magical thinking and one third magical smoke being blown up everyone's back end, but she'd never realized how nakedly obvious it was.

"That one," the vampire said excitedly, pointing at a stock that was currently taking a giant leap up. "Buy that one. It's going up."

"If you say so," Zinnia said ominously.

The trade went through with the ring of a tiny bell.

The stock immediately began to drop.

"Stop it," Zirconia said. "Stop it right now."

"Do you want to sell? Lock in your loss?"

"I don't know! Why's it going down? Zinnia, stop it. Make it go up again."

"That's not how it works," Zinnia said smugly.

"This isn't fair," Zirconia said. "You tricked me. I bet it was you who's been wiping my friends' memories, too."

Zinnia arched an eyebrow. "You have *friends*? This is a new development."

Zirconia growled at her sister. If the woman wasn't pregnant, Zirconia might have done more than just growl.

"Oh, get over yourself," Zinnia said, then she shooed her sister away from the computer. "I showed you the basics of stock trading. Now leave me alone. You ought to go back to the hotel suite and clean up the mess *your* offspring made there."

"I'm going to get the house money," Zirconia said with a defiant huff. "I'm going to get it all by myself, and you'll be sorry, because when we move in, you won't even get a bedroom. You'll have to live in the broom closet, with all the other dusty old things."

Zinnia feigned surprise. "I'll have to share a room with dusty old things?" She batted her eyelashes. "You mean you and I are going to be roommates again? Just like the old days?"

Zirconia didn't have to take this steaming heap of abuse.

She was in the right here, and Zinnia was in the wrong.

Zirconia was trying to provide a suitable home for the whole family, and, as usual, Zinnia was making it *all about her*.

The vampire got up and stomped out of her sister's private office. It was a relief to get away from all that garish floral wallpaper. The stuff actually had metallic glints. As if giant flowers weren't bad enough.

Out in the larger room, the menagerie of Wisteria Permits Department Employees stared at Zirconia with wide eyes.

"Get back to work," Zirconia snapped at them. "Taxpayers like me are paying your salaries."

The only man in the office that was halfways attractive said to her with a sneer, "You need a job first to pay taxes."

"I'm a consultant," she said.

He gave her an openly mocking grin. "Oh, yeah?"

She knew who he was, including his powers and his weakness. He was a gnome. His name was Gerome or something like that. Gerome the gnome.

More importantly, she was a vampire, and she didn't need to take his derision.

She used her vampire speed, and was at Gerome the Gnome's side before he knew it. She grabbed both of his knees, lifted his lower legs, and manually stomped his feet three times on the office floor.

His gnome powers activated, and he disappeared instantly.

Reboot.

Back to home base.

Gnome powers were comically simple.

Then Zirconia sped right back to where she'd been standing an instant earlier.

The woman who shared a desk with the gnome jumped up in alarm, knocking over her Diet Coke.

"Gavin?" The woman gave Zirconia an accusatory look. "Gavin's gone. What did you do?"

"Who's Gavin?"

The woman pointed one of her long, colorfully lacquered nails at the empty chair across from her. It was still rotating.

Zirconia barely glanced at the chair as she headed for the door. "Like a bad penny, I'm sure he'll be back," she called over her shoulder.

Unfortunately, activating the gnome's powers and using them against him hadn't cheered her up as much as she'd hoped.

Humiliation and failure still burned in her gut as she walked down the hallway.

She reached the lobby, where a pianist was playing a grand piano in the atrium.

Zirconia didn't even notice, even though it was one of her favorite classical pieces.

Why had she even expected her sister to help?

This was exactly why it was important to handle everything yourself and not get others involved.

Bitter failure hung around her like a storm cloud, obfuscating her perception of her surroundings.

It wasn't until she stepped outside of the City Hall building that she realized she was being followed.

It was one of the mixed nuts from the WPD box of chocolate weirdos.

He was trying to creep closer.

"I can smell you following me, Zachary," she said. "You couldn't be less covert if you were covered in salami and silver bells."

"It's Xavier."

"What's the difference?"

Without hesitation, the young man said, "Five out of seven letters."

"That was quick," Zirconia said.

She kept walking, but she turned her head and looked at him in a new light. Contrary to her earlier impressions, he was actually more attractive than the gnome. Over the past half-year, he'd had a minor growth spurt. He'd grown into his bravado.

The fellow had no powers, not even mage powers, but at least he was trying. People without powers only became Nothing People when they stopped trying.

The young man—Xavier Batista—grinned.

Zirconia said, "You may be slightly smarter than the other oddballs you work with. That means you may be under-utilized." She left out any acknowledgement that her sister may have been right. "Have you considered a career change?"

"Every day," Xavier said, trotting to keep up with Zirconia's fast strides. "I did some intern work for your daughter back before Christmas, but it didn't work out."

"It didn't work out," Zirconia said. "Didn't she murder you, and then resurrect you?"

He looked embarrassed. "She didn't mean it."

"But she did," Zirconia said. "It happened."

"It happened," he agreed.

"And yet nobody holds it against her," Zirconia said. "But when I murder and resurrect people, it's always such a big deal."

"You can murder me," he said eagerly.

"Too easy."

He looked around the side street they were moving swiftly along. The weather was what non-vampire people would deem a perfect day for a stroll, but they were moving much faster than a stroll. A few bystanders were regarding them with curiosity.

"Where are we going?" Xavier asked.

"Your place," she said.

He stopped in his tracks. "I, uh..."

"I assume you have a computer there."

"Oh, uh, yeah." He jogged to catch up with her. "I thought maybe you, uh..."

"You thought maybe I *what*?"

He squirmed, which was impressive, seeing as how he was also jogging.

Zirconia's outrage about her mistreatment at the office finally dissipated.

Oh, how she loved making people squirm. Especially when those people were men full of young, tasty blood.

Xavier coughed into his fist then said, "What do you need my computer for?"

"Making money. Do you like money?"

"Yes, ma'am."

"If you're not a taxi driver, I am not a ma'am. Don't ever call me ma'am again, or I will wear your entrails as a vest."

He nodded to show he understood completely.

CHAPTER 17

Two Hours Later

"This is going too slow," Zirconia said.

She couldn't bear the sight of the computer screen much longer, but the view inside Xavier's apartment was even worse. After only two hours there, she had come to despise every square inch of the place. It contained nothing of beauty. Only black faux-leather furniture held together with duct tape, and dusty electronics. It was the exact opposite of an inspiring space. The only thing it had going for it was thick blackout curtains to keep the blasted sun out.

"But you're up on your trades," Xavier said, pointing to the screen. "You're winning."

"If you think *this* is winning, you must leave this town at once, and see more of the world."

"But—"

He wasn't grasping the seriousness of the situation, so she picked up the computer and threw it against the wall.

Xavier reacted strongly. He reacted like it wasn't a regular thing for people to pick up his computer and throw it against the wall.

"We need more computers," Zirconia said. "If I could make trades on a dozen computers simultaneously, I'd be able to raise the funds for the house deposit by midnight." She waved at her protege. "Procure for me a dozen computers. I'll take my dinner break, then get back to it."

He seemed very distracted by the smoking wreckage of the first computer.

She snapped her fingers in front of his face.

Xavier jerked his head up. "Uh, even if we could get more computers, you won't be able to trade again until tomorrow, when the markets open." He checked the time on his phone. "They're about to close, in ten minutes."

She could have screamed, but there would be no point, because her sister wasn't there. The same sister who had failed to mention that there were time constraints. It was such a Zinnia thing to leave out vital details.

Xavier squirmed. "Do you want me to, uh, get you something to eat?"

"Not yet. Money first, celebrations later. Time for Plan B. How many guns and ski masks do you have on hand?"

His eyes widened. "We can't rob a bank."

She sighed. "You're right. They never keep that much cash on hand."

"You want this money for a house, right? I may not be a homeowner myself, but I know there's a period of time —escrow, I think?—where the buyer can get things in order. That is, assuming it's a... conventional deal."

"How much time?"

"It should say on the contract."

"I don't have a copy of the contract, and my agents have had their memories wiped by... my enemies."

"Wouldn't the seller have a copy?"

"Shh," she said. "I'm thinking."

Zirconia remembered a detail from the house tour. There had been a makeshift desk in one of the empty bedrooms. A folding table and some office equipment. That must have been where the owner's niece had been conducting business. A copy of the sales contract was probably sitting right on the desk, in plain sight.

She got up, picked up a motorcycle helmet, and tossed it at Xavier.

He barely caught it, and gave her a stunned look.

"You're so fast," he said. "I didn't even see you move."

"That's kind of the whole point."

He stared at her in awe. "What... what... what's it like?"

"What do you think it's like?"

"I don't know. That's why I asked."

"It's vastly superior to being slow," she said. "Put on your helmet, and let's go."

CHAPTER 18

Zirconia and her protege walked up to the house that was all corners.

"Wow. This place is so cool," Xavier said. "It's like the mansion that a comic book villain lives in."

"The villain? Why not the hero?"

"Heroes live in conventional houses," he said.

"Not always."

"Pretty much always," he said knowingly. "Pick up any comic book."

"Life is not a comic book," Zirconia said. "I want you to promise you'll stop reading those things. They'll rot your brain."

"Okay."

Zirconia did a double take. Had she used her persuasion powers on him? She didn't think so. And yet he'd agreed to her command so easily. It had to be a sign, a sign that he'd been in dire need of a wise mentor such as herself.

Xavier said, "I don't like reading, anyway."

"Atta boy." She patted him on the head like a dog.

They stepped up to the door, and she rang the doorbell. It made the electric buzz that she liked even better the third time. And nobody inside was yelling "doorbell!"

The door opened to reveal an old man in an even older suit and a bowler hat. The suit was of good quality, a dark wool, and he'd paired it with a dusty-rose shirt that brought color to his face, and a bright yellow cravat that brought a twinkle to his eyes.

He was Dorian Dabrowski, the owner of the house. He was the wealthy gentleman who'd bought the modern home as a long-term investment, then allowed it to sit vacant until now. He'd been preserving it for the Riddle family, and hadn't even known.

"Mr. Dabrowski," Zirconia said warmly, offering her hand. "Mr. Dorian Dabrowski."

Zirconia wasn't great with names, unless the owner of the name was wealthy. Those names, she remembered.

He shook her hand. "You look so familiar, Miss... ?"

"Riddle," she said.

"Ah. Any relation to the lovely redhead who works at the library?"

"She's my daughter."

Xavier, who had been silently standing beside her, cleared his throat. He got two points for technically waiting to be introduced, but lost five points for being impertinent. He was currently at minus three points.

Zirconia said with a flourish, "Mr. Dabrowski, this is my associate, Zachary Bonesaw."

She gave Xavier the slightest smirk to let him know she was joking about his name. She could make jokes. Her daughter Zara wasn't the only one who offered merriment.

Xavier shook the older man's hand and muttered his actual name, but very softly. It must have barely reached Dabrowski's ears, which were filled with white hair and resembled the ends of a rolled-up sheepskin rug.

Dabrowski asked, "To what do I owe the pleasure?"

"I'm the buyer of the house," Zirconia said.

"You are?" He seemed surprised.

"Yes. But I've misplaced my copy of the contract. I was hoping you could supply me with a copy."

"How unusual," he said, and he backed into the house, waving for them to follow him in.

Zirconia attempted to step over the threshold, but a force field stopped her.

How odd.

She could have used brute force to get through the home's defense against vampires, but there would be side effects. And besides, she shouldn't have to. She'd been invited inside the house two days earlier. The invite should have still been in effect. There'd been no issue yesterday.

"That's not right," she said under her breath.

Xavier, who'd already entered the house, noticed her hesitation. He stepped back out again.

Discreetly, he said, "What is it? Do you need an invitation?"

"No," she snapped at her protege. "I'll just stand on the front step all day like a traveling salesman."

Meanwhile, Mr. Dabrowski was using his pinkie fingers to jostle the white fur inside his ears. "What's that you're saying? Is there a problem?"

"No problem," Zirconia said evenly.

Xavier said to the old man, "You have to invite her in."

Mr. Dabrowski's eyes sparkled. "Like a vampire?"

"No," Xavier said, a little too quickly. "It's just, uh, manners."

"Very well, then," Mr. Dabrowski said. "Come in, come in."

The tension in the building's envelope immediately released.

Zirconia felt heavy, like she'd been in a swimming pool when all the water had suddenly drained out.

She was tired.

So tired.

How had she not noticed how tired she was?

She licked her lips. When had she last taken her artificial blood serum?

She really needed to settle this house purchase so she could focus on taking better care of herself.

Xavier grabbed her elbow and helped her over the threshold like she was an invalid. She gritted her sharp teeth, and allowed him to assist her. It never hurt to have people think you were weaker than you were.

They followed Mr. Dabrowski to the home's makeshift office, where he managed to produce—as much to his own surprise as anyone else's—a copy of the sales contract.

Zirconia looked at the first page.

She should not have been surprised to see what she did.

Given how the last couple of days had been going, and how everything that could go wrong had gone wrong, she should not have been at all surprised to see that the buyer listed on the contract was not her. Not her!

And yet she *was* surprised.

"Floopy doop," she said, followed by something a little stronger.

Not only had her unseen enemies erased the memories of her real estate agents, but they'd also managed to erase her contract.

This was going to take some effort to untangle.

CHAPTER 19

Several Hours Later

Zirconia and Xavier entered the lobby of the Cerulean Lagoon Hotel and Spa.

The Spa part of the name was a lie. The spa, such as it was, had been closed for several months. Something about an incident back in February involving some strange "birds" that set all the cedar panels on fire. Probably wyverns. But perhaps not. These days, it seemed like some establishments used any excuse to raise prices and decrease services.

Xavier said, "I need to hit the little boy's room." He headed in the direction of the hotel's cafe and bathrooms.

Zirconia pitied him for his small, human-sized bladder. One of the perks of being a vampire was increased efficiency in the digestive system. Gone were several unnecessary lengths of intestine, leaving more room for a bladder, or whatever else a vampire might need. They had very large spleens, all the better for management of new blood cells with superior mitochondria.

"I'll be in the lounge," Zirconia said.

He paused. "You want me to stick around?"

"Do you have somewhere better to be?"

"Nope. I'm all yours." He gave her two thumbs up as he hurriedly backed away to empty his Nothing Person bladder.

Zirconia entered the hotel's lounge by herself.

"What a surprise," said the young man working there.

He used a snarky tone that Zirconia didn't appreciate.

He went on, "It's a shocker to see you here when we're actually open for dr—"

She put her hand inside his mouth and squeezed his tongue between her thumb and forefinger.

He stopped talking and gave her a startled look.

People did that when a vampire had their tongue.

She released his tongue but didn't remove her hand.

He had to retreat physically, taking a step backward, and spitting out all of Zirconia's slender fingers.

He touched the amulet through his shirt and stammered,"You-you put your hand in my mouth. I was talking, and you— you just—"

"Let this be a lesson to you," Zirconia said. "That amulet may protect you from some magic, but there is no type of ward or protection that cannot be defeated by a clever foe."

"But you can't do that," he said. "It isn't fair."

"Life isn't fair," Zirconia said with a sigh. "If you insist on standing here and stating the obvious, I'll play. Yes, I put my fingers in your mouth. No, it wasn't fair. I have extreme speed, and slim fingers."

"You're a va—" He coughed again.

"Yes. I'm a vampire. Also, I'm thirsty. Put it together, and I'm a thirsty vampire. If only there were a place I could go to get a drink. Oh, what's this? We seem to be standing inside a well-stocked lounge." She walked up to the bar and scanned the mirrored wall of bottles. "Did I say well-stocked? I meant to say adequately stocked."

The young man, who knew he'd been defeated, ran behind the bar. He started filling glasses with ice cubes.

"That's better," Zirconia said. "Start with two Campari and sodas."

Xavier jogged up to join her, returning from the bathroom.

She turned to Xavier. "What's your poison?"

"Bad relationships," Xavier said.

The bartender snorted knowingly.

"Make it four Campari and sodas," Zirconia said to the bartender.

She and Xavier took a table near the piano just as the pianist stood to go on a break. The lounge was quiet. The air smelled of floor polish and the acrid sweat of whomever worked the floor polisher.

Zirconia nodded at the piano. “Do you play?”

“No.” His head dropped forward several inches. “I love music, and I love the idea of playing, but I never took a single lesson.” He looked down at his hands sheepishly. “I'm such a Nothing Person.”

“It's true.”

He looked up, startled by her honesty.

She shrugged one shoulder. “If you were my child, I'd be exactly as disappointed as I imagine your parents are.”

He looked around, like he was contemplating an escape, yet too intrigued to actually leave. She'd seen that look before. Plenty.

The bartender arrived with four tall glasses of pink fizzy drinks, and a platter of nachos.

“Fully loaded,” the young man said.

Before the bartender/waiter left, Xavier shoved nachos into his mouth with one hand, while holding the other hand up in a fist.

The two men bumped their fists together. They knew each other, apparently.

He said, “Kitchen screwed up, so you get free nachos. You're welcome, man.”

“I owe you,” Xavier said, spraying yellow cornmeal crumbs on the table.

Zirconia put two and two together.

She'd suspected that her granddaughter had been the one who'd supplied the young man with the anti-vampire amulet, yet the real accomplice had been under her nose the whole day.

After the bartender left, Zirconia said, “I see how things are. You pretend to be my ally, and yet you supplied my enemy with an amulet to use against me.”

“You and I barely knew each other before today,” he said, barely pausing to inhale air before inhaling more nachos. "How was I supposed to know he wanted the amulet to ward off... you?"

"You had to know. I'm the only vampire in town now that..."

Xavier stopped chewing and gave her a sad look.

The sadness hung in the air.

Xavier said, "Is he really gone?"

She picked up her first drink and finished it. Then the second one.

Within seconds, she felt better. The lights that had been dimming inside her brain flashed back on.

She was alive.

She was alive, and Bentley was not.

She didn't answer Xavier's question, but she did join him in eating the nachos.

They were fully loaded, with everything from ground beef to pulled pork and hot peppers. It was good—for low-class peasant fare.

The conversation turned to a review of their activities of the last several hours.

After getting the contract from Mr. Dabrowski, they had worked on tracking down the party that had wrongfully purchased Zirconia's dream house.

She planned to buy the contract for whatever price the other party named, but she and Xavier had been unable to locate the buyer. It was a wealthy businessman who had bought the place long distance, and then immediately jetted off to some part of the world that had no phone reception.

No phone reception. Ah, that was the life. Zirconia used to do the same, back when her family believed she was dead. Those had been the good ol' days. Being alive—such as she was—wasn't all it was cracked up to be.

"You'll find another house," Xavier said. "A better one."

"I want *that* house. It's perfect."

"Perfect doesn't mean what it used to," he said.

"It doesn't?"

"They're building a whack of new mansions at the edge of town. I bet one of them would be perfect."

"You can't buy a *new* mansion," she said with a snort. "If I were buying a mansion, I wouldn't look at anything under one hundred years old."

"But that house we saw today was pretty new."

"Exactly. It was a *house*. Not a mansion. Nobody in this country has built a decent mansion in a century. Everything new that they call a *mansion* is one french fry station short of being a fast food outlet."

Xavier stared straight ahead. "I'd love to have my own french fry station."

"That's the saddest thing I've ever heard."

Xavier picked up the menu. "Should we get chicken wings? They're on special." He showed her the picture on the menu. "It's Wings Wednesday."

"It's not Wednesday," she said.

"It's Wednesday," he insisted.

"Does everyone in this town have brainweevils? Today is Friday."

"Nu-uh."

"Right. Today is Thursday. I know it is, because I was at a bar yesterday, and it was Wings Wednesday."

He smirked. "Maybe you have brainweevils."

Indignantly, she said, "I do not have brainweevils."

"What's the first sign of brainweevils?"

"Today is Thursday, Xavier."

"You remembered my name. But it's still Wednesday." He pulled out his phone and showed her the screen with the date.

Zirconia threw her hands in the air. "So it is. You don't have to rub my nose in it. If I wanted to be humiliated and treated like I'm useless, I could be upstairs with my family."

His expression grew serious. "They treat you like you're useless? Welcome to my club."

"You're not useless."

He sat up straighter. "That's the nicest thing anyone's ever said to me."

She took his second drink before he could touch it. "You need to slow down. You're becoming maudlin."

"I don't know what that word means, but I am a pathetic wretch of a Nothing Person, so no big surprise there."

She finished the sweetly bitter Italian drink, and signaled for another round.

They ordered chicken wings, since it was Wednesday, after all.

As she ate the wings—ingesting bones and all—something chicken-like pecked at the back of her mind.

How could today be Wednesday if yesterday had felt like a Wednesday, and, come to think of it, the previous day as well?

The idea grew and grew in her mind until it was very large—larger even than her vampire-sized bladder.

If it had been Wednesday more than once, that meant...

She tried not to think of what that meant.

"To Thursday," she said, raising her glass in a toast.

The glass trembled. Her whole body was trembling.

She'd told herself not to think about it until tomorrow, but every cell in her vampire body was vibrating at the idea.

"Sure," Xavier said. "To Thursday, which is tomorrow."

"Unless it's Wednesday again," she said. "Which I believe it will be."

Xavier laughed as though she had made a joke.

She had not.

CHAPTER 20

PART TWO - Wednesday Number Four

Zirconia Cristata Riddle could not have woken up anywhere in the world because she had to—truly *had to*—wake up on a particular sofabed in a particular hotel room. It was where she'd woken up every Wednesday for the past four continuously occurring Wednesdays.

A single angry mattress spring stabbed at her heart from behind.

She sat up quickly, eager to confirm her theory. The bed frame made an unhappy sound.

Zinnia, who was making tea, quipped, "And I thought my joints were creaky."

Zirconia pointed at her sister. "What day is it?"

"It ought to be the day you fold your bed up for a change instead of leaving it for someone else to do," Zinnia said using the air of self-righteousness that came so naturally. What a burden it had to be, being perfect all the time.

Zirconia checked her surroundings. The hotel suite was arranged exactly the way it had been yesterday morning. It was not in disarray, the way it had been the night before.

It was as though all of time had rewound itself while she'd been sleeping.

Because that was exactly what time had done.

She kept pointing her finger at her sister. "My word is my bond, Zinnia Riddle, I will make you regret the next word you utter if it is not the answer to the question I'm about to repeat." She enunciated with vampire-strength enunciation, which was crisp enough to cut parmesan cheese. "What. Day. Is. It?"

"Wednesday," Zinnia said. "All day long. It's Wednesday today, you brainweeviled old bat." She rolled her eyes. "Somebody woke up on the wrong side of the coffin."

"For once, you're not entirely wrong."

"I'm not? Speaking of waking up, you should take the cot," Zinnia said. "It's just foam, no squeaky springs. I can barely sleep with this baby pressing on my bladder anyway. I'll trade you for the sofabed."

"Tomorrow. I have many things to deal with today."

The time looping vampire grabbed the clothes stacked neatly beside the bed—right where she'd left them on Tuesday night, several Wednesdays ago—and got dressed.

Zinnia frowned over the pot of tea she was brewing on the narrow bit of counter that wasn't covered in Riddle family personal items.

Confusion crossed her freckled face as she stirred in herbs. "Something is off. I feel like I'm forgetting something. Did you know I forgot my own birthday once?"

"If you forget your birthday, it doesn't count," Zirconia said. "In fact, you can subtract it from your age."

"I can?"

"You're such a rules follower. Don't you know we can make our own rules? Go ahead and take that year off. You don't look anywhere near your real age."

Zinnia blinked three times. "Why are you being nice to me?" Her hazel eyes narrowed. "You must want something."

"I'm in a good mood."

"Why?" Zinnia shook her head, gently fanning her long, red waves of hair. "I mean I'm glad for you. I've been so worried about everything lately. I ought to be more aware that I'm projecting my anxieties onto others." She glanced over her shoulder uneasily, as though there might be a ghostly child version of herself standing behind her, or a Pain-Body Cadodemon. Luckily for the Riddles, both had remained vanquished.

Just then, the cat jumped onto the counter, knocking down a stack of paperbacks.

The dirty, old books landed on the floor exactly as Zirconia had expected they would.

"Not on the counter," Zinnia said, half-heartedly shooing the cat away.

"Ham," said the cat, exactly as she had all the other Wednesdays.

"Find me," screeched the green budgie from its cage. "Find me! Find me!"

Zirconia began to giggle.

This prompted an extremely befuddled look from her sister, which only made her laugh harder. She had to hold both hands over her mouth to keep from falling into hysterics.

It was Wednesday. Again.

If only she'd recognized it sooner.

This had to be the fourth day in a row the day had repeated, and she'd only just noticed.

Oh, how the mighty could fall... when the mighty assumed the days were progressing in the natural order and never questioned the calendar.

If it was Wednesday again, that could only mean one thing.

Fate had given her one more chance to get things right. What a gift.

Zinnia sloshed tea into a mug and interrupted her older sister's thoughts. "Are you feeling okay? You don't seem like yourself. Would you like to try some of my new brew?"

"Too weak for my blood."

"But it's a new—"

"I need a computer. I'll take your laptop."

Without waiting for permission, Zirconia grabbed the leather bag that contained the laptop Zinnia used when she wanted to avoid talking to her family. She'd been using it a lot in the hotel. She claimed to be checking her work emails while actually playing anagram games.

Zinnia swelled up, mostly with air.

Zirconia sensed more than tea brewing. Family drama was on its way. She didn't have time for that. Well, she did, because she had a lot of time, but, like most people, she mentally used time as an excuse to avoid her responsibilities.

The vampire pulled the laptop bag onto her shoulder, and headed for the door.

"You're leaving? With my laptop?"

"Obviously," Zirconia said to her sister. "Do whatever you were going to do. Don't change anything on my account."

Zinnia picked up the white cat and said to it, "Boa, do you know what she's talking about?" She buried her nose in the cat's fluff. "Who's a good girl? You are, Boa. What's your Auntie Z up to?"

The cat writhed happily in the witch's arms.

Both of them were happy.

That wasn't good.

"Floopy doop," Zirconia said. "You're in a good mood now."

"I suppose I am," Zinnia said, cradling the cat like a baby. "I don't always realize it, but I'm glad you're here. It's nice having family around."

"No, no, no," Zirconia said. "This is all wrong. You should be annoyed at me."

"I should?"

Zirconia didn't want to deliberately hurt her sister's feelings—she did it so frequently by accident as it was—but she couldn't risk the alternative.

So, for the good of the day—the ends justified the means—she said what she had to.

"Zinnia, you're fat, and your career is no substitute for having a man who wants to marry you."

There was no satisfaction in being forced to tell the truth.

But it worked. Zinnia's eyes shone as they welled up with tears.

Zirconia's chest ached like an imaginary metal spring had shot through it.

She wanted to explain herself, to reveal what was happening, but she could not.

Full stop.

She. Could. Not. Tell Zinnia.

With a heavy, rusty, old-metal tang in her chest, Zirconia let herself out of the hotel suite.

She closed the door, and pressed her hand on the wood as she whispered, “You'll understand tomorrow.”

On the other side of the door, there was a POP. A puff of colored smoke seeped out underneath the door. It was not any single color, but all of them, all at once, but not a rainbow. If it had been a rainbow, Zirconia might have identified it immediately, had she even seen it.

Zirconia didn't see the colored smoke because she was already walking away.

CHAPTER 21

Zirconia made it to the hotel's front desk with plenty of time to spare before the Darnells came along to check out.

"Finally," she said under her breath.

Darren and Debbie ignored her, like they would an absolute stranger. It was to be expected, given they had no memory of the two Wednesdays the three had spent so many hours together. Even so, their blank stares in the vampire's direction still stung a little.

Both of them became concerned with the well-being of the young woman who should have been working at the front desk. She was slumped forward, her forehead resting on the marble desk.

Debbie prodded the girl on the shoulder—not that it would do any good. The sleep induced by a vampire's kiss was deep, restful, and difficult to break.

Darren quipped with a laugh, "It's like the Hotel California. You can check out, but you can never leave."

Zirconia said, "It's actually a lot like that."

Darren gave her a second, warmer look, and offered his hand. "I'm Darren, and this is my wife, Debbie."

Zirconia said, "Any chance either one of you knows how to write up a real estate contract?"

Darren yanked his hand back and produced a business card. "At your service," he said with a flourish.

His wife laughed and swatted him playfully. "Darren's a silly goose," she said to Zirconia.

"Honk, honk," the man said. "Wait. Am I a goose or a swan? Honk, honk."

Debbie said, "Don't you dare go running to the lagoon to see your friends, you silly goose."

"Honk, honk," he said again.

The couple were quite comfortable being themselves around Zirconia. She was pleased that their new "first" meeting was going well. But why wouldn't it? People weren't that difficult, if you weren't related to them.

They would all celebrate with drinks and chicken wings after the house was hers.

Darren composed himself. “Are you serious about buying a house?”

“Deadly serious,” Zirconia said. “There's a house I need to make a bully offer on.”

“Ooh. A bully offer,” Darren said with a triple eyebrow waggle. “I do like an aggressive lady client.”

Zirconia replied, “Few ladies are as aggressive as yours truly.” She grabbed Darren's warm forearm and gave it a playful squeeze.

Debbie flinched, her eyes wide as she stared at the vampire's pale white hand on her husband's bare arm.

Zirconia released the man and chided herself. The couple had a powerful bond. They were that rare thing—true soul mates. She would need to treat them as one instead of two, for energetically that was what they were. Lucky for them.

“Let's talk about this bully offer,” Darren said. “It's a shame the lounge isn't open yet. Maybe they'll make an exception for us.”

“Coffee might be better,” his wife said.

“I defer to my wife,” Darren said. “She truly is my better half.”

“I can feel that,” Zirconia said. And she could. If Darren hadn't found his soul mate, his ambition might have driven him to madness or evil, which were nearly the same thing.

“It's not the best coffee, but it's nearby,” Debbie said, leading the group into the hotel's coffee shop.

They ordered beverages, and got started on the paperwork for the house offer.

There was little time to spare. If Zirconia was to beat the other potential buyer, it would be best to close a deal before the businessman's offer even came in.

She wasn't afraid of getting into a bidding war, but the whole point of a bully offer was to avoid such an undignified situation.

Darren typed away at the laptop he'd pulled from his packed suitcase. “And the address of the subject property is...?”

Zirconia didn't know it. She had an excellent memory, but, even so, her brain wasn't a supercomputer.

She reached into her pocket to pull out the flier with the address, only to find she didn't have it.

But of course she didn't.

This was a new Wednesday, and she hadn't yet been to Dreamland Coffee to pull it off the corkboard.

“I don't have the exact address,” she said.

Darren said, “If you have the street name, we could look it up online.”

“Or the neighborhood,” Debbie said.

Zirconia searched her memory, but all she found were the emotions she'd felt each of the three times she'd visited the property.

She could have described the exact height of the doorbell, the pale gray color of the interior walls, the way the concrete slabs subtly choked and restrained the sun's harsh rays. She could have flawlessly described any number of aspects of the house, except the number above the door. Or the street.

“I can get you the address,” Zirconia said. “We'll have to drive over to another location so I can get it off a community corkboard.”

Debbie, who'd been regarding the vampire with suspicion ever since the arm-grab, leaned over and whispered to her husband, “I have a bad feeling about all of this.”

Darren began sweating. He mopped his brow with an old-fashioned handkerchief.

Debbie had transferred her bad feeling to her soul mate. Either that, or he'd been suspicious on his own.

Zirconia hadn't noticed until now, but she should have known.

"The address is a mere formality," the vampire said. "You can stay here, and keep working on the offer, and I'll get the address. I could telephone Humphrey. He's just standing around right now, flicking his tongue at flies."

These facts were true, but not the right facts to put the Darnells at ease.

Darren said, "I'd like to refer you to a colleague who works locally. I, uh, just remembered I'm not licensed to work in this state."

Zirconia would have to cast a mind control glamour over the duo.

She gave them fair warning, saying, "We can do this the easy way, or we can do it the hard way. I will make my bully offer today."

Debbie whispered to her husband, "Code Red."

Darren mopped his sweaty forehead and whispered back, "Give me a minute."

"I can hear you both," Zirconia said. "I'm right here." She crossed her arms. "I'm so very disappointed. I thought you were better than this. I wouldn't go on a road trip with you two if you were the last couple on earth."

"I guess we're fired," Darren said. "Do you still want that referral?"

No. She did not want a referral. She still liked the Darnells, even if they didn't like her back. Curse them for being so charming.

She would have to use her powers.

Before she could give the Darnells the first taste of a glamour, trouble approached with loud boot stomps ringing out on the hard floor. The stomps had an uneven sound, as though one boot might be a different shape from the other.

Zirconia rotated her chair. It wasn't a rotating chair, but vampires could do cool stuff like that.

Trouble was there, all right.

In the form of a red-haired witch in the prime of her life.

Not Zirconia's sister, but her daughter.

Zara Riddle.

Her uneven-sounding boots were, indeed, mismatched. That was never a good sign. A wearer of mismatched footwear was rarely packing a purse full of decorum, let alone sanity.

Zara bared her teeth and growled, "What did you do to Aunt Zinnia?"

Zirconia held up her hand. "Zarabella, I'll deal with you after I've—"

"Mother, you'll deal with me now."

There was a loud snap.

It was Darren Darnell's suitcase closing up. He was breathing heavily as he backed away.

Debbie stood behind her man, using his larger body as a shield while she spoke for both of them. "I am so sorry, but our babysitter just called, and we have to get home immediately."

Zirconia knew there was no babysitter, but she had to let the couple go. Her daughter wouldn't allow a simple glamouring to take place without interfering. Zara didn't believe in choking people. Never mind that the woman frequently shot fireballs at innocent people, which was far worse than a subtle neck squeeze. Zara made her own set of rules for herself, and she was too powerful for anyone else to rein in.

The Darnells left.

Zara watched the couple scurry away, casting the occasional fearful glance back.

She said to her mother, "I see your people skills are as good as ever."

Her words shot straight through Zirconia's heart.

She wished, in that moment, that she could be dead once more. Dead forever.

Zirconia felt every year of her age, which included every repeated day. How old was she, if she counted all the time loop days? Two hundred years old? Three hundred? It had to be more. It felt like more.

Zara must have known she'd gone too far, as she softened her stance slightly. Fire still danced in her eyes as she returned to her first question.

"What did you do to Aunt Zinnia? She's inconsolable."

"It doesn't matter," Zirconia said weakly. "She'll be better tomorrow, when I show her the new house I'm buying for all of us to live in."

Zara didn't react.

Speaking slowly, Zirconia said, "I've found us the perfect house. Did you hear me? Today is a good day."

"I don't need a house," Zara said. "I've got an apartment."

"A hotel suite is a far cry from an apartment. And it's no place to raise a family."

"You're not listening to me," Zara said. "I've got an apartment. It's..."

Zirconia cocked her head. She'd been listening the whole time, but now she was *really* listening.

"I'm leaving," Zara said. "I'm leaving Wisteria."

CHAPTER 22

"You can't leave," Zirconia said to her daughter, continuing the argument seamlessly even as they changed locations.

The two were walking up the carpeted stairs, returning to their floor and their suite to argue in private, somewhere the other hotel guests wouldn't stare at them with open mouths. You'd think people had never seen a family discussion before.

"Of course I can," Zara said, still fuming and walking at an impressive pace.

They reached the door of their suite. Ozone lingered in the air.

Zara used her magnetic keycard on the door's lock. It didn't work.

That wasn't unusual; the keycards were always sputtering out, particularly in Zara's hands. Her moods often stormed around her, out of control.

Zara tried the keycard again.

It still didn't work.

She tried a third time.

The third time was not the trick.

The thirty-three-year-old witch howled in frustration, like a petulant child.

Zirconia said, "Must you be so dramatic?"

Zara continued to be dramatic.

"Zarabella, there should be no such thing as a locked door, but you've been lazy."

"I have not. You-know-who took our powers."

"Just one power. And it happened months ago. You should have been making better use of your free time to learn alternate means, such as unlocking spells."

Zara made a throaty noise halfway between gagging and growling.

"Don't you dare give me a boil," Zirconia said. "I'll give you one twice the size. Right on the tip of your nose."

Zara stewed silently.

To move things along, Zirconia used her own keycard to open the door. The electronic gadget flashed green and unlocked.

Zara pushed in ahead, not thanking her mother.

The budgie greeted them with a cry of, "Find me! Find me!"

The hotel suite reeked of ozone, and was even more of a mess than it had been an hour ago.

Zirconia tripped over a pile of clothing, jewelry, and makeup.

The pile rippled, and the cat shot out from underneath. A pink shawl was looped over the cat's neck, forming a superhero's cape over the white feline as she shot under the sofabed.

Zirconia said, "What happened here? Did your aunt do this? She used to throw the most spectacular tantrums when she was ten years old. Some people never change."

Zara ignored her mother and went to coax the cat out from under the couch.

Zirconia checked the bedroom for her sister. Zinnia wasn't there. The bedroom was empty, and looked strange without anyone in it. Zoey and her sickly-pale friend were usually camped in there during the day. School was out for the summer, and while both of the girls claimed to have summer jobs, they were never at them.

The bathroom door was closed, as it had been earlier.

She knocked on the door. "Zinnia? Stop overreacting."

A voice on the other side said, "Don't come in, Gigi!" Gigi was what Zoey called her grandmother, who preferred not to be reminded she was a grandmother.

"You don't have anything I haven't seen," Zirconia said, trying the handle anyway. It was locked. Not just locked, but magically locked.

Zara came over to the door, holding the cat as she extracted it from the pink shawl.

"And there you go again," Zara said. "Typical."

"Whatever do you mean?"

"That's not what you're supposed to say to kids." In a mocking tone, she repeated her mother's phrase. "*You don't have anything I haven't seen.*" Zara shook her head emphatically as she set down the cat. "We don't say things like that any more."

"We don't? Why not?"

Zara rolled her eyes and walked away, disappearing into the bedroom.

Zirconia left her granddaughter to whatever she was doing in the bathroom—naked or otherwise—and followed her daughter into the bedroom.

Zara furiously sorted clothes into a suitcase. Her method of "sorting" was to pick up an article of clothing, sniff it, then either toss it in a random direction or cram it into one of the case's compartments.

The vampire mother said, "I hope your memorization of unwrinkling spells has been more of a priority than your door-unlocking spells."

"I can use an iron," the witch said sullenly.

She continued to pack, and Zirconia continued to watch, until finally she said, "Is there anything I can say or do that will make you stay?"

"No."

"Nothing?"

Zara bit her lower lip. She was caving in, just a little. There *was* something that would make her stay.

"You can tell me," Zirconia said. "If there's *anything* that would convince you to stick around a bit longer, let me know."

"It's too late."

"It's too late today, but tomorrow's another day. Especially if tomorrow is today again."

Zara stopped packing. "Huh?"

"A lady doesn't say huh." Zirconia used the pause in packing to take her daughter's hand.

Zara jerked her hand away and growled, "Don't you dare touch my cuticles."

"I wasn't going to touch your cuticles. Must you always be so dramatic? I don't know who you got it from. Probably your father, and his mixed-up shifter blood."

"You are the worst. The absolute worst."

"Zarabella, if you keep joking around on this tired theme in which we are to imagine that I am not a sufficient parent, I may start taking it personally."

Zara's posture shifted. "Thank you." The rage was gone, the storm passed.

"For what? Don't tell me you're finally ready to thank me for everything I've done for you."

"No. Thank you for making it very clear to me that the correct decision is to get as far away from you, and this town, as possible."

"Don't be silly. We'll be moved into our new house in a few weeks, as soon as the paperwork's settled. You'll be glad you stayed. You'll see. This time around, it will be better."

Zara crossed her arms. "It never gets better. We always fall into our old patterns."

"What about Christmas? Remember when we camped out in that dilapidated old house? That was nice."

"It was just one night, and it didn't last. Two days later, I caught you and Ribbons shredding clothes straight from my closet."

"We had to shred them. If I threw them away, you'd retrieve them from the garbage. I was only doing what was best for you." She added, "Well, Ribbons was taking revenge for something to do with maple syrup, but I swear I was only doing what was best for you."

"What about what I want?"

"You don't want what's best for you? I'm so confused. Our relationship would be so much easier if you simply explained exactly what it is you want from me."

Zara closed the suitcase—a seemingly impossible feat—which it would have been, if not for witchcraft.

She snapped the buckles closed, and picked it up. She was ready to go.

She was still wearing two different types of boots. Zirconia used an admirable amount of restraint not to mention the boots.

Zara thanked her by saying in a cold tone, "I have no interest in being part of your redemption arc."

Then, with her freckled nose in the air, she marched out of the hotel suite.

A minute passed.

Zirconia said to no one in particular, "She'll be back."

CHAPTER 23

Wednesday Number Five

"You can't leave," Zirconia said to her daughter, continuing the same argument exactly as she had the previous Wednesday.

The trick to being a successful time looper was to only make small changes, one at a time. So far, Zirconia had been following the same pattern as the previous day.

As she had yesterday, or today the previous time around, Zara took the carpeted stairs two at a time.

"Of course I can," Zara said.

They reached the door of their suite. Ozone lingered in the air.

Zirconia tried the first change.

Rather than allow her daughter to become frustrated over her keycard not working, Zirconia quickly slipped her own card through the lock.

The gadget flashed green and unlocked.

Zara stomped her foot. "What are you doing? I can open a locked door. You don't have to treat me like I'm a baby. That's... that's what you do. You infantilize me."

"Zarabella, must you be so dramatic?"

"Mother, must you be so... infantilizing?"

Without waiting for an answer, she pushed open the door and marched in.

The budgie greeted them with a cry of, "Find me! Find me!"

Zirconia tripped on the pile of clothing again. The cat shot out from underneath, once again wearing a pink shawl as a cape.

"Poor kitty," Zirconia said. "Let me help you with that. Here, kitty kitty."

She reached under the couch, only to get yowled at as well as scratched by the cat.

"Wretched creature," Zirconia said. "It doesn't know when to shut up and let me help it."

She sucked on the wound to keep her precious blood from being wasted, along with her wise mothering.

Zara scowled. "What did you do to Boa?"

"I'm the one who's hurt." Zirconia waved her wounded hand as explanation. Unfortunately, the cut had already healed at vampire speed, which really undermined her stance as the victim.

Zara pushed her mother out of the way, and coaxed the cat out from under the couch.

Zirconia glanced at the closed bathroom door—Zoey would be on the other side—and asked, "Where's your aunt, anyway?"

"At work."

"Right. I knew that. She's in her office when I go to ask her for help. Unlike you. You're not at work today because you called in sick."

Zara said nothing as she finished extracting the cat from the pink shawl.

Zirconia said, "What time is your flight?"

Zara gave her mother a sidelong look. "Who told you?"

"The piles of clothing told me. I recognize your suitcase-packing style when I see it." She tapped her forehead. "Give your mother a little credit."

Zara narrowed her hazel eyes. Oh, she was in a mood that morning. "Did you really tell Zinnia she was old and fat, and nobody would ever marry her?"

"No. I didn't say she was old. As for her career, I said it was no substitute for a man who wanted to marry her."

Zara's cheeks reddened. "That checks out. The nastiness really rolls off your tongue, doesn't it?" The ozone scent in the air turned to the aroma of scorched tires as the witch's anger rose up. "I guess you've had a lot of practice saying stuff like that to me, over and over."

She put her hands on her hips. By the look of it, it was a safety maneuver to stop herself from shooting fireballs at her mother.

"I only speak the truth," Zirconia said. "I do not interpret it."

Zara left for the bedroom, where she got back to flinging clothes anywhere but the suitcase.

Zirconia went to the door. She stood there and said gently, "Is there anything I can say or do that will make you stay?"

"No."

"Nothing?"

Zara bit her lower lip. "It's too late."

"It's never too late." The vampire held out her palm. "May I hold your hand? I promise I won't touch your cuticles."

"No." Zara slammed the suitcase shut. "Don't you dare use your vampire glamours on me, or I swear I'll move so far away you'll never find me again, and you can forget about seeing your granddaughter."

Zirconia held her hands up. "I wouldn't glamour you."

"How am I supposed to believe you? You also said you just wanted to borrow a sweater, but then I found you and Ribbons shredding half my wardrobe."

"That was all his idea."

"It doesn't make it any better that you were his accomplice." Zara shook her head. "It never gets better. We always fall into our old patterns."

"I shouldn't have listened to him." Zirconia entered the room in spite of the unwelcoming energy.

She sat on the bed, and patted the spot next to her.

Zara said, "Now what?"

"Sit down, and let me give you the good news. I'm buying a beautiful house for all of us to live in."

"With what? You don't have any money."

"Zinnia showed me how to manipulate the stock market to make money out of nothing, like rich people do."

Zara was so taken aback by this news that she took three actual steps back in her mismatched boots.

"You have to see this house," Zirconia said. "I'll let you have the first pick of the rooms, as long as you don't pick the one in the north east corner."

Zara thanked her mother by saying in a cold tone, "I have no interest in being part of either your redemption arc, or your greed-fuelled downfall."

Then, with her freckled nose in the air, she marched out of the hotel suite.

A minute passed.

Zirconia said to no one in particular, "She'll be back."

CHAPTER 24

Wednesday Number Six

"I would *rather* you didn't leave," Zirconia said to her daughter, trying a different approach.

Zara took the carpeted stairs two at a time.

"Of course I can," Zara said.

"You're not listening. I didn't say you *couldn't leave*. I said *I'd rather you didn't*."

Zara managed to audibly stomp her mismatched boots on the carpeted stairs.

Zirconia braced herself for failure. The third time wouldn't be the charm. She should have known.

Sometimes a time looper's changes were too small to affect anything. Days had a stickiness to them. A sort of inertia. Days didn't want to be changed.

They reached the door of their suite.

As Zara fumbled through the mess of her purse, Zirconia handed her daughter her keycard. "Try mine. Your cards are always losing their magnetic charge. Through absolutely no fault of yours."

"You are up to something," Zara said angrily, despite successfully opening the door.

The budgie greeted them with a cry of, "Find me! Find me!"

Zirconia sidestepped the pile of clothing.

"Careful," she said to her daughter, pointing at the tripping hazard.

"Careful of what?"

Zara tripped and fell on top of the pile.

The cat shot out, wearing its pink shawl as a cape, and now also yowling about having been fallen on.

Zara was still windmilling on the now-magically-animated pile, struggling to get free of it.

The pile was agitated about having been given life in the first place, and, like most monsters, tried to take revenge on its creator.

The witch let out a streak of curse words that caused the peeling wallpaper inside the hotel suite to roll down further.

The cat raced around the room, white fur flying under its pink superhero cape.

"Poor Snake," Zirconia said. She stepped over her daughter to pick up the cat—was it named Snake?—and extracted it from the cape. The cat meowed in protest.

Zara said, "What are you doing to Boa?"

Boa. The cat's name was Boa.

"I'm helping her. I'm helping... Boa."

Zara finally broke free of the pile, and got to her feet. "That sounds about right. You're a real helper." Sarcasm dripped off her words the way the old wallpaper dripped off the walls.

Zirconia glanced at the closed bathroom door and asked, "What's Zoey doing in there, anyway?"

Zara snorted. "I know you've been a creature of the grave for a while, but have you already forgotten how human bodily functions work?"

"I can't win with you, can I?"

"Are you kidding me?" Zara gave her mother a sidelong look. "You're like the house at a casino. You always win."

"Speaking of houses, I've bought us the perfect one. You can still fly off to your job interview. I'm not going to stop you. But when you get back, I'll take you to the house. You can have whichever room you want, even the northeast one."

"You bought a house?"

"I'm in the process of buying a house."

"A big one?"

Zirconia nodded. "It's not a mansion, but it will do."

Zara crossed her arms. "Don't bother buying a big house with guest rooms on my account. After I leave this cursed town, I'm not even coming back to visit."

"What about Fred? And Katie? And all your other little friends at the bookstore?"

"*Frank* and *Kathy* work at the *library*."

"That's what I said."

"That's not what you said."

Zirconia waved her hand. "Names are just *words*. Don't get so hung up on the exact things I say. You spend far too much time around all those dirty old books full of old, dead words. You actually think they matter."

Zara's cheeks reddened. "Maybe I will get a job at a bookstore. No. I'll *buy* a bookstore and name it after you. Zirconia's Old Dead Word Emporium." The ozone in the air turned to the aroma of burning lima bean casserole. The witch's humorous ire was rising, storming around her in a new pattern. "What do you think about that, *Mother*?"

Zirconia knew better than to answer a rhetorical question. Zara knew darn well what her mother thought of that.

Zara put her hands on her hips. A sizzling sound came from her palms. The burning lima bean casserole scent intensified. Anyone who didn't know Zara was a witch might have guessed she was burning up actual food to sicken the guests at a potluck.

Zirconia might have said something that would defuse the situation.

She might have. Given enough Wednesdays, she surely would. But not this one.

Instead, she said, "Zarabella, must you make every single one of your life choices based on the criteria of what would antagonize me the most?"

Zara, satisfied at having made her mother lose her composure, left for the bedroom.

She got busy flinging clothes and hairbrushes—why did she have so many hairbrushes?—anywhere but the suitcase.

Zirconia followed her in, careful to dodge the volley of hairbrushes.

The vampire mother wisely said, "Deep down, you know your life is here. You belong here. You are *needed* here. One must not walk away from that." She spoke a truth so true it almost hurt. "Not everyone is so lucky as to be needed."

Zara bit her lower lip. "It's too late. I've already decided, and you can't make me change my mind. Being in this cursed town has brought nothing but pain and suffering to everyone I love."

"But I've had a wonderful time catching up with you here."

Zara's eyes burned with anger. "I said I've brought pain and suffering to everyone I *love*."

Zirconia felt that one. It shot straight through her like a burning, poison-tipped arrow.

She kept herself calm, her voice calmer. "You're only saying that because I occasionally go too far. I should not have cleaned out your closet. I realize now it was wrong of me to do so. I should not have listened to the wyvern."

"The wyvern." Zara shook her head. "You two are like the bookends on a shelf full of bad stories."

Zirconia sat on the bed. She patted a spot next to her. "Sit down. Let's talk this through like civilized adults."

"I'm not feeling very civilized." Zara looked down at her mismatched footwear. "Why didn't you tell me I'm wearing two different boots?"

"It's very hard for me to tell you anything, Zarabella."

The witch shuddered visibly. "Don't call me that. Nobody but you calls me that."

"It's your name."

"Just stop." She kicked off both boots, and put on a matching set of sandals that were more appropriate for a summer day. "Stop calling me Zarabella. Stop calling me anything. Don't talk to me, and don't send any of your creepy birds to spy on me."

"I cannot abide by your request because..."

Because I'm your mother and I love you unconditionally, was what she might have said.

Instead, she said, "Because it's the most foolish thing you've ever said, and that's saying a lot, Zarabella."

Zara said, "I liked you better when you were dead."

Then, with her freckled nose in the air, she marched out of the hotel suite.

A minute passed.

Zirconia said to no one in particular, "That could have gone better."

And then, in the silence, she sat with her thoughts.

After a while, she thought about doing something she'd never, ever, ever considered doing before.

She would try something everyone had been suggesting for years.

She would... visit a therapist.

CHAPTER 25

Wednesday Number Seven

The sign on the door read:

Tallulah Swiftwater

Therapist Specializing in Families of All Kinds

Zirconia entered a small waiting room decorated in shades of pumpkin and beige, mostly pumpkin. The walls were an *interesting* shade of orange. *Walls shouldn't be so interesting*, she thought.

The sign on the reception desk read:

Please be seated. I'll pop my head out of the other room when I'm ready to see you.

- Tallulah

Zirconia puzzled over the sign.

It was an intentional sign, not a hastily written sticky note. It had been professionally designed and permanently printed on a piece of white plastic.

Why, then, did it include the phrase "I'll pop my head out?"

That wasn't very professional. Or was it? Zirconia didn't know what was considered professional for a therapist. Maybe this was how they did things.

There was a creak on the floorboards in the adjoining room. The door handle to the adjacent room turned.

Every cell in her body protested being there, in the orange room, about to see a therapist.

Not one single cell wanted to stay.

Zirconia used her vampire speed to leave the waiting room.

She made it out before she could be seen.

From the safety of the hallway, Zirconia heard a woman—Tallulah Swiftwater, presumably—say, "Hello? Is anyone here? Are you invisible?"

What an idiot, Zirconia thought.

She left the building as quickly as she could without setting off any fire alarms.

CHAPTER 26

Wednesday Number Eight

The seventh Wednesday had been a complete waste of time, what with the pointless trip to the therapist, but the time looping vampire would make better use of her eighth Wednesday.

She was back in the hotel stairwell with her daughter, who'd just located her in the cafe and yelled at her for upsetting Zinnia, who'd already left for work anyway.

"You can't make me stay in this cursed town," Zara said, moving quickly in her mismatched boots.

"I wouldn't dare try," Zirconia said to her daughter, trying yet a different approach. "It's probably the right decision for you to leave town."

She was pleased with herself for the delicate phrasing. She could solve this puzzle herself. Who needed a family therapist like Taffy Bilgepump—or whatever her name was—anyway?

Zirconia had all the time in the world, or at least a lot of it, and she would fix things with her daughter or die trying.

Zara, however, wouldn't make it easy for her mother. She raced up the carpeted stairs at record speed. The vampire actually had to exert herself to keep up.

"Don't you dare," Zara said with a snort.

"Don't I dare *what*?"

"Don't you dare try reverse psychology on me."

"I'm not," Zirconia said, which wasn't at all true. Reverse psychology worked quite well with someone as stubborn as Zara Riddle, which was exactly why she used it whenever she could remain calm enough to do so. And on this Wednesday, she would remain calm. Zen calm.

They reached the door of their suite.

Zara tried her keycard, and got a red light on the device.

She turned to her mother and snapped, "What did you do to my keycard?"

That was it.

Zirconia's zen calm left her.

She threw both hands up. "If you insist on believing that everything bad that happens to you is my fault, then I don't know what I can possibly do that won't earn me your disdain."

Zara rolled her eyes. "Overreact much?"

"I can't win with you."

"You're like the house at a casino. You always win."

At this point in the conversation, they were still in the hallway. All of the previous Wednesdays, by now they'd been inside the suite, amidst the chaos of the pile, the cat, the budgie, and the lingering aroma of whatever Zinnia had been brewing in the teapot.

This was different, but was it progress?

Zirconia regained a pinch of zen calm, and spoke carefully. "Speaking of houses, I wanted to surprise you in a few days, but you could use the good news now. I've bought the perfect house for all of us to live in."

Zara didn't react. Her face was a mask. She appeared to be frozen in time.

Zirconia went on, emphasizing the points she'd planned in her head. "Zoey will benefit the most. There's room for a study, where she can do her homework, plus plenty of room for her friends. The rooms have high ceilings, so we can put in one of those full-sized bunk beds."

Zara's face remained a mask.

Zirconia couldn't help but smile at how well she was delivering this speech. "With all the space, and the beds, young Amnesty can stay over all the time, and not be in the way."

Zara's face unfroze, and scrunched up. "Ambrosia," she spat out.

"That's what I said. Ambrosia. Lovely girl. Could use a little guidance, so once we're settled, I'll assist you in mentoring her. I suggest we start with a makeover. That girl's eyeliner—"

"You bought a house?"

"I will have, once I... finalize the paperwork."

By *finalize the paperwork*, she meant she would retrieve the Darnells from the janitor's closet—where she'd placed them for safekeeping—and wake them up to complete their tasks.

Zirconia might have used a hundred Wednesdays to learn about real estate contracts, but she hadn't seen the need. It was difficult for her to see the utility in any goal when the process of getting there held so little intrinsic pleasure.

Zara, cautious like a wise old fish nibbling on bait, asked, "What neighborhood?"

"I believe it is within walking distance to your bookstore, where you work with Frances and Karla. I can't wait to see your face when you see the house. It's absolutely perfect."

"Is it a character home?"

"In a manner of speaking."

"There's something you aren't telling me. What's the catch?"

"You'll have to stay here in Wisteria because that's where the house is."

Zara frowned. "I'm flying out today for a job interview."

"But... you don't hate me? You're not going to curse me, or tell me that you liked me better when I was dead?"

Zara's eyebrows flew up. "I would never say that. And I don't hate you. I... love you."

Zirconia let out a huge sigh of relief. "There. Was that so hard?"

She took out her own keycard, unlocked the door, and nudged her daughter into the suite.

Zara said, "I'm still going to the interview. I haven't changed my mind." The unspoken addition of the word *yet* hung in the air. She hadn't changed her mind *yet*.

Zirconia knew that an unspoken *yet* was as good as things could get on sticky Wednesdays like these.

Mission accomplished!

"Pack your suitcase and have a good flight," Zirconia said. "Don't forget to change your boots. And don't trip over that pile of clothes. Snake is hiding in there."

Zara tilted her head. "There's a snake in the room?"

"The cat. It's under that pink shawl."

Zara leaned over and lifted the pink shawl, pulling it safely off the cat.

The white feline lazily rolled onto its back, all four paws in the air.

For a moment, everything was calm.

And there it was. The eighth Wednesday had been the charm. At least when it came to the business between the two of them.

But, as with all treaties, it could end quickly.

Zirconia backed away, away from the doorway, blowing a kiss.

She was like a seasoned gambler who knew when to leave the table.

Zara said, "You're going?"

"We'll talk more when you get back from your interview. I hope you'll let them down easy."

"I..." The witch was actually speechless. It was a very special Wednesday, indeed.

As the door between them slowly closed, Zara gave her mother an uncertain wave goodbye.

CHAPTER 27

Zirconia was in a celebratory mood at the end of that Wednesday.

She didn't dare return to the hotel suite and mess things up with her family, so she went to see a lover.

Nick Lafleur, a zookeeper with minor magical powers, lived in a rustic cabin at the top of the mountain behind the zoo.

He was attractive, agreeable, and knew how to celebrate.

But when the rustic cabin door opened, Nick looked anything but pleased to see his vampire lover.

"It's been far too long," Zirconia said. "I know, I know. But you have to forgive me. I come bearing gifts." She held up the gift bag full of Nick's favorite snacks—peppered beef jerky and a type of chocolate bar that was difficult to come by in a small town due to its short shelf life.

He leaned forward to peer into the gift bag, but remained in the doorway, blocking her entry.

"You can't come in," he said. "It's not a good time. You're uninvited."

Uninvited. The energy shifted, and not in her favor.

"Who's in there? The cheetahs?"

He didn't budge or answer her question.

"Oh, Nick. Don't be silly. You can invite me in. You know I don't mind the big kitties."

He stepped outside, and closed the door behind him so she couldn't see in.

It was a warm summer night in town, but here on the mountain, the breezes were chilly. Zirconia might have shivered, if she'd been anything but a vampire.

"You should have called first," he said.

"Since when do I need an appointment?"

He tilted his perfect face, and puffed out his cheeks. Unlike Humphrey the komodo shifter, Nick's good looks were distinctive, superior to those of a catalog model. Nick could have been a movie star.

In fact, Hollywood had tried to make him one. He'd worked on a few feature film sets, handling the trained animals. It was interesting work, but he'd had to leave the job because the directors couldn't take the rejection of Nick declining all their offers for him to replace the current leading men.

Nick said solemnly, "You can't just float in and out of my life whenever it suits you."

"I don't float. Nick, you know—"

"I'm a living person. I have feelings."

"And I don't?"

"Not like me."

There was a sound on the other side of the door. Someone was in the cabin.

"Nick, who's in there?"

"Nobody," he lied.

"I know someone's in there. And don't tell me it's just zoo animals. A man doesn't put on fresh cologne to hang out with baby hippos." She added, "At least not any man I would consort with."

"I am sorry, but I'm not available for consorting with." He lifted his movie-star chin. "You can't come inside. You're uninvited."

Uninvited. She'd heard him the first time. Now he was just insulting her intelligence.

But she was nothing if not forgiving.

And he looked so forgivable in the starlight.

She flipped her hair over one shoulder and gave him a come-hither look.

"I don't need to come inside," she said. "Come to me, you delicious beast."

"What?"

"Don't play coy. Come here, and give me a little nibble to tide me over."

He stayed rooted where he was, and looked up at the night sky.

The mountain was far enough from town that the streetlights couldn't interfere with a perfect view of the stars. A cloudless, too-hot day had led to a night full of stars.

Nick continued to look up at the sky, exposing his throat. Every major vein and artery pulsed with rich, wonderful blood—much more than any regular human could offer.

"It's hard to resist you," he said.

"Then give in. That's all people want. To give in. They don't need temptation. That's everywhere. Nick, it's me. You can give in."

"I won't."

"Then stop tempting me with your exposed neck," she said. "It's very rude."

He tucked his chin quickly. He hadn't realized what he'd been doing.

"That's better," she said. But it wasn't much better. Her senses were full of him now. She wanted him so badly, it made her skin hurt.

He nodded at the cabin, and stuffed his hands in the pockets of his jeans. "Thanks for dropping by. If you'll excuse me, I need to get back to reading my book."

"You don't read books," she said.

"It's an audiobook."

"You're lying."

"Fine. It's a podcast." He glanced behind her. "I trust you can show yourself back down the mountain safely?"

"Yes. There's just one thing I need to do. I'd like to be prepared, in case I find myself here tomorrow."

He did a double take. "What now?"

His confusion gave Zirconia a sharp pain behind her ribs. When Nick Lafleur played dumb, he was downright beautiful.

She was serious about the research, though.

She easily dodged around him, and kicked the door of the cabin.

The wood and metal gave way immediately, no match for her vampire speed and strength.

She was uninvited, so the home's force field dissuaded her from entering, but she didn't need to go inside to see what she needed to see.

There, in the living room, looking extremely guilty about being caught there, was the pretty young detective. The fox shifter. Rhys Quarry's other daughter.

"Hello," Zirconia said icily, as though they were mere acquaintances, and hadn't bonded through the shared endurance of Zara's family dinners.

The dark-haired woman said, "Hi," and quickly disappeared. A small, black fox hung in the air for an instant before landing on all four paws on the sofa. The fox held still, her powerful hind legs coiled, ready to run.

Zirconia turned back to Nick and sniffed.

She said, "How could you?"

"You and I are not together. This was your idea. You're the one who broke up with me."

Had they broken up? She couldn't remember. How long had it been since they'd seen each other? A while. But only because she'd made her family a priority.

This was the thanks you got for trying to help people who didn't want to be helped. The beautiful things that actually gave you pleasure had a tendency to wander off when you weren't paying attention.

Nick Lafleur, a beautiful thing that gave her pleasure, had wandered off.

She said bitterly, "I don't know why I'm so surprised to find you carrying on with *that* girl."

"I should have told you," he said.

"How long has it been going on?"

"Honestly? Not long. It's not like we're official or anything." He glanced into the cabin at the black fox. "Uh..."

The black fox didn't have eyebrows, yet she managed to raise an eyebrow his way.

"Oh, Nick," Zirconia said. "You silly boy. You can't have your cake and eat it, too. Not without a lot more powers than you currently have."

The black fox trotted over to a purse, picked it up with her sharp canine teeth, and retreated to the cabin's only bathroom.

Nick rubbed the back of his neck. "Now I'm in trouble," he said huskily. "Do you want to... stick around?"

"Not like this," she said.

She handed him the gift bag of beef jerky and imported chocolate bars. There was also a new type of mustard in the bag. Nick liked mustard.

"I should go talk to her," he said.

"A word of advice, Nick? Don't chase what you don't want, and don't kill what you can't eat. No good can come of it."

And with that, she left.

She used vampire speed until she was out of sight of Nick, and then she slowed to catch her breath.

So much for a pleasant ending to a stressful day.

It was for the best that she didn't end up in Nick's arms. She might have gotten too comfortable, too complacent.

Something rustled in the bushes.

Zirconia called out, "Who's there? Show yourself."

A creature stepped out of the shadows. It walked on four legs, as most wild creatures on that mountain did. The animal was stocky, smaller than a deer, and covered in shaggy, light-colored fur.

It was a woolbird. A cute but deadly creature that was neither a sheep nor a goat.

The creature lowered its head and turned to the side, showing off a coat that begged to be touched.

Zirconia knew a trap when she saw it.

Woolbirds seldom traveled alone. Where was the other one?

The woolbird made a soft, lowing sound.

"Stay back," she warned. "I could break your neck and drain your blood before you break your stride."

The animal shuffled two steps closer, as though subtly herding her.

That was one of the tricky things about woolbirds. They looked like grazing herd animals but thought like predators.

Zirconia took stock of her surroundings. The mountain had plenty of deadly terrain. It was a mountain, after all. She stood dangerously close to the edge of a cliff. It wouldn't do her well to fall off a cliff like that. She was tough, but she was not immortal.

"Back off," she said with a low-pitch growl that animals and other lowly creatures such as parking ticket attendants understood better than words.

The woolbird finally took two steps back, head bowed in defeat.

Zirconia didn't notice the creature's accomplice, another woolbird, sneaking up behind her.

It struck her on her hips.

The skinny vampire flew up—ah, the perils of being at one's goal weight—and over the cliff.

Zirconia fell down, down, down, into the crevice.

When she landed, she suffered fatal injuries.

Great, she thought as blood gushed out of her compound fractures and the lights inside her mind faded into darkness. *And now I'm dying again.*

CHAPTER 28

Wednesday Number Nine

Zirconia Cristata Riddle, who had died the previous day, woke up on a sofabed.

As her consciousness returned, the resurrected woman felt gratitude.

She had died, yet she was not dead.

She was grateful for the creaky bed, right down to the spring that poked into her back.

Her situation wasn't ideal, but it was preferable to not waking up at all.

She sat up. The bed squeaked louder than it had the previous Wednesdays—louder than she thought a bed could squeak.

"And I thought my joints were creaky," said Zinnia, in the kitchen as usual.

"I was dead," Zirconia said.

"Nice try. You were snoring."

"I died last night. I was pushed off a mountain by a hairy goat thing."

"And yet here you are. We ought to add 'hairy goat things' to the list of perils that are no match for your healing abilities."

"It was a woolbird."

"Were you up at Nick's last night?"

"That's none of your business."

"The only woolbirds that exist are on that one mountain." Zinnia sprinkled herbs in her tea. "I thought you broke up with Nick."

"Since when do you care about my love life? You should worry about yours. You should be visiting Baby Bearclaw's father regularly. Believe it or not, the same thing that got you into trouble can also provide some relief at this stage."

Zinnia looked horrified.

"Don't be such a prude," Zirconia said. "You need to embrace what powers you have, while you have them. Life is a long hallway full of doors that are always closing. It gets very dark at the end."

"Sure," Zinnia said, barely listening as she rubbed her belly. "I can barely sleep with this baby pressing on my bladder. Do you want to trade beds? If I take the sofa, I'll be closer to the bathroom and won't have to climb over Zoey at night."

"You say that so smoothly." Zirconia got up and began dressing. "I know you're using trickery to get me to trade beds for your own benefit, not for mine."

"You have a strange definition of *trickery*." Zinnia raised an eyebrow. "Someone woke up on the wrong side of the coffin."

"You're fat."

"Nice try. I'm pregnant. This is a normal weight for this stage of the pregnancy."

"You don't know how old you are."

"I'm forty-nine."

"Are you sure?"

"What's gotten into you? I ought to call up your blood bag, Nick, and tell him to lay off whatever recreational drugs he's been enjoying. They're making you loopy."

"Loopy," Zirconia said with a snort. "I'm loopy, all right." Loopy as in time-loopy. Not that she would reveal that fact to her sister. But did she even have to? Had Zinnia figured it out? Was that why she'd used the word *loopy*?

Zinnia made her tea without breaking eye contact.

This was a new game, mixed in with the old. The day was shifting, evolving. The days were sticky, and resisted changes, but in spite of that, were never sticky enough to stay perfectly on track. They had an evolution.

It was mostly likely a failsafe—a deliberate flaw in the programming of the magic so the world could not lock itself into an infinite loop and get hung up there forever.

Zirconia didn't know all of the rules—or who had made them, but she did know that even if retraced her steps exactly, she would never end a Wednesday the exact same way as a previous one.

The cat jumped up, knocked down the books, and said, "Ham."

The budgie shrieked its usual nonsense.

The sisters continued to stare at each other.

They used to play staring games all the time as children. It could go on for hours.

Zinnia would win, because she always won. She could stare forever. It was a useful side effect of not having as much activity in her head as Zirconia had.

Zinnia took a slow sip of tea, maintaining eye contact, then said, "Your move."

"Blink once if you called me *loopy* for a specific reason."

Blinking was allowed during their staring contests, so this wasn't a trick.

Zinnia blinked once. "I did. Brainweevils."

Zirconia's suspicion settled down.

Zinnia didn't lie. She was weirdly secretive about her romantic life, and she sat on the juiciest bits of gossip, but she didn't outright lie to her sister.

Zirconia relaxed and looked away, letting her sister win. She finished buttoning her blouse, and moved toward the door.

Zinnia said, "Don't leave. Zara wants to talk to you about something."

"I know. She's planning to leave town, and she's got a job interview today."

Zinnia spat out a mouthful of tea. "Who told? Was it Ribbons? If it was him, we ought to pretend you don't know." Zinnia looked sad. "She'll be so hurt by his betrayal. First he helped you shred her closet, and now this."

Zirconia hesitated at the door. "It feels odd to start a day without an argument with you."

The mischief glinted once more in Zinnia's eyes. "With the way my hormones are, I'm sure you can do something to set me off."

Zirconia said, "I know you're pregnant, so you may not technically be fat, but you do *look* fat."

The statement of truth was sufficient.

Zinnia gasped in outrage. And, she was back in the agitated state that would keep the day's events roughly in line with previous ones, so Zirconia could get the outcome she devised.

Zirconia left the hotel suite and walked down the hallway.

Behind her, the smoke emerged under the door, unnoticed by the time looping vampire.

Something else was different that morning.

The back of her head ached right where she'd landed on it the night before.

The ache was a layer of bone forming, making that patch of her skull stronger. It was only one cell thick, but it was real. She was evolving, like the day.

She walked down the stairwell, rubbing the back of her head and thinking about how nice it might be to talk to someone about the changes she was going through.

She couldn't talk to Zinnia about the time loop, which left her with few options.

A stranger would do, if they were equipped to handle it.

Perhaps she would pay another visit to that therapist, and get further than the waiting room.

CHAPTER 29

The Office of Tallulah Swiftwater, Therapist Specializing in Families of All Kinds

Zirconia sat in the small waiting room that was decorated in shades of pumpkin and not enough beige.

She tried closing her eyes to block out the orange walls, but they remained in her mind's eye.

She would never, ever, ever put such a ghastly color on walls. The only good walls were gray, cream, or white walls. Unless the walls were in a proper mansion that was over a hundred years old. Mansions were like elegant women; they could be dignified in any color.

The time looping vampire had no interest in the magazines on offer, as they were several months old, so she read the irritating sign on the counter. She read it over and over.

Please be seated. I'll pop my head out of the other room when I'm ready to see you.

- Tallulah

The sign's unprofessional wording turned into a silly song in Zirconia's head.

I'll pop my head out. Pop, pop, pop. Pop goes the weasel. Pop goes my head. My head goes pop, pop, pop when I'm ready to see you.

There was a creak on the floorboards in the adjoining room. The door handle to the adjacent room turned.

Zirconia fought the urge to use her vampire speed to leave before being seen.

A woman entered the waiting room.

She was earthy, with that bohemian look that lazy, middle-aged women fell into when they stopped making the effort to look presentable in public.

She had long, chestnut hair that would have looked nicer if it wasn't half gray and half the shade of dirty dishwater. Her loose clothes draped and rippled like curtains. The many layers would be appropriate elsewhere—such as the desert, where the temperature might change dramatically within a few hours. These were not the clothes for wearing inside an air-conditioned office building.

The woman put her hands together in a prayer position, bowed, and said, “Bless you for coming in.”

Bless you? For coming in?

First the sign, then the clothes, and now a blessing? It was the third strike.

“No, thank you,” Zirconia said.

She left the waiting room.

She left so quickly that a draft knocked over the irritating sign and riffled the pages of the outdated magazines.

From the hallway, Zirconia heard a woman—Tallulah Swiftwater—say, “Hello? Is anyone here? Have you turned yourself invisible?”

What an idiot, Zirconia thought.

She left the building so quickly, she set off two fire alarms.

CHAPTER 30

Wednesday Again

Zirconia was in the lobby of the hotel, luring the Darnells into a janitor's closet when something unexpected happened.

Xavier Batista, the eager young man who so desperately wanted to be near magic, came running into the lobby.

His dark hair was lopsided, like he'd gotten out of bed and come straight there without brushing it. Or maybe it was a trendy style the young people were doing.

"There you are," Xavier said, red-cheeked and breathing hard. He did a double take when he saw Debbie and Darren, swaying on their feet in a glamour.

"You're not supposed to be here," Zirconia said.

"Yeah, I should be at work." He ran his hands through his nearly-black hair, which only made him look more disheveled.

"I must have caused an unintended shift in the cards," the time-looping vampire mused to herself. "I'll fix it next time around. Which one of my family members contacted you and told you to come here?"

"I came here on my own. I need to talk to you about —"

"In a minute. Can't you see I'm busy?" She indicated the swaying Darnells. "You have two safe choices. Help or get out of the way."

He actually was in the way. He had positioned himself between the real estate team and the janitorial closet Zirconia had been about to stow them in.

Xavier stepped out of the way.

He watched with big eyes as Zirconia walked the Darnells into the closet, made sure they were comfortable, and put them fully to sleep.

She closed the door and turned to interrogate the stray wildcard. "Who told you to come here? You couldn't have thought of it on your own."

"Something strange is happening," he said. "I can't deal with it on my own."

"This sounds like something we should discuss over a beverage." She steered him toward the lounge. "I'm actually glad you're here. I like this version of events." She patted him on the back. "You might be a key that unlocks a door."

They entered the lounge.

The young man who guarded the liquor from thirsty guests was there as usual.

He did a double take when he saw Xavier.

The two exchanged fist bumps.

"Dude," he said to Xavier. "I told you I'd handle it myself. You didn't have to—"

Zirconia cut him off by putting her hand in his mouth and pinching his tongue.

He was just as surprised as he'd been the previous time she'd silenced him that way. As far as he knew, today was the first time.

"Two greyhounds," she said. "And whatever *the dude* wants."

"Light beer," Xavier said. "I need to keep my wits about me today."

"Uh, okay," the reluctant bartender said.

Success! Xavier really was the key. He could unlock the lounge. She'd have to keep him around, once she figured out the chain of events that had brought him to her.

They took a seat at a table.

The lounge was very dark, due to being closed. Drinking in a lounge when it was closed to the public was one of Zirconia's favorite things. She liked it more than most people liked puppy kisses or tax refunds.

Xavier leaned in over the table. "You're not going to believe this, but... I'm caught in a time loop."

Zirconia put together the clues and came up with the conclusion that Zinnia knew about the time loop. The witch must have been faking ignorance that morning. How long had she known?

Zirconia said, "What did my sister tell you to say?"

"Who?"

"Zinnia. She put you up to this, didn't she?"

"Who?"

"Zinnia Riddle. She must have phoned you this morning from the suite. She must have..."

Zirconia couldn't think of a good reason why her sister might have involved a third party.

Except to cause chaos.

Was that it? Was Xavier an agent of chaos?

He said, "I don't know what you think is going on, but I'm not joking. And I haven't talked to Zinnia since yesterday, at work. We took our coffee break together." He glanced down at his hands. "Only because I thought she was taking a nap under her desk when I went for my break."

If he wasn't working under Zinnia's direction, that meant he was...

She looked at him in a new light.

His eyes were shining with new knowledge. A person couldn't fake that.

"Go ahead," she said. "Tell me what you think is going on."

He held up one hand as though taking an oath. "My word is my bond, I'm telling the truth. Today keeps repeating."

"Interesting."

"I go to sleep, and when I wake up, it's Wednesday again. Every day."

CHAPTER 31

PART THREE

"I know it sounds crazy," Xavier said.

Zirconia didn't say anything.

"The day keeps repeating. It's a genuine time loop, like in the movies. I'll prove it. Look at this." He pulled a pencil from his pocket and broke it in front of her. "I've broken this pencil every day for three days now. Four now, including today. And every morning when I wake up, it's whole again."

Zirconia didn't say anything.

He said, "Well?"

Still, she said nothing.

Hollowly, he said, "I guess snapping a pencil in half doesn't prove anything." He muttered, "Note to self. Get better proof next time." He forced a smile. "Tell me something about yourself that nobody else knows."

Silence.

He tried again. "Okay. Ask me a question I couldn't possibly know, but that I could research today, and tomorrow I'll give you the answer when we go through this all over again."

He leaned back, looking pleased with his strategy.

The young man arrived with their drinks. The two men exchanged more fist bumps.

Zirconia took a few sips of her pink beverage.

A pleasant unwinding sensation wove through her body, and it wasn't coming from the alcohol.

She was... enjoying herself.

Who knew having Xavier show up to tell her about the time loop would be so enjoyable?

It was like watching a version of herself. A warped, much less clever version of herself.

Still, what Xavier lacked in sophistication, he more than made up for with his youthful enthusiasm. Ah, had she ever been that young?

Xavier pulled a pocketful of change from his jeans, and dumped it on the counter.

"New game," he said with excitement. "Pick a coin, and flip it three times in a row. Then I'll tell you... wait. No." He frowned.

If he'd been a robot with gears on his face that indicated internal thinking, all the gears would have been turning rapidly.

"That won't work." He looked around the lounge. "I need a pen and paper."

Zirconia felt the tiny muscles that controlled the ligaments in her toes loosen. Those ligaments never loosened. This was the most she'd been entertained in a long time.

Opportunities like this didn't come around often.

She had to play along. *Had to.*

She batted her eyelashes in fake confusion. "What do you need a pen and paper for? Are you going to write down a number between one and ninety-nine before I pick it?"

"That's a good idea. I was going to say between one and ten, but yours is better. Let's do that. Tell me your number."

"But we don't have a pen and paper. You haven't written anything down."

He waved a hand. "I don't need it this time. I'll write it down next time."

"But that won't work. Your hands are empty right now. If what you're saying is true, and we're caught in a loop, then we might have a different conversation tomorrow. Even if just a few words are different, might that not affect my mind, and the number I pick?"

He narrowed his light-green eyes. Xavier had dark skin and light eyes. He had a too-long face and a too-broad nose, but the features balanced out. He could have been attractive. Not to Zirconia, but to other women, maybe.

He kept giving the vampire a suspicious look, as though recording her every twitch in his mind for future analysis.

"You know what's going on," he said evenly. "You know, and you're messing with me."

"Of course I'm messing with you. I'm playing along with your silly thought experiment." She blinked repeatedly. She didn't need to blink, not with the vampire oils that formed a film over her eyes, but she did blink when it suited her.

"My thought experiment," he said hollowly.

"You and I both know time travel isn't real, but if it were, logic would still apply."

The light-green eyes narrowed again.

Zirconia had the unpleasant prickling sensation of being seen when she didn't want to be seen. The ligaments in her feet tightened up again.

He said, "Humor me. Pick a number."

"Ninety-nine," she said.

He blinked hard as he nodded, like a genie in an old TV sitcom. "Got it. Thanks."

"Now what?" She couldn't keep her amusement from her voice, but that was fine. A version of her who didn't know about time loops might be amused in this situation.

"You'll see."

"Oh, will I?"

"You'll see tomorrow."

"What if it doesn't work? Then you'll have wasted a whole day on one idea."

He frowned.

She said, "If I were you—and I'm glad I'm not, because I prefer sanity—I'd come up with a second idea. Something else you can use to convince me that time travel is real. Something good."

"Pick another number between one and ninety-nine."

"That's just the same idea," she said.

"It'll work," he said. "Pick."

"Ninety-nine."

He snorted. "Not the same one."

"Why not?"

He was genuinely stumped, which was good. He'd stopped seeing her when she didn't want to be seen. Her toes relaxed again.

She said, "What about the winning lottery numbers?"

"Yes!" He pointed at her. "I can tell you what today's numbers are before they're drawn."

"That would certainly prove something." She leaned in. "I could use the funds. Tell me, what are the winning numbers?"

He puffed out his cheeks in frustration. "I don't know them yet. I'll have to tell you tomorrow."

"Ah." She twirled her finger. "Because you control time. Like a science fiction villain."

"I'm not a villain."

"Don't forget to look up the winning numbers today before you go to bed."

He scowled, just like a villain. "You're making fun of me."

"I'm being helpful. I'm actually quite helpful. Unfortunately, my family doesn't see it that way."

"No. They do not," he said knowingly, with a dark laugh.

His amusement was like a barbed wire running through her center.

"My sister has told you things?"

His dark laugh got louder. "So many things."

The barbed wire of familiar betrayal was so jagged.

"Family matters shouldn't be discussed outside of the family," Zirconia said coolly.

"I agree," he said. "That's why I usually avoid the break room when Zinnia's in there."

Zirconia didn't like the sound of that. Her sister shouldn't have been spilling secrets at the workplace. At least not in a boring Zinnia fashion that diminished any interest her coworkers might have had in Riddle family gossip. It was a disservice on so many levels.

Xavier drained his light beer, then dropped the glass on the table loudly.

"Oh, what's the point? You don't believe me," he said sullenly. "Even if I do give you the winning lottery numbers, you'll say I just got them from Dawna."

Dawna?

He had to be referring to the card mage who worked at his office. The woman did have some talent with the cards, but she lacked training and thus focus.

Zirconia said, "If you know someone who can give you the winning lottery numbers, why do you work in the permits department?"

He exhaled loudly. "I didn't say she *would* give them to me, just that you'd think... never mind." He rose from his seat with a groan. "I'll try again tomorrow. Forget all this."

"Sit down."

He sat, on her command, with a loud thump.

"Ow. My tailbone," he said. "Was that magic?"

She didn't answer. She couldn't remember if she'd used glamour magic or not. It came so naturally.

He rubbed a spot at the center of his collarbone. "Next time you see me, I'll be more prepared." He had to mean he'd be wearing the bartender's amulet.

They could play the game again tomorrow, but she did want a bit more information on this round.

"Let's say you were caught in a time loop," she said. "Why would you come to see me about it? And after so few iterations. Aren't there at least a dozen other people you have a stronger bond with?"

He let out a huge sigh. "I don't even know how many days I've been looping." He put his face in his hands.

Zirconia recognized the signs of an incoming Pity Party.

"I'm such a loser Nothing Person," Xavier said.

And there it was.

He went on, sounding upset, but—to her relief—not crying. "I didn't even notice I was living the same exact day over and over."

He hadn't even noticed? What an idiot.

She had missed it for a few days herself, but that was different. She'd been living in a sort of loop for months, which had camouflaged the actual loop.

"Focus, Xavier. I need to know why you came to me."

"You do?" He peeked at her between his fingers. "Why?"

Why, indeed? She couldn't tell him much without tipping her hand and letting him know that she was, as he'd originally suspected, in on the time loop.

"It might be a clue," she said. "If you want me to help you with this thought experiment of yours, I should know everything. Full disclosure."

He rubbed his head, sending his dark hair in every direction.

"Tell me," she said, with authority but not with magic. Too much glamour right now would only make him more suspicious.

He spoke slowly. "I came to you because of something that happened. We hung out together, in one of the loops. You don't remember because the day disappeared for you when it started over."

"How interesting. Why were we, as you say, *hanging out*?"

"It hasn't happened yet, but later today, you're going to come to the Permits Department to get someone to help you do something on the computer." His light-green eyes brightened. "You'll want help trading stocks to make money. Does that ring a bell?"

"No," she said coolly. "That doesn't sound like something I would do."

"Maybe it's Zinnia's idea," he said.

"Regardless of the circumstances, let's say you and I are fated to 'hang out.' What did I—or what will I—say to you about time travel?"

"Well, you poured us—you will pour us—a long row of shots and tell me to drink up because we are living in a time loop, and there will be no hangovers."

"You must have misunderstood me."

"No." He shook his head. "I asked you to explain, and you talked to me for an hour about time travel." He patted the table as though looking for something. "I wish I'd kept those napkins. You drew diagrams and everything."

"I did?" A faint, booze-soaked memory came back to her. She had drawn on napkins. Cartoons, and diagrams about... time loops.

Her toes tightened again.

How could she have been so careless? Even as she asked herself, she knew why. It was Xavier's fault. The young man was so desperate to be near magic, he must have dragged it out of her, like a body preservationist in ancient Egypt, dragging a dead pharoah's brains out through his nose.

"You're a good teacher," Xavier said.

"Obviously it was all a joke," she said, even as more memories crystallized in her mind.

"I thought you were joking, too. Alcoholics will say anything to get other people to drink with them."

She shook her head. "I don't understand. Who are these alcoholics? Were other people present?"

"When I woke up the next morning, I remembered what you said. I remembered it because I didn't have a hangover." He picked up his empty glass and swirled the dregs and foam. "Then I got up and went to work. I didn't think I was in a time loop. I figured the real reason I didn't have a headache was because you gave me something. Like an anti-hangover potion."

"If only," she said. "If only those potions were easier to come by."

"I know," he agreed.

"But then, a couple of days later, I had a funny feeling."

"How many days later?"

"I don't know." He waved a hand. "It's irrelevant. Anyway, I looked at my alarm clock a few days later, and I thought about how I'd been drinking every night, and how I hadn't had a hangover any of those times."

"Your liver must have finally gotten up to speed."

He kept going. "I got this whisper of an idea to smash it. *Smash the alarm clock*, it said. Smash it."

"The alarm clock spoke to you?"

"No. It was my brain. I think. But it sounded like somebody else. Does that ever happen to you?"

"I'm not crazy."

"So, I smashed my alarm clock, finished my beer, and then I went to bed." He leaned forward, raising the suspense. He was a good storyteller. "And then... in the morning, I wasn't hungover, and the alarm clock was whole again."

"Your alarm clock fixed itself overnight?"

"Yes." He squeezed his eyes shut and shook his head. "No. It was never broken. I checked the date, and it was Wednesday, the same as the day before."

Then he held out his hands, indicating that he'd reached the end of his tale.

Zirconia waited a full minute before saying, "You have quite the imagination."

His light-green eyes twinkled. "I'll be more convincing tomorrow. You'll see."

"Why are you trying so hard to convince me of anything?"

"Because I think you know. Maybe not today, but on other days. Why else would you tell me about it?"

"You think I'm aware of the time loop, but only some days?"

He shrugged. "Maybe. I didn't have it all figured out, to be honest."

"I hadn't noticed." She pressed her lips together.

He looked down and rubbed at some spilled wax on the table with his thumb. The wax peeled up in white flakes.

"As a Nothing Person, I can't do much on my own," he said. "If I'm supposed to save the world or whatever, I'll need allies with actual powers."

"You're planning to save the world? From what?"

"From whatever keeps ending it," he said matter-of-factly. "Why else would time keep rebooting?"

Zirconia didn't have any response for that. Had the world been ending? She hadn't noticed.

Xavier abruptly stood. "If you'll excuse me, I'm off to do my research. When you see me tomorrow, I'm going to knock your socks off. It's too bad you won't know."

"It is too bad," she agreed.

He pointed at her. "Ninety-nine," he said.

"Ninety-nine." She pointed right back. This was too easy. "Plus the lottery numbers."

"I didn't forget," he said, tapping his forehead.

Then he left her to her drinks and the rest of her day.

CHAPTER 32

Wednesday Again

Zirconia was in the lobby, luring the Darnells into a janitor's closet when something she'd expected might happen, happened.

Xavier Batista ran into the lobby with messy hair.

"There you are," Xavier said, red-cheeked and breathing hard. He nodded casually at Debbie and Darren, who stood by, swaying under a glamour.

"You're not supposed to be here," Zirconia said, trying to say it the exact way she had the previous day. She had a good memory for these things, but it wasn't perfect.

Xavier ran his hands through his dark hair, making it look tidy this time instead of messier. "Yeah, I should be at work, but I'm not."

She forgot a few lines but carried on. "Which one of my family members told you to come here?"

"I came here on my own. I need to talk to you about —"

Cutting him off mid-sentence came instinctively. "I'm busy." She indicated the swaying Darnells. "You have two safe choices. Help, or get out of the way."

He stepped aside, and watched calmly as Zirconia walked the Darnells into the closet then put them both to sleep. Darren's mind resisted more than Debbie's.

"Something magical is happening to me," Xavier said. "I need your help. Let's discuss it over drinks. I'm sure it's five o'clock somewhere."

She patted him on the back. "I thought you'd never ask."

He gave her a wary look. "Have we had this conversation before?"

"That's an odd question." She was perfectly safe deviating from the script now that he was.

His eyes narrowed to cartoonish dashes. "Does any of this feel familiar to you?"

He watched her closely. So closely, in fact, that she worried he might have already seen something.

Had she slipped up?

She would have to be more careful. The boy could be clumsy, but he was not unintelligent. He had come to her, after all. More tellingly, he'd woken up to the time loop. Few people could do that, even when given ample opportunity.

She shrugged casually. "Of course it feels familiar. I've been at this cursed hotel so long, the days are all running together. Sometimes I forget what day it is."

"It's Wednesday," he said. "Does that seem odd to you?"

She led the way to the lounge. "Wednesday does come around once a week or so. Nothing odd about that."

As they walked up to the bar, the bartender gave Xavier the same double take. "Dude. I said I would handle it myself," he said to Xavier. "You didn't have to —"

Xavier cut off his friend by poking at the amulet through the shirt. "Sorry, dude, but I need that back. Just for today."

Xavier took back the charm that would protect him from vampire glamours.

The vampire pretended to be more concerned with ordering beverages.

"Two greyhounds," she said. "And whatever *the dude* wants."

"Light beer," Xavier said. "I need to keep my wits about me today."

They took their usual seat in the darkened lounge.

They waited in silence until their drinks arrived.

Once they were alone, Xavier said, "You're not going to believe this right away, but I'm caught in a time loop."

"Is this a prank? Did my sister put you up to this?"

"I'm not joking." He held up one hand. "My word is my bond, I'm telling the truth. Today keeps repeating. It's a genuine time loop, like in the movies. I'll prove it."

"Oh?"

He pulled a folded piece of paper from his pocket and held it between his fingers.

"Pick a number between one and ninety-nine."

"Seven," she said.

He winced. "A different one," he said.

"Thirty-three."

"One more try," he said. "I'm new at this."

"Another number? Hmm. How about your emotional maturity? Twelve."

He gave up, putting the folded paper—the one that had ninety-nine written on it—back in his pocket.

She clapped her hands like a giddy child. "Why are we stopping already?"

"I messed it up," he said. "You were going to say ninety-nine, but I messed it up." He smacked his forehead.

"Is that all you've got?"

His cheeks flushed. His dark skin didn't show much pink on the surface, but Zirconia sensed the blood rushing to the surface as easily as a regular person might sense the presence of raspberry jam on scones, or dirty thumbs on that jam.

The new time looper asked sheepishly, "Would you be impressed by today's winning lottery numbers?"

"I might be, around seven o'clock tonight when they're drawn."

He wrinkled his nose. "Seven o'clock, huh?" He scratched his head. "And is there a place they're announced, or would I be able to find them online?"

She tilted her head to the side. “Did you forget to check them last night?”

“No.” He abruptly stood. “Maybe.”

He looked at the exit, groaned, and sat back down again.

“Yes,” he said. “I forgot to check for the winning numbers. How did you know?”

“Your blood doesn't lie.”

He clutched at his amulet like an old lady clutching her pearls at a burlesque show.

“Relax,” she said. “I'm not going to bite you.”

He grabbed his light beer for a drink, then slammed it on the table in frustration. Zirconia recognized that emotion. She'd been awkward on her first loop as well. Not as awkward as him, mind you, but she understood how he was feeling better than anyone could.

“You really do believe this delusion of yours,” she said. “Did you know there are spells that cause people to experience life as one continuous déjà vu?”

It was true. It happened to people sometimes after brain injuries. Magic didn't even need to be involved.

“That's not what this is,” he said. “What's happening to me is real.”

“I'm sure it feels real.”

“Déjà vu doesn't make you plan ahead.” He took the paper from his pocket and unfolded it to reveal a tidy handwritten 99. “You were supposed to pick ninety-nine.”

“Was I?” She sipped her greyhound. It was such a lovely shade of pink.

“You're being difficult,” he said.

“Now you sound just like my family,” she said.

He groaned.

“Let's say you were caught in a time loop,” she said. “Why would you come to see me about it?”

“We hung out together recently, in one of the loops. Yesterday, and a few days before that. You don't remember, but you told me to drink up because we were living in a time loop and there were no hangovers."

She snorted. "Obviously I was joking."

He leaned forward and grabbed her by both wrists. "You remember," he said, squeezing her wrists aggressively.

Zirconia didn't react well to people grabbing her let alone squeezing her.

She flipped the interaction—her hands were now around his wrists—and sunk her fangs into his pleasantly muscled forearm before he even realized he was in danger.

She yanked her head away, licked her lips, and released him.

His arm was bleeding. Her teeth hadn't retracted yet.

He pulled backward hard, desperate to get away. Without the resistance of her grip, he fell off his chair.

He got to his feet, sputtering incoherently.

He stared at his bleeding arm in disbelief, then clutched his amulet.

"You bit me," he said. "You bit me. With your fangs and everything."

"I barely scratched the surface."

"I'm bleeding like a stuck pig. I could die." He squeezed the skin below the wound like a tourniquet. The wound had already stopped flowing freely. "You could have killed me."

"If I'd wanted to bleed you out, you wouldn't be standing there right now, with that indignant expression. The entitlement you must have, to look so indignant. Young man, you got exactly what you deserved for grabbing a lady the way you did."

"I wasn't going to hurt you. I just... I just..."

"You just made a mistake," she said. "And you won't make it again."

He backed away, both hands up. "I... I won't."

"Good," she said.

And then he turned and ran.

Zirconia wiped the metaphorical dust from her hands.

Well, that was that.

Xavier had learned his lesson.

He hadn't been able to convince her about time travel, and he wouldn't be back again to mess up her day.

She was wrong.

CHAPTER 33

The Wednesday Zirconia Killed Xavier

Zirconia was in the lobby, luring the Darnells into a janitor's closet when something unexpected happened.

Xavier Batista came running into the lobby with messy hair.

But she didn't see him, because he came in a few minutes later than he had the previous two times.

This time, her back was turned to the front doors.

This time, he ran up quietly, on the tips of his toes.

She could have heard him if she'd been listening, but she hadn't been listening. She had been overconfident about having scared him off.

Not knowing she had an audience, Zirconia walked the Darnells into the closet, and put them to sleep.

So far, everyone was going according to plan. This time, without Xavier distracting her, she would get everything perfect. Today was the day that would lead to tomorrow.

Suddenly, there was a body against hers. Arms wrapping around her. Arms squeezing her.

It was Xavier. She knew instantly.

The next thing happened almost instantly.

She would have had enough time and awareness to control her reaction to his attack.

She didn't have to throw him across the lobby.

But she did.

He landed on a couch, where she'd meant for him to land.

It knocked the wind out of him.

“It's just me,” he said, gasping to refill his lungs. He held up both hands as he righted himself. “It's me, Xavier. I work with your sister.”

"What are you doing here?" She didn't have to act surprised. She was surprised. Most people who got bitten by a vampire were... what were the lyrics of that song? *Once bitten, twice shy.*

He moved toward her instead of fleeing. Apparently she had not bitten him or flung him across the lobby hard enough.

"I need your help," he said.

"No," she said. "Go away."

"You have to help me."

"Go away." She put a strong wave of magic into her command. "Be gone from my sight."

He kept closing in on her.

He wore the amulet.

He was late to their rendezvous because he'd stopped by the lounge and gotten the protective necklace from his friend already.

"Leave now or I will bite you," she said.

"That's exactly what I want," he said.

She was speechless.

He got close enough to grab her wrist, and he did. He squeezed it as he looked into her eyes.

"I consent," he said. "Turn me. I want to be like you."

She yanked her wrist away easily.

He wore the amulet, so he wasn't susceptible to her enchantments, but she still had her other skills. He was a strong young man, but he had nothing on her supernatural strength.

"Turn me," he said.

"No." She picked him up and flung him onto the lobby couch again. Harder this time.

He got up and came right back at her.

"I want this," he said through gritted teeth. "Come on. Don't you want to taste my blood?" He held his forearm to her nose.

He was nervous. He smelled acrid, of sweat, but his blood was rushing to the surface and it did smell good.

"You don't want this," she said. "Leave here now, and don't come back again."

"I won't go." He crossed his arms and stood tall in front of her.

She wove around him, but he lunged, grabbing her around her shoulders again, in a tackle.

She pushed his arms away hard enough to hurt him. She heard the pop of a tendon.

His face twisted in agony, but he didn't scream.

"Bite me," he said. "We could be an amazing team. We could save the world."

She picked him up and flung him as hard as she could. No holding back.

He shot over the couch and hit a wall like a bullet.

He hit it hard enough to get knocked out, which was good. *Good*, she thought. That would teach him a lesson. He'd wake up later with a concussion, and he'd remember that the next time he tried to make demands on her.

There was just one problem. She couldn't leave him lying on the floor of the lobby. That would mess up her whole day.

She grabbed him by the arms, and dragged him into the same janitor's closet where she'd stashed the Darnells.

Mr. Darnell was starting to wake, and gave her a dazed look.

"That actually explains a lot," Zirconia said to Mr. Darnell. "You've been waking up every time, haven't you? No wonder you two aren't here when I come back for you."

Darren Darnell looked over at Xavier's limp body, and opened his mouth to scream.

She put him to sleep again, this time with enough magic to keep him stashed away until past midnight. More than enough time.

She was about to leave when she noticed something didn't look quite right with Xavier. His head tipped to the side at an odd angle.

She checked his pulse, which she could do without even touching him.

There was no pulse.

"Oops," she said.

He was dead.

So much for everything going to plan today.

She checked the Darnells one more time, then she left the three bodies—two sleeping and one deceased—in the closet.

"You idiot," she said to the air around her. "If you can hear me, wherever you are, I want you to know that you did this to yourself."

Then she went about her day.

CHAPTER 34

A Dozen or So Wednesdays Later

Zirconia was in the lobby, luring the Darnells into a janitor's closet when something unexpected happened.

Xavier Batista came running into the lobby with messy hair.

He didn't say anything, but his light-green eyes, blazing with fury, said everything.

Zirconia was so surprised, she momentarily forgot her lines.

She had lived about a dozen Wednesdays since the one in which she'd accidentally killed the young man.

Evidently, he had woken from his death with his memories intact, as she'd figured he would. And he'd steered clear of her, as she'd figured he would, but not forever. Not even long enough for her to accomplish her goals.

If she wanted to get rid of him again, it was of utmost importance that she keep him convinced that she wasn't aware of the time loop. Therefore, even if she didn't get her lines exactly right, she did have to act surprised to see him.

She did a double take in his direction then said, "Zachary, what are you doing here?" She congratulated herself for intentionally getting his name wrong. It was a nice touch.

Xavier spoke in an oddly flat voice, as though reading from a teleprompter. "I should be going to work right now, but I'm not."

She said, "Are you here to give my sister a ride to work at the insurance place?" She knew darn well it was the Wisteria Permits Department, but calling their sad office an "insurance place" was yet another nice touch.

"I came here on my own. I need to talk to you about —"

"I'm busy." She indicated the swaying Darnells. "You have two safe choices. Help or get out of the way."

"I don't think either of those options is safe." He pulled something from his pocket and handed it to her. It was the amulet he'd worn on their last interaction.

"What's this?" She feigned confusion. "It's a pretty little bauble, but not really my style."

"You know exactly what it is." He stuffed his hands in his pockets and lifted his chin at the Darnells, who were still swaying in their glamour. "Put them in the closet, and we'll talk."

"The closet?" She played dumb. "Oh, sure. I guess the janitor's closet is nearly as good as their hotel room. You have a devious mind, Zebediah."

He winced at the name, but didn't speak again until they were in the lounge, seated in the usual darkened corner, sipping on their usual drinks.

"You know why I'm here," he said over his light beer.

She blinked at him. "I'm getting the strangest feeling. Have we had this conversation before?"

"Not like this."

"Do you need my help dealing with my sister?" She waved her hands in fake submission. "I can't help you there. That woman is impossible. She's so stubborn, and arrogant."

"I've been following you," he said.

The chilly blood running through her veins turned to ice water.

She tilted her head and pursed her lips to hide her fangs, which were emerging as a defensive reflex.

"I've followed you for nine days in a row now," he said. "Every day, you start off with the same routine, but then, at some point, you vary from your routine. You're conducting experiments. You're tweaking things here and there to see how it affects the outcome."

"Stalking a lady is a serious offense." She kept playing dumb and fake-sighed. "I suppose I have fallen into a rut lately. I've been trapped at this cursed hotel for far too long. The days are all running together."

He pointed to the amulet, which now sat on the top of the table between them.

"I gave you that as a peace offering. No more deception. I want us to be honest with each other."

She grabbed the amulet and crushed it to powder, her hand moving so quickly it was a blur, even to her.

In a low, serious tone, she said, "You need to mind your own business, and leave me alone."

He shook his head. "Why can't you admit that you know what's going on? Is it because you're too proud to ask for help? Be honest with me."

She signaled for the bartender to bring her two more greyhounds. She drank both pink beverages.

Alcohol always helped people to be more honest, and the vampire was no exception.

She gave in to his request.

In a soft, unguarded tone, she said, "How did you know that I know?"

"You killed me," he said. "You picked me up, and you threw me against a wall so hard, you killed me. I heard my neck snap." He shuddered. "It was... the worst thing that's ever happened to me."

"You've been killed before. My daughter killed you at least once that I know of."

"Not like that. Zara had to kill me. She had no other choice. You killed me because I was... because I was..."

She finished the thought for him. "A nuisance."

He shuddered again, and gazed wistfully at the pile of dust that had been the protective amulet.

"I knew you wouldn't stay dead," she said.

"The words you're looking for are 'I'm sorry I killed you, Xavier.'"

"But I'm not sorry. In fact, I'm tempted to kill you again right now."

He gave her a bewildered look. "Why?"

"To teach you a lesson."

"You wouldn't—"

He abruptly stopped talking.

And who could blame him?

It was difficult to form words when a vampire was ripping out your throat.

CHAPTER 35

The Very Next Wednesday

Zirconia was putting the Darnells into the janitorial closet when Xavier entered the lobby at a regular walking pace.

"I'm all charmed up," he said, waving to a collection of necklaces around his neck. "You can't bite me. You can't even touch me."

"You got me." She raised her hands in a truce position, and led the way into the lounge.

Rather than go straight to their usual table, she led him to the grand piano. She took a seat on the bench.

Xavier stood on the other side of the large musical instrument and rested his elbow on it.

"This is nice," he said. "I'm glad you've seen the light and decided to play nice."

"You call this nice?"

She took hold of the piano and gave it a shove with her full vampire strength.

Xavier, crushed against the wall by the piano, sustained life just long enough to give her an accusatory, hurt look.

She almost felt bad.

CHAPTER 36

Another Wednesday

Xavier managed to dodge the chandelier Zirconia dropped on his head.

As the crystals spun around his feet, he said, "Aren't you getting tired of this routine?"

She replied, "Aren't you?"

"I have no other choice," he said, artfully dodging the fire extinguisher she'd lobbed at him. "Can't you see we're supposed to be working together?"

"Says who?" She tossed a marble-topped side table in his general direction. It didn't even come close to hitting him.

Xavier looked at the side table with confusion, then down at himself. "Is it my imagination, or am I getting better at combat with you?"

"This is *hardly* combat."

"But I am getting better. Even you have to admit it."

"There's a saying we have. What kills you makes you stronger."

"You mean, what doesn't kill you makes you stronger."

"Not in the magical world. Not in these time loops. In here, what kills you makes you stronger."

He gave her a surprised look. "You're making me stronger." He pointed at her. "You."

"Technically, it wasn't me. It was the piano, the front desk, the sliding front doors, the Darnells' car, the ceiling, the swan pond, and..." She looked around. "What else?"

"There was something that exploded," he said.

"Right. The grenade."

"Where did you get a grenade?"

"Never mind my grenades."

He took a seat on the sofa. She'd tried to kill him with it once, but it had been too soft to do a good job.

"I thought Zinnia was stubborn, but you're so much worse," he said.

"Thank you."

"How is Zinnia?" He glanced in the direction of the stairs. "Maybe I'll pay her a visit. I miss seeing her at the ol' office."

He jumped up from the sofa and headed to the stairs.

Zirconia cut him off with her own body.

"I won't let you go up there," she said.

"What's the harm? She won't remember anything tomorrow."

She continued to stand in his way.

"Oh. You're hardcore serious," he said. "You really don't want me to talk to her, do you?"

"Leave her out of this."

He gave her a sidelong look. "Does she know?"

"No. And you're not going to tell her because if you do, I will injure you the next instant I see you, and it won't be a fatal injury. You'll stay alive for several excruciating hours. You will beg me for death."

He took a few steps back. "Why don't you want me to see her? She's my coworker. I could just go to work, like normal, and see her there. Maybe she can help me brainstorm—"

"Don't," Zirconia said. "You can't talk to her about this."

"Why not?"

Zirconia muttered, "It's bad luck."

He tilted his head. He was onto her. "You don't believe that."

She was on the spot. She didn't have a single explanation that sounded reasonable in her head, let alone out loud.

Xavier pointed at her. “Something happens when you tell people about the time loop,” he said. “It changes things.”

“Of course it does. Everything you do differently changes things. That's called causality.” She crossed her arms. “Killing you is making you stronger, but not mentally.”

“Being mean is your defense mechanism.”

“It is not, you worthless Nothing Person.”

“I think... when you tell someone they're in a time loop... it wakes them up.”

She had just enough respect for Xavier—he'd earned it—that she didn't argue.

She did, however, find a side of the sofa that was firm enough to kill him.

CHAPTER 37

Many Wednesdays Later

Zirconia had to look outside for Xavier.

She found him sitting on a bench in the bright sun.

"There you are," she said. "I've been waiting inside for you." She'd devised an elaborate method of killing him, using the lobby chandelier, but not in the expected way.

He stretched his arms along the back of the bench. He looked about as relaxed as a person could be around the vampire who'd savagely killed him several days in a row.

"Funny thing. I'm in no particular rush to go in there and get killed by you."

"We're done with that," she said with an eye roll, as though it should have been perfectly obvious. She had always been going to stop after the chandelier finale.

He said, "We are?"

"Games only last so long, even the good ones. I wasn't going to kill you anymore."

"Swear?"

"After today. My word is my bond."

"Good," he said. "That last one, with the couch, was brutal."

"I didn't enjoy it much, either."

He snorted. "Poor you."

She took a seat next to him on the bench.

The black and white swans swam around in the lagoon in front of them, looking perfectly content. The large birds had no idea they were also caught in a loop, endlessly eating the same aquatic vegetation day after day, only to reboot and eat it again.

The vampire and her—was he a friend?—stared out over the water.

The sun was still too bright, but it was somehow more tolerable on this particular Wednesday.

She wasn't alone in this loop. Plus she had increased her powers through the playful exercise of killing Xavier all those times.

Xavier said, “So, run me through the rules.”

“There are no rules.”

“You know what I mean. Why is time looping? What makes it stop? What are we supposed to do?”

She listed off the answers on her fingers. “I don't know. I don't know. I don't know. But I use the time to set things right in my life, so that when it does stop looping, I'm ready.”

He gave her a stunned look. “You don't know?”

“I don't know.”

“But... but...”

“It takes a smart person to admit when they know nothing about a particular topic.”

“And it doesn't bother you that you don't know?” He squeezed his eyes shut. “I can't believe this. You talk about it like it's got nothing to do with you. You talk about it like it's weather.”

“As far as I know, it is just weather. A simple storm front of time that comes in for a bluster before moving on.”

Xavier put his face in his hands and hunched forward.

She patted his back.

“I was once like you,” she said. “Once upon a time, I thought it was personal, that it had something to do with me. But I came to my senses. I may be self-absorbed from time to time, but I'm not so egotistical as to believe that the world and time itself revolves around me.” She stopped patting his back and held her hand to her chest. “I don't believe I'm the center of the universe.”

Xavier sat up straight, all the better to let gravity help the news travel down his digestive system.

He chewed his lip a moment, then asked, “Is there a special way you have to tell people about the loop so they wake up?”

“Probably.”

“You don't know?” He shot her a disrespectful look. “Come on. Seriously?”

She thought about biting him. He wasn't wearing the amulet. She could bite him. She probably should. It would teach him to be more respectful to his elders.

He said, “Come on, lady. Give me something to work with.”

She didn't like the way he said *lady*, like it was a slur.

She would have to bite him.

He edged away from her on the bench, as though he knew what she was planning.

“I'm sorry,” he said, just in time. “If I come across as... whatever... it's only because I'm frustrated with the situation.”

She retracted her fangs.

He said, “Why do you think I woke up after you told me? You told Denver that night, too. And I've told him a whole bunch of times, but it doesn't stick.” He thumbed in the direction of the hotel and added, “Denver is the bartender that you call Denim. He never wakes up.”

“Magic has a mind of its own,” she said. “Sometimes people wake up. Most of the time, they don't.”

“So, I could tell Zinnia, and the odds are—”

“Don't,” she said. “Don't tell Zinnia.”

“Why? You said so yourself, most people get reset.”

Zirconia picked up some loose pebbles then tossed one into the pond.

“Zinnia's different,” she said. “If one of us told her, she'd believe it. She's been in them before. That's why you can't tell her.”

“But don't we need all the help we can get?”

“I can manage just fine without her. And without you, for that matter.” She tossed more pebbles in the pond, earning a scathing look from the swans. "We can't tell Zinnia. I swore I'd never wake her up ever again."

"Why?"

"Do I really need to spell it out? Why do you think?"

Xavier shrugged.

"No. You tell me," she said. "Why do you think she made me swear to never tell her?"

"Probably because something bad happened once," he said.

She pointed at him. "Two points for Xavier."

"When? Was it when you were younger? Like, a lot younger?"

"Two more points."

"Did you kill her like you killed me?"

"No."

"But other people got killed."

She nodded. A lot of people had gotten killed.

"But so what? Everybody got over it, didn't they?"

"Yes and no," Zirconia said. "My sister is extremely sensitive. She never got over seeing what she saw. Her mind couldn't turn the memories into what they were. Imaginary possibilities."

She picked up more pebbles. The rocks were gritty, covering her fingers in an orange dust that threatened to stain her clothes.

"Huh," he said. "And she couldn't let it go? Even though it wasn't real."

"Back then, she wasn't like you, Xavier. She never knew about magic. She didn't want it. The family actually thought the gift had skipped her over, until..."

Xavier was leaning forward, staring intently at her, not the swans in the lagoon.

Zirconia waved her hand for him to stop being so interested. Family business belonged within the family.

"Never mind," she said. "My sister wouldn't want me to tell her coworkers any of the details."

"The details don't matter. I get the picture," he said.

They went back to watching the swans, and the ripples in the water from the pebbles Zirconia kept tossing in.

"That's a good metaphor," Xavier said.

She turned to him. Was he hearing things? She hadn't spoken.

"The ripples." He pointed to the pond. "Everything we do, every action we take, it ripples out from us. It affects everything. Everyone."

"Some people more than others."

He flinched. "Is that your way of calling me a Nothing Person?"

"I suppose it is."

"Thanks," he grunted.

She looked him over, seeing him in a new light.

"Except you aren't a Nothing Person. You woke up. You may have some dormant mage powers after all."

"Yeah," he said with a hollow laugh. "We're totally going to find out I'm a superhero in disguise when it comes time to save the world."

He abruptly stood.

"Have a good one," he said as he backed away.

It was the first time in a long stretch of Wednesdays that he was ending their interaction by doing something other than dying.

She didn't like it.

There was a glint in his eye. He was up to something.

She said, "Whatever you're thinking about doing, don't do it." She got to her feet to look more authoritative. "Don't go around telling a bunch of people. It's more trouble than it's worth. Trust me."

"What's the harm in trying?"

"You have no idea."

"Yeah, well, I'm not like you. I'm not going to sit back and let it happen. I'm going to test some things. What's the worst that could happen?"

"The worst thing that could happen is that every person you wake up becomes a wildcard. You can't plan anything around wildcards."

"But what if every person I wake up wakes up ten more people? And so on? And so on? It could go viral."

"We're not supposed to do that."

"What? We aren't? You told me yourself. There are no rules."

He went to a motorcycle that had been parked on the lawn, and jumped on it. He started pulling on a helmet but then stopped.

"I guess I don't need this," he said, tossing the helmet aside.

He started the motorcycle, and used the back tire to kick up a jet of green lawn.

And then off he rode.

CHAPTER 38

After Xavier rode off on his motorcycle to conduct his independent experiments, Zirconia expected he would be back that day.

But he didn't come back.

The next day, which was another time loop Wednesday, Xavier still didn't return to the hotel.

He didn't make an appearance the following one, either.

Or the next hundred Wednesdays.

On a Wednesday when she'd lost count of how many there had been, Zirconia stared across the lobby thinking about Xavier. Specifically, that she didn't care that Xavier was doing his experiments without her, and that she didn't care that she had no companion to share her day with. She didn't care at all.

The shadows in the lobby shifted. There was movement outside the hotel entrance.

Someone was coming!

Her vampire heart soared. Literally. Vampire hearts had the ability to physically move upward in the body. Only about an inch, but that inch made a huge difference when a vampire hunter was trying to stake you. They'd be hammering in a wooden stake, feeling pretty good about themselves, then BAM. Lunch. The hunter became the prey.

Was that Xavier approaching? Had he finally come to his senses? It was about time.

The hotel lobby door opened.

It was just the groundskeeper.

He must have deviated from his usual routine due to some noisy guests throwing potted plants out of an upper-floor suite. The guests who'd chucked the plants were the

Riddle family. Zinnia Riddle had reacted particularly poorly to that morning's insults.

Zirconia's vampire heart sank back down to its usual location.

She shoved the Darnells into the janitor's closet, and then went through the motions of her day.

Her Wednesday was close to perfect, even without Xavier's help, which she didn't want anyway.

She would wake up, and have the usual fight with Zinnia, who sometimes tossed houseplants out of the window. Zirconia would take care of the real estate and money situation before noon, then talk Zara out of moving away, and still have plenty of time for leisure activities.

She finished her business at the Cerulean Lagoon, and headed out in search of entertainment.

The groundskeeper was outside, complaining to a delivery driver.

Zirconia lingered to listen to their conversation.

"I hear they're witches," the groundskeeper said. "Those plants they chucked out the window weren't regular plants. Can you believe that?"

"Yup," said the delivery driver.

"One of the plants bit me," the groundskeeper said. "I'm sick of it. We would have kicked them all out months ago, but, you know how it is."

The delivery driver took a long puff on his smoking device. "Yup."

"Do you ever feel like we're the extras in somebody else's movie?"

"Yup," said the eloquent delivery driver.

"It's like we don't even matter. It sucks being a Nothing Person."

"Yup."

A moment of silence passed.

"But it beats the alternative," the groundskeeper said. "I wouldn't want to have powers. No way. Too many responsibilities."

"Yup."

"I don't even read comic books, or watch superhero movies," he said. "I feel bad for those guys. Always running around, saving the world. Coming home to find their loved ones stuffed in the refrigerator. That's no kind of life."

"Yup."

"No kind of life at all." The groundskeeper sucked on the finger where Zinnia's plant bit him.

"Yup."

"I'm heading up to Becky's Roadhouse tonight. She's rolling out a new beer. Made right here in town with local grains. A real farm-to-table kinda deal. Plus there's darts. You in?"

"Yup."

"All right. Now we're talking."

The conversation turned to beer, which felt like a commercial break in the tepid soap opera Zirconia was watching. She'd had enough. Plus she was extra thirsty, thanks to the mention of beer.

Zirconia left the hotel in search of a drink. Becky's Roadhouse wasn't her favorite destination, so she took a vampire taxi—a car driven by a random person—up the coast to Westwyrd.

Traffic was light, so the trip would take less than an hour.

She settled in the back seat and tried to nap but could not.

Her mind raced.

She thought about the groundskeeper and delivery driver's conversation. Those two Nothing People weren't wrong. Having powers was a burden. If she could have renounced her witch powers and still survived to see her grandchild grow up, she would have. Gladly.

Instead, she was... this.

Her stomach grumbled.

She was this... this beast that was never not hungry.

This beast that was never not thirsty.

Well, *never* wasn't quite right. She could be sated. But it never lasted.

The car pulled up to Castle Wyvern.

She didn't step out right away.

The driver of the car, a middle-aged woman, had a pleasant scent, and the vampire didn't want to leave the vehicle alone.

She tapped the driver on the shoulder and asked, "How would you like to spend the day at the spa being pampered? My treat."

The driver turned and gave her a confused look. "What? Who are you?" She grabbed her phone. "Oh, no. I'm late to pick up my kids."

"Never mind," Zirconia said.

She left the car and went into the castle alone, wishing she wasn't alone.

She didn't have to be alone.

She would arrange her day differently when she got the chance to do it all over again.

CHAPTER 39

The Next Wednesday - Spa Day

Zirconia gave a handful of cash to the not-a-taxi driver.

"Don't forget to pick up your kids," she said helpfully to the pleasant-smelling woman.

Then she and her companion got out of the vehicle.

The woman squealed her tires in her rush to get back to her children's school.

Zara clucked her tongue as both women watched the car drive away.

"Mother, you should have let me drive," Zara said.

"Nonsense. We're having a mother-daughter relaxation day," Zirconia said.

"I could use a face treatment." Zara rubbed at her eyes, which were swollen from the tears she'd shed during their argument earlier. The argument that Zirconia had won by a landslide.

There was a loud engine sound as a motorcycle approached. The rider was a young man with no helmet, his nearly-black hair tousling in the wind.

Zara said, "Was that Xavier Batista?"

Zirconia sniffed the air. "Yes."

"He should be wearing a helmet."

"Or make sure his organ donor card is up to date."

Zara shot her mother a horrified look. "Must you be so morbid?"

"He could save someone else's life. Isn't that what he wants? To be a hero?"

Zara frowned. "Not like that."

"Of course not. Nobody wants to be a hero if it requires a great sacrifice. They just want the glory without the cost. People like that should become actors, so they can play heroes without the..."

Zara burst into tears.

Zirconia realized her mistake.

CHAPTER 40

The Next Wednesday - Spa Day Two

Zirconia gave a handful of cash to the not-a-taxi driver.

"Now pick up your kids and don't speed," she said to the woman as she and Zara got out of the vehicle.

The woman squealed her tires even louder in her rush to get away.

Zara said, "Mother, you should have let me drive."

"Nonsense. We're having a mother-daughter relaxation day, and you could use a face treatment for your eyes."

Zara rubbed at her eyes, which were swollen from crying. Zirconia had gone easier on her that afternoon, but Zara had cried in the car ride over anyway.

There was a loud engine sound as Xavier rode by on his motorcycle.

Zara said, "Was that Xavier Batista?"

"Yes."

"He should be wearing a helmet."

"I agree."

"That boy won't ever be a hero if he dies young," Zara said. "He'll never get to sacrifice himself..."

Zara's voice choked off as she burst into tears.

Zirconia resolved to get there a few minutes earlier or later on the next round, to avoid Xavier. She didn't want to see him anyway.

CHAPTER 41

The Next Wednesday - Spa Day Three

Zirconia and Zara arrived at Castle Wyvern at the exact same time, in spite of the time-looping vampire's plans.

They had taken a different not-a-taxi, and embarked at a different time, yet the day's stickiness had trapped them like flypaper. They'd wound up at the same place and time as the previous two days.

They exited the vehicle, and Zirconia waited expectantly for Xavier to roar by on his motorcycle.

But he didn't.

Zara said, “Should I start with a facial, or a massage?” She was bubbling with eagerness. No crying on the ride over.

“Facial,” Zirconia said. “Your eyes look atrocious.”

“Mother!”

They entered the castle. It was, unlike most castles on the continent, authentic, having been shipped over and rebuilt there, stone by stone.

Zara stopped at a tall, arched mirror and leaned in, turning her face from side to side. “You're right about one thing today. My eyes look exactly like two cats' buttholes.”

Zirconia's stomach turned at the idea. She'd seen their white cat's back end more than enough times to imagine a pair of them perfectly.

That was one of the worst things about words and phrases—they put ideas in your mind that you never would have imagined on your own.

Zara squeezed one eye shut, and then the other.

“Meow,” she said to herself in the mirror. “My hazel eyes look like brown-eyes.”

"Zarabella, you have the worst way with words. Considering you sell books all day, you should have learned by now how to phrase things more delicately."

"Meow, meow," the witch said, still winking at her reflection.

"Why?" Zirconia had no other words except, "Why?"

"Because you have to laugh," Zara said. "You have to let it out. It's either laugh, cry, or crush it down into a little ball of venom, like you do."

Zirconia couldn't argue. She *did* crush her negative emotions into venom. It was just basic vampire physiology.

The two Riddle women stopped at the front desk.

Zara said to the receptionist, "I know we don't have an appointment, so we don't expect—"

The receptionist said, "Zara Riddle? We have you booked for the whole afternoon. In fact, you have every one of us here at your disposal."

Zara gave her mother a suspicious look. "Just a little spur-of-the-moment fun, huh?"

"I called ahead," Zirconia said.

"How many other people's appointments did you cancel?"

Zirconia patted her daughter's shoulder. "It's a spa treatment, dear. It's not elective surgery."

The witch grumbled, but she wasn't irritated enough to walk away from spa treatments.

They enjoyed a hot stone massage, and then settled in for a mud treatment.

Both were coated in a layer of mud from head to toe, except for their eyes, which were covered in the stereotypical cucumber slices.

In the quiet darkness—the cucumber blocked what little light remained in the dim room—Zirconia's mind turned back to Xavier, her erstwhile companion.

Why had he rode his motorcycle by the castle on two days in a row but not three?

What was he up to?

She thought about what he'd said at their last meeting, by the swan-filled lagoon. About breaking the time loop through their own actions. Taking control of it instead of waiting for it to pass by like weather.

What if he was onto something?

What if they could set off a chain reaction of waking up more people who then went on to wake up more people?

Then there would be so many wildcards in play that a time looped wouldn't be all that different from regular days.

Except the weather would be exactly the same. And nobody would give birth, or get older, or die. Not permanently, anyway.

A voice came through the darkness, startling Zirconia.

"Penny for your thoughts," said Zara.

Zirconia had become so accustomed to being alone that she'd nearly forgotten she wasn't.

"Just thinking about what an interesting day it's turned out to be."

"What do you mean?"

Zirconia considered telling her daughter about the time loop. She played it out in her mind, along with a vivid scene of her daughter not taking the news well. It was extremely difficult for Zirconia to tell her daughter anything at all.

Worst of all, if the news blew up in Zirconia's face, Zara might wake up—fully wake up—and remember everything the next day.

Zirconia would not get a second chance to do it better.

No.

She couldn't let that happen. With a daughter like Zara, a mother needed all the second chances she could get.

Zirconia diverted herself away from the dangerous topic.

"I'm so glad we could do this," Zirconia said. "It's nice seeing you in a toga again."

"A toga? Oh, you mean these big robes. I guess they look a bit like togas."

"When you were little, I always put you in the prettiest dresses for social functions. You would be so pleased with yourself, in your ruffles and lace, the belle of the ball. But then you would, I don't know, get bored, and go looking for trouble. I should have given you a sibling to keep you entertained. You know what they say. Only children are lonely children."

"That's not true. Zoey has plenty of friends." There was a pause. "Now. Now that she has Ambrosia."

"I'd be at a party, a nice one, and I would hear a commotion. Where's Zara, I'd think. Where's my daughter? Then I would see you, and the pretty dress would be gone. Everyone would be looking. There you would be, my only child, my little Zarabella, dressed in nothing but a toga you'd made for yourself using the bathroom guest towels."

"What? You're making that up. I don't remember that."

"You were very small."

"Hmm. But not too small to make myself a toga out of some stranger's towels."

Zirconia suddenly found the mud covering her body to be too dense, too restrictive. She was trapped, and the worst part was she'd trapped herself.

Zara's voice came through the darkness, tiny, like a child's. "You wiped my memories."

"It didn't do any good," Zirconia said with a reluctant sigh. "Every time we went somewhere, you'd go back to the same thing, like a dog to its old buried bones. Some things can't be changed or skipped over."

Zara went quiet.

A few minutes later, she was softly snoring.

Zirconia sat up, removed the cucumber slices from her eyes, and looked down at her mud-covered daughter on the mud-covered plastic treatment table.

Her stomach clenched in with the usual hunger and thirst, plus another thing. Guilt.

She had used her vampire glamour to put Zara to sleep. The two of them had an agreement to not use magic on each other unless it was absolutely necessary.

Zirconia struggled to convince herself that a nap had been necessary. And it had. Poor Zara's swollen eyes really did resemble the rear exits of two felines.

An attendant came in to check on them.

"My daughter's sleeping," Zirconia said in a whisper. "She doesn't sleep well at night, so we should leave her to rest when she can."

The attendant said, "And what about you?"

"Let's get this putrid mud off me and treat my insides to a tall glass of beer. You do have beer on the premises, do you not? Something light?"

"You're in luck. We just got a keg from Becky's Roadhouse Bar and Grill."

Zirconia sighed. Sometimes the day chose the strangest things to be sticky about. What could she do? Magic had a mind of its own.

* * *

After Zara woke up from her nap, the two decided to stay the night rather than hitch a ride back to Wisteria.

They went to a nice room on the top floor, still in their spa robes, and ordered room service.

The room service menu at Castle Wyvern wasn't perfect, but it was far superior to the Cerulean Lagoon, where the chef considered hamburgers with mushrooms the height of cuisine.

Zirconia ordered a hamburger with mushrooms. She happened to like hamburgers with mushrooms, but more so when she also had the choice of other things.

"Mmm," Zara said when their meals arrived. "Hang-a-burgers. I do love me some hang-a-burgers."

They sat and ate.

Zirconia found herself thinking about Xavier again. Where was he? Had he crashed his motorcycle over a cliff? If so, she understood. She had gone through a phase of ending the day on her own terms as well. It was only dumb luck that she hadn't done so right before time pulled itself out of the loop.

Zara said, "You're awfully quiet. Are you talking to Ribbons, too?"

"No," Zirconia said. She hadn't even noticed the telepathic wyvern was nearby.

"Just thinking? Penny for your thoughts. What are we up to now? Two cents?"

"What do you think of Xavier Batista? Your aunt's young coworker?"

"Oh, gross." Zara's face scrunched. "He's way too young, even for you." She stuck her tongue out.

"Not like that. Must you always take a straight line toward the most upsetting interpretation of my words?"

Zara didn't say anything. She kept making rubbery faces. She'd gotten that from her father. Rhys was always contorting his face to make new, never-before-seen expressions. Zara was, at times, the spitting image of her shifter parent.

"Don't make faces," Zirconia said. "If you're doing that when the clock strikes, it'll get stuck that way."

Zara giggled.

Then she laughed.

The laughing took a turn. A bad turn. The laughs became sobs. The happy outburst seamlessly turned into a sad one.

Zara slipped off her chair like a camisole off a hanger, onto the carpet. She rolled onto her side, into the fetal position, where she sobbed uncontrollably.

It was grief.

This was Zirconia's fault. Not Bentley dying—that had been nobody's fault but the devil himself, but Zara's rapid descent into a crying jag was Zirconia's doing.

She should have known better than to push too hard for perfection. One could only bend reality so much within a single day, even with the fullness of time in a loop.

This wasn't the first time Zara had gone from joy to pain in these loops. It happened more often than not.

Grief was a sneaky thing. You'd think you were free of it, only to have it roll up behind you and run you down.

Zirconia went to her daughter and sat next to her on the carpet.

Zara curled tighter into a ball.

"It's okay," Zirconia said. "Shhh. It's all going to be okay. Time heals all wounds."

Except time wasn't healing Zara's wounds. It was keeping her trapped in her grief, day after day without any progress.

Zirconia's heart sank a full inch.

The time loop wasn't helping her daughter.

If anything, Zara's grief seemed to be getting worse.

CHAPTER 42

Another Wednesday

Zirconia didn't give up on trying to save her daughter from her grief, but she did try an entirely new direction.

She went in search of her fellow time looper, to find out if he had discovered anything useful about the magic they were caught in.

She checked all the obvious places, and found him at last when she stopped into the local bowling alley in search of a refreshing beer that didn't come from Becky's Roadhouse.

Shady Lanes Bowling and Ales was dark inside, still closed for the day.

Xavier was there, sitting cross-legged on top of a table, deep in concentration.

A trio of robotic vacuum cleaners whirred and rolled around the carpeted lounge next to the lanes.

Xavier wore the same clothes she'd seen him in previously, but no shoes. His feet were bare, sockless. His toenails needed trimming. He had hairy toe knuckles.

He looked up, saw her, and waved frantically with one hand.

She waved back.

One of the round vacuuming robots bumped into Zirconia's boot, then ricocheted off merrily.

"Noooo," Xavier groaned. "You've messed it all up."

"It's nice to see you, too," she said icily, turning to leave.

So much for that relationship.

"Wait," he said. "You might as well stick around, now that you've messed it all up."

"I see you've been using your time to polish your hospitality skills."

"I might have been happier to see you if you'd jumped up on a chair like I asked you to."

"You didn't ask me to jump on a chair. The first thing you said to me was that I'd messed something up."

He made the waving gesture again, palm up, fingers flipping upward repeatedly. "That's what this means. It means *jump up on a chair*."

"No. That gesture means *let's go*."

"Why would I say *let's go* to someone who just walked in?"

"How should I know?"

He groaned. "Haven't you ever played that game where you pretend the floor is hot lava?"

"I've seen plenty of hot lava, and it's no game."

He jumped off the table, and kicked one of the robot vacuum cleaners with his bare foot. It made a pitiful sound that might have tugged at Zirconia's heart strings, if she'd had any.

Then he kicked it again, using the side of his foot to protect his bare toes.

"Stop abusing that device," she said.

"Why? It'll be fine tomorrow morning." He pulled his bare foot back to kick it again.

Zirconia used her speed to intercept him.

She whisked the round, flat vacuum cleaner to a safer spot, and put it down. "Go play with your friends," she said softly.

Xavier stared at her in disbelief. "You can murder me in cold blood, over and over, but you've got empathy for a piece of electronics?"

"He's just trying to do his job."

"He? Wait. Are those things sentient?"

"I hope not," she said. "I just happen to like them. I have a soft spot for servants that know their place and do their jobs without complaint."

He nodded and waved a finger. "Yeah, okay. That checks out."

She'd never seen the bowling alley empty before. The repetition of the lanes were odd when viewed without people on them. Like an optical illusion. Her eyes didn't know what to make of it. The alley was large and cavernous, like a ballroom, but a ballroom didn't have lanes and gutters.

It wasn't a bad place to be. She'd enjoyed some pleasant evenings there, socializing and throwing balls at pins with her sister's colorful collection of coworkers.

It was a shame the day being repeated was Wednesday and not Friday, the night the league bowled.

She kept looking around, though she couldn't see, smell, hear, or sense any explanation for why Xavier might be there.

"I'm conducting experiments," he said, as though reading her mind.

Was he reading her mind? Had killing him made him that much stronger?

She said, "What am I thinking about right now?" She thought about the beer from Becky's Roadhouse. Too hoppy.

Xavier said, "The number ninety-nine."

"Wrong," she said. "Never mind. What are you doing in here?"

"Experiments," he said again. "These little robots are a clue."

One of them meandered across the carpet between them. It was the one Xavier had kicked—badly dented, but still working. Zirconia admired the little guy's work ethic. Carrying on with one's job in spite of an injury was a mark of excellence.

"There's a variation in the pattern they use to vacuum," he said. "I come in every day at the exact same time, and sit in the exact same spot. After a while, their pattern changes. It's not the same as the day before."

"That can't be."

"Come back tomorrow. You'll see. But take off your shoes and socks, and don't step on the carpet."

Walk barefoot on the carpet of a bowling alley lounge? Who did he think he was talking to? Someone who wanted to acquire new strains of foot fungus?

Xavier said, "One time I had sock lint between my toes, and one of them circled back to get all of it. So now I wash my feet before I come in."

"Where do you wash your feet?"

"There's a hose outside."

She nodded for him to continue.

"I step in the exact same spots on the carpet," he said. "It's a low pile, so it probably doesn't matter, but I step in the same spots just in case. Then I use the tables and chairs, like the floor is hot lava."

Zirconia could already see where he was going with the story, and was already bored of it, but let him finish anyway.

Xavier explained, in great detail, that he'd noticed a variation from day to day. It was subtle, but with the trio of robots interacting with each other, gently bumping chairs and nudging them into different positions, the variations compounded over time, rippling out with greater effects.

He concluded with, "That tells me the days aren't exactly the same."

"And you find this exciting."

"Wouldn't you?"

"Is it more exciting each time?"

He gave her a wary look. "Yeah? I guess so."

She pointed to the empty bags of cheese-crusted snack products that sat next to him on the table.

She asked, "Did you eat all three bags of those crusty cattle-feed things yesterday?"

"Only two."

She shook her head.

Indignantly, he said, "So what? Who cares? When I wake up tomorrow, I won't have eaten them. I could smoke three packs a day and it wouldn't matter." He waved one foot in the air. "It doesn't matter how short I cut my toenails, they've grown back the next morning." He wiggled his big toe independently. "I'm getting really sick of this one. There's a snag that catches on my sock. Do you have any tricks for stuff like that? It drives me nuts. Wouldn't that drive you crazy?"

"No. Your personal hygiene doesn't concern me."

"Then why do you care what I eat?"

Zirconia said, "I don't care what you eat."

"That would make you different from every other woman I've ever met."

He crumpled the snack bags into a ball, and tossed them at the circulating vacuum cleaners. The bags unfolded themselves and floated themselves out evenly, so that one landed on top of each robot.

"Woah," Xavier said. "That was a one in a billion shot. Did you see that?" He looked up. "It's on the security cameras. I can rewind it and show you."

"I saw it."

"Doesn't matter. I'll do it again tomorrow."

"You won't."

"Wanna bet?"

There was a manic zeal in his eyes. Poor Xavier had been going a bit nutty on his own. It wasn't just the snag on his toenail, it was everything that was driving him to madness.

He picked at his toenail, and then ripped off the overgrown tip. "Ouch." He sucked in air between his teeth. "That's a bleeder." He pointed at the vampire. "Don't get excited. Hold your breath or whatever."

She stared at him for a moment, taking in all the signs of madness. All things considered, he did seem mostly sane, which was good.

He ripped off another toenail, having not learned his lesson from the first time. Again, it tore off too much, and he howled about the injury to his skin.

"Whatever," he said, throwing both hands in the air. "The important thing is I got proof. The days aren't the same."

"Xavier, you should be smarter by now."

"Huh?"

"Don't you see it? The days only vary for you because you are the wildcard," she said. "You are the variable that changes the robot algorithms."

"No way. I barely step on the carpet. It's three steps. No toe lint."

"No matter how hard you try, you can't control every single atom. You can't even control your metabolic rate. You ate three bags of crusty cattle-feed today because you were hungrier than yesterday."

He frowned at the bag-covered robot vacuums.

"The variable could be your body heat," she said. "Or the moisture in your breath. Or both. You being here affects the outcome of the programming far more than you think."

He jumped off the table, and kicked a chair. He was still barefoot, so the chair won. He hopped up and down holding his abused foot.

"You could have told me," he said grumpily. "I've been wasting my time here, and you could have told me."

"I could have told you plenty, if you'd come to me instead of jumping on your motorbike and riding off like some sort of... like... like a mountain hermit."

The mountain hermit metaphor wasn't quite right, because it wasn't like the world was frozen or gone. There were still the usual number of people around for Xavier to interact with.

And yet, because those people would reset the next day with no memory, they were, from the perspective of a time looper, more like the robot vacuum cleaners than they were like people.

Perhaps that was why she had empathy for the little robots. Her brain confused living and nonliving things.

Xavier said, "It's funny you should call me mountain hermit. It does feel like I'm living this day all alone in my own bubble. That's a perfect metaphor."

"Thanks." And she was thankful. "It's nice to be able to share this with someone." She waved at the empty bowling lanes. "Where are all the legions of friends you were going to wake up? Couldn't you get anyone to believe you?"

"Not for lack of trying. I tried a whole bunch of people, even my ex-girlfriend."

"Laura Fitbit?"

"Liza Gilbert," he said.

"That's what I said. Lisa Bilbert."

"I tried to wake her up a bunch of times. You'd think someone who's gone through time and visited another world would believe something like this, but no."

"You two were the ones who lived with the sandworms?"

His expression crumpled like a foil snack bag. "Lived with? We were their captives. It was a living nightmare." His crumpled face elongated as an idea came to him. "That's what we need to do! We have to go through the elevator to the other world, and back again. It's like this world is slipping gears or something. We can get it back in gear."

Zirconia shrugged. "We can give it a try. Do you have an elevator key?" Elevator keys were magical items that had strange time-looping properties of their own. They were difficult to come by.

His shoulders slumped. "No." He dropped into a chair heavily. "And forget about asking the mayor. You'd think she knows, since she's a time paladin or whatever, but every time I busted into her office, she had me thrown in jail." He hugged his arms around himself. "And not the regular jail."

"Time paladins don't know that much about time," Zirconia said. "They're like the economists who work for the government."

Xavier looked sadder than ever. His pity parties had no bottom floor.

Zirconia took a seat on the chair next to him.

They watched the trio of robots bump and whirr their way around the lounge.

It was soothing, like viewing a coral reef from her sister's friend's weird little submarine.

"Liza laughed at me," Xavier said.

"She's your girlfriend?"

"Ex."

"Did you trick her into getting back together with you?"

"No!"

They watched the robots for another minute.

Xavier said, "Yes. We got back together. But it didn't last."

"Don't waste any more time on it."

He shot her a dark look. "Liza's not an *it*. She's a person. You're horrible." He didn't hold back his anger. "I can't believe I'm going to be trapped for eternity with you. You're a monster. You're a demon. This is Hell, isn't it? I'm in Hell. I died and my soul doesn't know it yet."

Zirconia didn't need to take that. Not from him, a weakling whose windpipe she could crush without breaking a sweat.

She got up from the chair, and turned to leave. She would spare his life today.

"Wait," he said. "You're not a monster."

She stopped, still with her back to him. Looking in his eyes would be too much. She hadn't faced someone who was awake in many weeks. If she looked into his soul now, she would see the void, and he would be able to see into her own dark abyss.

With a gravelly voice, he said, "How many times has it happened to you?"

"I don't know. I lost track."

She heard him get up and walk away, then sit on a different chair. A barstool, by the sound of it. The best kind of stool.

She joined him at the bar, where she tapped her fingers on the counter.

The long, unblemished surface was cool and hard, not natural stone but not entirely fake. She scratched it with a hardened fingernail—unlike Xavier, she had perfect control over her nails. What was that material? Would it be suitable for a kitchen renovation?

Xavier said, "Ballpark it for me. Did it happen more than ten times? More than a thousand? Somewhere in between?"

"In between. They weren't always a big deal. Sometimes it was only a couple of days, barely noticeable. It happened at least ten times after I had Zara. I used to drive her nuts redecorating the house every time I came out of a longer one. She couldn't have possibly understood what it meant for me to wake up and have my surroundings look different, even if it was just a paint color. She had no idea what a relief it was for me to step out of bed onto new carpet, or gleaming hardwood."

Xavier was listening with far more interest than any other man had, at least for a discussion about interior decorating.

"It's like we're kinda-sorta cursed," he said.

"Oh, young Xavier. Don't you see it? We are absolutely, definitely, one hundred percent cursed."

He shuddered. "You think?"

"Why do you think I renounced my witch powers?"

He stared at her, his light-green eyes drooping with despair. These last hundred Wednesdays had taken a toll on him. The flesh never showed the passage of looping time, but the eyes did.

"We're cursed," he said glumly.

"Being cursed isn't all bad."

"It's not?"

She sprung from her barstool and over the bar in one leap. She grabbed the bottles, and started pouring.

"There's an upside to everything, even curses," she said. "No tomorrow means no hangovers."

"This can't be everything," he said.

She pushed a paper cup full of alcohol toward him.

He took a sip. "This cannot be what life is for."

"Says who?"

"There should be more," he said. "More than... bowling, and drinking, and trying to figure out what it's all for."

"Good idea," she said. "We're in a bowling alley, so we can bowl."

He finished his paper cup and visibly relaxed. "Okay," he said. "Since we're here anyway, let's bowl."

CHAPTER 43

Another Wednesday

They could only drink and bowl for so many days—eleven of them—until they grew bored of it.

Today, they would embark on a more noble mission.

Research.

Followed by drinking and bowling later.

They were at the library.

Zirconia held back while Xavier charged ahead up the sidewalk toward the lunky, solid building.

He stopped and turned to look at her. His light-green eyes sparkled in the sunshine. That was the only good thing that came from the hot sun—it made everyone's eyes brighter, and shook away the dark shadows of knowledge.

Xavier said, "What's wrong? Is this a bad time to be here today?" He looked straight up at the sky, as though a construction crane holding a boulder might have snuck up silently.

The boy could be jumpy when they were out in open spaces. Perhaps she shouldn't have killed him quite so many times back when they were playing their first game at the hotel.

Meanwhile, the big ol' library continued to rudely impose itself on innocent space up ahead. *Come on in*, the library said, more a dare than a welcome. *Step right up and drink your fill of the pathetic scratchings left behind by mortals struggling with their futility. It's free.*

"Just give me a moment," she said.

Xavier continued to glare up at the completely blue sky with suspicion.

"I need to fortify myself," she explained. She took a sip of her purple-hued takeout coffee from Dreamland. "All the dead words in there give me a headache."

"You sure need to fortify yourself a lot. Alcohol, caffeine."

"You sure speak your mind freely for someone who is a walking blood bank."

He frowned. "You *wouldn't.* I mean, we're friends now."

"We are?"

"I paid for your coffee," he said.

She leaned on a concrete planter box that was already too warm, scorched up by the sun.

At least she had her coffee, which she savored. It did taste better, having been paid for by someone else.

Xavier said, "I noticed you don't have a lot of friends."

"I have more friends than you can even imagine."

"I followed you around a bunch of Wednesdays, and I never once saw you visit a friend."

"My friends don't live in this town."

"Then why are you buying a house here?"

She crumpled the empty coffee container, tossed it in the garbage, and walked into the mouth of the lunky building, barely shuddering as she entered the spooky book tomb.

She went directly to the counter and rang the silver bell.

Frank, the well-dressed man with snowy white hair and a designer suit appeared. He gave her a friendly but crooked smile with his crooked mouth.

"Hello, gorgeous," he said. "You're looking lovelier than ever. What have we done to deserve your company today?"

"Hello, darling." She leaned over the service desk and air-kissed his cheeks. "I've popped in to do some research."

Frank said, "I hope Zara is feeling better soon. We miss her." He fidgeted with a giant plastic spider. "We want the old Zara back."

"We all want her back. That's why I'm here. Fetch me all the books you have on time travel."

He led her over to a rack of paperbacks with dog-eared covers. They had evidently been touched and fondled by countless people—probably in bed, and also in the bathroom. The horrors.

Frank said cheerfully, "This is the science fiction, and over there is the fantasy."

"Not fiction," she said. "I'm specifically looking for real information about time."

Frank nodded, and led her in a different direction.

He handed her a copy of *A Brief History of Time* by Stephen Hawking.

"Oh, Stephen," she said, running her thumb over her old friend's photo on the jacket.

Frank said, "Is that what you were looking for?"

"It's a start," she said. "I can take it from here."

He continued to stand there, even though their transaction was complete.

In a grave tone, he said, "I'm concerned about Zara."

This conversation again, she thought. She'd covered it before, but it was still the same day for Frank.

"We are all concerned about Zara," he said.

She felt the sting again, as she had on a previous visit. *We are all concerned.* We, as in *they*. The people who worked there. *They* were concerned because they thought nobody else was. They believed she hadn't been taking care of her daughter.

"Thank you for your concern," she said. "If tomorrow ever comes, I'll see that Zarabella is back at her post."

"No rush," Frank said. "We don't need her weeping in the alcoves. It's heartbreaking. And it's not good for the books." He gave her a meek, still-crooked smile. "Because of all the moisture from the tears."

She wagged a finger at the man. "You should be ashamed of yourself for putting these books ahead of your coworker."

"It was just a joke. A bad one." His cheeks reddened. "Even my sense of humor has suffered in her absence." He ducked his head, looking scolded. "Well, you are her mother, so I'm sure you know what's best for her." The white-haired man backed away, bowing slightly.

"Riddle women are tougher than we look," she said.

Xavier joined her, arriving as Frank left.

"I like that," Xavier said. "*Riddle women are tougher than they look.* Zinnia's always saying it."

"She shouldn't," Zirconia snapped. "It's *my* saying."

"But it's about all of—"

She cut him off by pushing her old friend Stephen's book into Xavier's chest. "Less chit-chat, more research."

Xavier took the book to a table, sat, and started reading.

Zirconia selected some slimmer volumes from the same section of the shelf, and joined him.

They read for a very long time before Zirconia stood up to take a break and check the time.

Ten minutes had passed.

She could have sworn she'd been reading for hours.

She sat down and read some more. She read until the dead words started to blur, and her head got very heavy. She began to drift into sleep.

For every hour she couldn't sleep at night, there was an hour on the other side of the clock where she couldn't stay awake. Aging could be so heartless about sleep, rearranging it hither and thither, like a bad housemaid.

Xavier shook her by the shoulders.

She brushed his hands aside, and kept from biting them. "What was that for?"

"We're a team. You can't sleep on the job."

She closed the book and tossed it aside.

"I don't even know what we're looking for." She looked around at the towers full of books. "Such a ghastly building. I don't know why the local residents don't request their tax dollars be spent bulldozing this place and burying the contents."

"Maybe books would be nicer to you if you were nicer to them."

She grabbed a slim volume with a red cover and stroked it tenderly. "Such a pretty book. Won't you tell me something helpful?" She flipped it open to a random page and started reading.

She'd done so as a joke, but it had worked.

The page had terminology she didn't understand, but some of it was written in plain, direct language. She understood it. Sort of.

She snapped the book shut triumphantly.

"Quantum entanglement," she said to Xavier. "That's it."

Across the table, he rested his chin on his palm, unconvinced.

"I must be entangled with someone else," she said. "They are the one who keeps stopping time."

"You think?"

"There must be *some* explanation. Things don't happen for no reason. And I know I'm not the one stopping it. Therefore, it's the person I'm entangled with."

"What about me? How do I figure into this entanglement?"

"You're not part of it. You're a bystander."

He sniffed. "Typical." He went back to reading his book.

"You don't have to do that." She pushed her books aside. "We're done here."

He peered at her over his book. "Just because you have one glimmer of an idea, that doesn't mean we're done researching."

"It's not just a glimmer of an idea," she said. "I know what it is, and I know who it is."

He slowly put his book down. "Who?"

She pointed to the photo of the author on the book jacket.

Xavier wrinkled his nose. "Stephen Hawking? I'm sorry to break the news, but he's no longer with this world."

"Not Stephen," she said. "I'm talking about our mutual friend. That's who I'm entangled with."

"Does this friend have a name?"

"His name is Rhys Quarry. He's Zara's father."

Xavier leaned back and crossed his arms. "Sell me on it. Does he have time-bending powers?"

"No. He's just a shifter, but it's him," she said.

"How do you know?"

"Because he's the only person I could never find whenever I was in a loop. Not once. And trust me, I tried."

"You tried?" Xavier leaned forward. "Why? Did you want to hook up with him? You know what they say, *what happens in a time loop stays in the time loop*." He chuckled at his joke. "I just made that up."

"Don't be ridiculous. I could have had any man I wanted."

"Then why were you looking for your ex?"

She didn't answer.

Xavier's eyes grew round. "You wanted to wake him up to keep you company."

"Nobody wants to spend eternity alone."

"Not many people would choose to spend eternity with their ex. You like him."

"There was no point in waking up someone I liked. They'd only get on my nerves. It's better to wake someone you're neutral on. Someone you could take or leave."

"Uh, I'm right here."

"I wanted to wake Rhys because he might have been able to keep me sane, at the very least."

"Sane? Are you saying we could go insane in here?" He shook his head. "That couldn't happen. We reset every day. My toenails are back how they were."

"But you have your memories. That's a physical thing. Memories are written in our brains. It's very, very small handwriting, but it's written there."

He tilted his head. "Your brain has handwriting in it?"

"Doesn't everyone's? That's why one must always practice good penmanship."

"What?"

She waved it off. She'd had years to ponder it, and it would take ages to bring Xavier up to speed on her theories about neuroscience.

"Focus," she said. "We need to find Rhys. Maybe I can finally track him down, with you helping me."

"I'll do what I can."

She waved at the pile of books on their table. "If we want to crack this thing, we have to work smarter, not harder."

"What are you thinking?" His eyes were shining brightly, full of life and the clarity of his young, fresh mind.

She liked that gleam in his eyes.

They would be a good team.

Together, they would find her quantum entanglement, Rhys Quarry—there was a clue right there, with the Q in his last name—Q as in Quantum—and they would solve this thing.

CHAPTER 44

Many Wednesdays Later

Shady Lanes Bowling and Ales hadn't opened for the day, as usual, which made it an excellent location for what Zirconia and Xavier called Time Looper Headquarters.

The place was as busy as a beehive today.

Xavier was bowling, perfecting his technique. He soon would be able to play a perfect game—nothing but strikes.

Zirconia was relaxing with a magazine about bathroom renovations. The house she was still in the process of buying had never been lived in, but trends didn't care about wear and tear. The bathrooms were already dated, so she was researching tile patterns.

All around her, the trio of robot vacuum cleaners were doing their usual bee-dance around the carpeted area of the lounge.

Sitting at a row of tables that bowlers used for eating nachos, the twelve human vacuum cleaners were diligently working as well.

They weren't *actually* human vacuum cleaners.

They were research assistants. Zirconia and Xavier called them human vacuums as a joke, because they did vacuum information from the books into their minds. They summarized their learnings in an oral report at the end of the day.

Time Looper Headquarters was a hive of activity because time loopers knew how to work smarter, not harder. So many things got easier when you had unlimited money to pay your human resources, since pay day was always *tomorrow*.

At one point, Xavier had asked Zirconia if it was ethical to employ people in this manner. He'd used the word *enslave*. She'd replied by asking if it had been ethical for him to trick Liza Gilbert into getting back together with him on some of the day's iterations. He'd dropped the subject.

One of the smartest human vacuums, a woman with braided hair, raised her hand and asked, "Are we allowed to take short breaks, or are you going to deduct the time from our day rate?"

"You'll get your full pay." Zirconia waved for Braids to go ahead and leave her station for the bathroom.

The woman, a physicist who'd happened to be passing through town, would be gone for seventeen minutes. Seventeen minutes was the amount of time she'd used the women's room every previous Wednesday since being employed by the time loopers.

Zirconia also knew Braids would spend ten percent of the time using the restroom and ninety percent of the time shopping on her phone for the car she planned to buy with the day's reading fees.

There was no point in putting a stop to the long break. Some time would be wasted, but Braids always worked harder after selecting her dream car.

Humans were like horses heading back to the barn when they had specific rewards waiting for them. Faster, stronger, better. At least when it came to rote tasks. Not so much for creative endeavors. Brains were funny, with all their handwritten ways.

Human Vacuum Cleaner Number Two raised his hand.

"Yes, you can leave ten minutes early," Zirconia said tiredly.

Number Two got back to reading, not noticing that he hadn't asked a question.

The man was a math teacher at the local high school, and he always lied to her, claiming he had to pick up his dog at doggy daycare.

The truth was much weirder: He was obsessed with getting a rotisserie chicken from the warehouse grocery store. If he didn't get there right on the dot of five o'clock, they would be sold out. No amount of payment for the day's research could get Number Two to forget about the rotisserie chicken. Zirconia had tried. If she offered too much, he'd get scared off, and that was a shame. He wasn't any better at summarizing research than the others, but his voice was the most pleasing. And he had nice hair. If Number Two weren't so obsessed with rotisserie chicken, she might have had other assignments for him.

The door to the bowling alley banged open.

Blythe Delores Boomer, whom everyone called Boomer, came stumbling in.

"I found him," Boomer said, breathing heavily.

Boomer carried some extra weight, and breathed heavily even when not rushing around.

She was a lawyer who'd recently moved to Wisteria and set up a practice. She was in her thirties and unmarried. Her hair was neither feminine nor masculine —chin-length, fair, and curly. She wore a men's suit with a pink bowtie that day.

Boomer said, "This one was a real humdinger, but I did it. I found your Mr. Rhys Quarry."

"It's about time," Zirconia said.

The lawyer held her dimpled hand to her chest. "I beg your pardon? I've only been on the case for three hours. I know you're paying quadruple my usual rate, so I tried to make it speedy, but three hours is nothing a bullfrog would hop over to bump its butt on the grass. Especially for finding a man with as many aliases as your friend."

"He's more of an acquaintance," Zirconia said, reaching for the folder.

Boomer clutched the folder to her chest, and nodded in the direction of the research assistants.

She said only, "Who? What? Why?"

"It's complicated."

"You appear to be farming research assistants to assist you with," she picked up one of the books, "time travel?"

"Apparently it's not that complicated," Zirconia said.

"My grandpappy always said we're all traveling through time. The problem is, we only know how to go one way." She looked up at the ceiling, a grid of acoustic tiles. "Except for owls."

"Owls?"

Boomer twitched one shoulder. "My grandpappy had a thing for owls. We don't talk about it. I wouldn't tell you, but you have client confidentiality."

"That's not how client... oh, you're joking. Because you're in a good mood. Did you really find Rhys, or just a strong lead?"

They'd had plenty of false positives. Zirconia recycled all Boomer's dead ends back to her at the start of the new day, attributing the information to a made-up third party private investigator named Jiminy Whoozat. She'd let Xavier pick the name.

Boomer said, "I don't know what your other investigator was doing besides billing you for road trips and nights on the town because finding your guy wasn't that hard."

Just then, the wooden pins at the end of a lane crashed loudly. Two pins stayed standing. Xavier cursed them loudly—not that it would do any good, since he had no powers.

Boomer looked over at the lanes. "You folks sure know how to have a good time on a weekday."

Zirconia snapped her fingers with some magic to get Xavier's attention. He came running over.

He slapped Boomer on the shoulder and said, "Better luck tomorrow."

"She's off the case," Zirconia said. "She found him."

Xavier took a step back. "Oh."

Boomer said, "What's the matter? You look disappointed. Did you want me to take longer so you can get real good at throwing a perfect game?"

Xavier rubbed the back of his head. "Yeah. Kinda."

"Your grip is all wrong," Boomer said. "What you need is a coach. There's no point doin' the same thing wrong over and over. My grandpappy was the best fiddle player in town only because that's what my great-grandpappy taught him."

Now that Boomer was talking about bowling, she handed the folder of research to Zirconia like it was an afterthought.

Zirconia held the folder closed between her palms.

She should open it.

She didn't.

Xavier said to Boomer, "How are you at bowling?"

"Better than you," she said.

Zirconia kept holding the closed folder.

If she was right about her quantum entanglement with Rhys Quarry, then all she had to do was go to him. He would put a stop to this. Then the days could go back to normal.

Xavier said to the lawyer, "Care to put a little cash on the line?" He nodded toward the lanes.

Boomer slapped her hands together and rubbed them gleefully. "What are you thinking? A hundred bucks?"

"I could take a hundred bucks off you, sure."

She laughed. "Oh, honey. You're about to get whooped, and you don't even know it. You're like an old chicken who's stopped laying on Sunday morning."

"We'll see who's the old chicken."

The two of them headed toward the lanes, stepping over the whirring robot vacuum cleaners.

Zirconia stared at the folder in her hands. All she had to do was open it, and time could start rolling forward again.

Just one more repeated day, maybe two, and then it would be Thursday.

On Thursday, she could fight with her sister and not know how it would end.

On Thursday, her daughter would do what she wanted, and there was no way Zirconia could stop her.

On Thursday, the bowling alley would be Shady Lanes again, and not Time Looper Headquarters.

Over on the lanes, Xavier gave Boomer tips about which balls were optimal. He'd named all of them.

Braids, the physicist, returned from the women's room, smiling about the new car she was going to buy.

Chicken Rotisserie Guy popped a piece of spearmint gum in his mouth and kept making notes.

Zirconia set the folder on the table and left it there.

She went to the head of the long table of research assistants, and clapped her hands.

"Good news, everyone," she said. "We've solved our research project."

They exchanged confused looks. Chicken Rotisserie Guy checked the time.

Zirconia said, "You can take the rest of the day off, with pay, but there's a catch. You can't leave this bowling alley without bowling. I'll be the captain of one team. Braids, you can be the other captain."

"My name is Mary."

"You can pick first, Braids."

The collection of teachers, scientists, and engineers broke out in smiles and laughter.

They formed two teams, including Boomer and Xavier, and spent the rest of the afternoon bowling.

When the alley opened for regular business in the evening, everyone stayed. Even Chicken Rotisserie Guy.

The time loopers ordered in catering, and threw an impromptu party for the Shady Lanes owners and staff, the twelve research assistants, and anyone else who happened to wander in.

Eventually everything reached the end of the day, and blinked back to how it had been the previous day.

Zirconia woke up on the sofabed in the hotel.

Her memory of all the previous Wednesdays was still handwritten in her brain.

This time, she didn't sit up suddenly, and the bed didn't squeak.

She lay there quietly, listening to Zinnia hum as she made her pot of tea.

Zirconia Cristata Riddle was in no hurry for the day to start, because she was in no hurry for it to end.

CHAPTER 45

The Wednesday Zirconia and Xavier Fell Out

The lawyer/investigator/bowling coach did provide the exact location of Zirconia's presumed quantum entanglement. He wasn't in town, but he could be reached within the day.

The two time loopers put off going to see him. Not indefinitely. Just one Wednesday at a time.

What was the rush? There were plenty of things to do in Wisteria, if you had a companion. Eternity was only long when you didn't have a friend to share it with.

That Wednesday was shaping up to be an excellent one. The days weren't all winners—cooking lessons had been an absolute nightmare, and tango classes had resulted in a blood bath—but this particular Wednesday of skydiving had been perfect so far.

Zirconia and Xavier lay on their backs on the grassy hill, staring up at the sky.

Even the sunshine was bearable for the vampire, thanks to Zirconia's designer sunglasses, which matched the new designer clothes she'd picked up to complement her parachute. For time loopers, there was no excuse to not be impeccably dressed and ready for any occasion.

It was peaceful on the grassy hill, with their spent parachutes draped over the ground all around them. They would have taken photos, if the photos would have lasted. Instead, they stuck self-made images on the refrigerator doors of their minds the old-fashioned way.

"That was the best jump yet," Xavier said. "Did you see me almost stick the landing? It was almost perfect."

"I saw."

"I tripped on a rock. Next time I'll do better. I'll get it perfect when we do the skydiving package again the day after tomorrow."

"Why not tomorrow?"

"It's your turn to pick. Whatever you want. We can even go shopping for tile backsplashes again. I know it's been on your mind."

"Oh, Xavier. You'll make someone a fine husband someday."

He sighed. "Someday."

She rolled to face him, propping her head up with one arm.

The young man was feeling sorry for himself, as she'd predicted. Worrying about the future gave his smooth face worry lines.

She poked him in the shoulder. "Skydiving isn't enough for you?"

He opened his eyes and rolled in to face her. His breath reminded her of petrichor—the scent of fresh rain on dry land—for no reason.

No. Not for no reason. There was dirt on his lips. He'd eaten some earth and grass on his almost-perfect landing.

Kids were so messy. She plucked a green blade of grass from the corner of his mouth. It felt good to mother someone.

Xavier's worry lines got deeper.

A butterfly flitted over them. A bunny chewed on sweet purple clover nearby. A black fox watched them from the nearby woods. Zirconia felt all of the life around her, all of the circulatory systems doing their jobs in creatures large and small.

He hadn't answered her question, so she said, "We can go to Rhys and stop this thing tomorrow if you're already bored of having unlimited resources and godlike powers."

"Godlike powers?" Xavier laughed hollowly. "I don't have any powers, let alone godlike. All I've got are a bunch of Nothing Person skills. Nothing Skills."

He chewed his dirt-stained lower lip and stared at her mouth. He wasn't wearing sunglasses, so it was very easy to see what he was thinking about. He was back on Zirconia's least favorite topic again.

He said, "But I don't have to keep on being a Nothing Person. I mean... what if you—"

"I'm not turning you into a vampire," she said. "End of discussion."

He didn't take her rejection any better than he had the previous hundred times.

His light-green eyes blazed with fury.

Zirconia was once again reminded that Xavier was not her toy, not her pet—not even when he chewed on grass. He had no supernatural abilities, but he was still a full-grown man, with a full-grown man's rage and little wisdom to temper it.

He spat words into her face. "I thought you were different. I thought you weren't like the others."

"I am different."

He scowled.

Her simple acknowledgement of reality hadn't earned her any points. Nothing new there. The entire Riddle family hated it whenever Zirconia told them the truth.

She said, "Let's not—"

"When it all got started, this thing between me and you, it had a real will-they-or-won't-they vibe, but you know what? Forget it. I'm not interested. I wouldn't be with you if you were the last woman on earth."

Zirconia was more surprised by this than she had been the time he'd tackled her from behind, early in their relationship. Was he actually referring to a potential romantic liaison between them?

She shouldn't have been so surprised. Xavier was a young man. For him, every relationship with a woman would have a will-the-or-won't-they vibe.

Even so, she hadn't thought of him that way. He wasn't her type. She liked powerful men.

Xavier said, "I'm not going to be one of your grave groupies. I don't even think you're hot, now that I know what you're like. No amount of silky black hair and smooth skin can make up for a bad personality."

She felt the fire of anger that could only come from an undeserved rejection, but she did what that kitschy vampire poster said to do: Keep Calm and Don't Choke Anyone.

Carefully, she said, "If you think I'm going to be hurt by your rejection of me as a romantic partner, you must have brainweevils. I'm fifteen years older than you, and furthermore—"

"Try thirty," he said with spite. "You're at least thirty years older than me. You're a dried-up old hag, and nobody wants you."

Dried-up old *hag*? That wasn't fair. She wasn't even a witch anymore.

With deliberate cruelty in his voice, he said, "I think you woke me up on purpose because you knew that was the only way you could get someone young to hang around you, to make you feel young. You're such a vampire. You're an emotional vampire. You suck up other people's energy."

"You can't possibly believe that—"

He stood and threw off the harness for the parachute noisily. His movements scared away the bunny, as well as the fox, which was a regular fox and not one of the local shifters.

"Forget you," he said, only he didn't use the word *forget*. "Do whatever you want tomorrow, and the next day. I don't ever want to see you again. I'd rather be a hermit."

And with that, he stomped off.

Zirconia stared after him. He didn't look back.

Had he really accused her of being an emotional vampire?

He had.

What an awful thing to say to someone, even if they were an actual vampire.

And completely untrue.

An emotional vampire was someone who took joy in taking away other people's happiness.

Zirconia never did that. Never intentionally, anyway. She did deliver tough love, and it occasionally made people less happy in the moment, but that effect was transitory, and besides, it was always for their own good. People understood that. Deep down, they understood that the ends justified the means.

She rolled onto her back.

You're a dried-up old hag, and nobody wants you.

The sun was brighter at that hour, or it must have been, since her sunglasses were no longer blocking the harsh light. Her eyes stung and watered.

Had Xavier really said all those nasty things?

Yes. He had.

And after everything she'd done for him.

He was the emotional vampire, not her. He was always trying to manipulate her into sharing her powers with him. Him.

Had they even been friends? Had their good times been genuine? Had this stretch of Wednesdays been nothing but a long con?

Starting tomorrow, she would be on high alert.

Xavier only wanted one thing from her. Power.

Like a dog to its old bones, he would try his original strategy. He would attack her physically in a pitiful attempt to force her to bite him.

Or he might take a few days to come up with something else. Manipulation? He was showing some improvement in that area. He had a good teacher.

She held her hand over her chest. Her vampire heart was heavy in her chest as it sunk to new depths. For a Nothing Person, Xavier Batista certainly was good at hurting her.

CHAPTER 46

The Wednesday Zinnia was Extra-Mean to Zirconia

Zirconia woke up on the sofabed feeling different.

Why wouldn't she? She was friendless now. Truly friendless. Alone. A mountain hermit in a world of people with no memories.

The spring in her back didn't bother her.

She was actually glad she could feel it, that she could feel anything at all after Xavier's cruel betrayal.

She sat up slowly. The bed gave a slight squeak, little more than a whisper.

"And I thought my joints were creaky," said Zinnia as she brewed her tea.

"You can't be serious," Zirconia said. "It barely squeaked."

The witch gave her vampire sister a mischievous smile. "You're right. Your old bones barely squeaked. You'll have to give me the formula for the magic grease you've been using to lubricate your hip joints."

"Maybe I will," Zirconia said stiffly. "You can use it to finally get that baby out of there. How long have you been pregnant now? Two years?"

The mirth fell off Zinnia's face. "What?"

"It's a joke," Zirconia said, even though it wasn't.

Zirconia made the bed, and folded it back into a couch. Doing so took some guesswork and spatial problem solving, as it was the first time she'd ever attempted such a maneuver.

When the bed was all put away, her sister said, "I was thinking, you should take the cot. It's just foam, no squeaky springs. I can barely sleep—"

"Sure."

Zinnia blinked. "Sure?"

"Whatever you want. You know me better than anyone, so you know that I'm nothing if not perfectly agreeable."

Zinnia raised an eyebrow. "Someone woke up on the wrong side of the coffin."

Zirconia changed from her silk pajamas into her usual clothes, then took a seat at the stool next to the counter.

The cat, Boa, jumped onto her lap and curled up. The budgie chirped happily on top of its cage. The pile of novels sat by, undisturbed.

Zirconia said to her sister, "Am I a monster?"

"Yes." Zero hesitation.

"I mean, am I a bad person?"

"You'd have to be a person first to be a bad person."

"Zinnia. Be serious."

The witch frowned. "What's going on? Everyone's acting so strange this morning."

"They say you are exactly what someone thinks you are, to them. In your mind, I'm a monster. And I happen to know you're an excellent judge of character, so, therefore, I must be a monster."

"Don't say that. Don't call yourself a monster. That's exactly what lazy people use as an excuse to never change."

"So, I am a bad person?"

The witch softened. "Nobody is all good or all bad. Everyone's a mix."

"How bad is my granddaughter? What percentage?"

"That's not fair. Zoey is different."

At that moment, Zoey could be heard giggling on the other side of the bathroom door. She must have done so on the previous days but been drowned out by all the commotion with the cat and budgie.

Boa was still on Zirconia's lap, gnawing on the vampire's fingers whenever the petting slowed down. All the little cat wanted was love. Unless there was ham available. Ham was better than love.

Zinnia lifted her tea to her lips. "Any plans for today?"

"Nothing specific. How about you?"

"Work."

"Sounds boring. Call in sick, and we'll go skydiving instead."

Zinnia stepped back and pulled her belly upward, then gently rested it on the countertop in the small kitchenette.

"That little bump can't stop us," Zirconia said. "I'll glamour the pilot if he's being a stickler for the rules."

Zinnia tilted her head to the side. "Is there anything going on that I should know about?"

"Like what?"

"You know exactly what I mean." She whispered, "A time loop."

Zirconia laughed and waved her hand. What a preposterous idea!

"Those stopped when I changed powers," the vampire said. "You know that." She didn't offer to swear on it.

"But if one *were* to happen, you absolutely, positively have to... *not* tell me."

"I've kept my promise."

The pregnant witch's eyes widened in fear.

"Relax," Zirconia said. "It was easy to keep my promise when they stopped happening." She pointed to the teapot. "Yes. I'll have some."

"I wasn't going to offer you any."

Zirconia struck the air with her pointer finger. "And *that's* how you know we're not in a time loop right now."

Zinnia pursed her lips as she poured the tea. "That's not funny."

"You know what else is not funny? You would rather curse me to live endless days without a companion than take the risk of waking up yourself, and making a few unpleasant memories of things that didn't happen."

"That is an accurate assessment of my wishes."

"This isn't going anywhere," Zirconia said with a sigh.

She compelled the cat to leave her lap, got up from the chair, and went to the door of the hotel suite.

"Wait," Zinnia said. "You didn't drink any of your tea. And Zara wants to talk to you about something."

The vampire stopped with her hand on the doorknob.

Zara.

Zirconia's mind threw together a slideshow of all the times she'd let her daughter down, all the crying spells on all the Wednesdays. All the anguish. The pain and grief she couldn't move past.

The vampire's brain bogged down in the sorrow, then whipped around to anger, like a roller coaster on a hairpin turn.

It was Xavier's fault that time hadn't moved forward yet. He'd been so intent on enjoying his godlike powers, and then whining about it, too.

Without looking back, Zirconia said, "Tell your niece, your coworkers, and everyone else to go ahead and do whatever they want. I'm tired of the thanks I get for trying to help people."

Zinnia huffed. "Fine then. Just leave." She dropped her teacup, and didn't catch it with magic before it smashed on the floor. Her voice bordered on hysteria. "Just leave already."

"I will, but remember I'm only doing what you asked."

"Just go already. You're good at that. Go find yourself a dark, dingy bar to hang around in. Everyone knows you prefer the company of strangers with alcohol over your own family."

Before that moment, Zirconia had assumed she didn't have any feelings left to have hurt, and yet she did.

She did not defend herself to her sister, nor seek retribution. The latter was something a bad person did, and the former was pointless.

She left the cursed hotel suite without another word.

A puff of colorful smoke seeped under the door behind her, unseen.

CHAPTER 47

The Office of Tallulah Swiftwater, Therapist Specializing in Families of All Kinds

Zirconia sat in the small, orange-hued waiting room.

Why *was* it so orange?

At least now she knew how a candle might feel, sitting inside a hollowed-out pumpkin.

All the room needed were triangular windows to see out of. And there were triangles, on a quilted wall hanging that gave her sensitive eyes some relief.

She tried not to look at the sign on the reception desk, but the words still got into her head. A childish song played over and over in her mind.

I'm Tallulah, and I'll pop my head out. Pop, pop, pop. Pop goes the weasel. Pop goes my head. My head goes pop, pop, pop when I'm ready to see you.

The floorboards creaked. The door handle turned.

Pop, pop, pop. Pop goes the therapist, shrinking your head.

The interior door opened, and out stepped Tallulah Swiftwater in a swirl of skirts, and shawls, and turquoise jewelry.

The swirling, whirling woman put her hands together in a prayer position, bowed, and said, “Bless you for coming in.”

Zirconia didn't run away. Though it irritated her greatly, she put her hands together in the same manner.

“Bless you for seeing me,” she said.

“You're not Jason,” the therapist said. “Unless... you are Jason?” Tallulah Swiftwater was a supernatural herself, and knew all about the magical world.

"Jason willingly gave up his appointment today," the vampire said. "I'm a new acquaintance of his. He said I could take his place."

Zirconia waited for a response.

It was not the first time she'd gotten this far.

Tallulah Swiftwater always had four clients scheduled for sessions that day. Zirconia had tried taking the place of three of them so far, with more elaborate explanations. Each time, Tallulah had politely but firmly declined to see a new client without an appointment.

This time, Zirconia was playing it simple, close to the truth.

She'd intercepted Jason fifteen minutes earlier, and given him an expensive—priceless, really—gold watch in exchange for his appointment slot.

Tallulah's many layers of clothing swirled around her, as though an invisible tail was twitching and swishing under there. Tallulah Swiftwater was a shifter who took the form of an Appaloosa horse. Some of that animal's energy, if not the actual tail, clung to her human form, causing her clothing to ripple.

"This is highly unusual," Tallulah said. "What do you mean, he gave up his appointment?"

Zirconia explained, "I gave him a gold watch as a bribe because I really needed to see you."

The woman nodded as though this sort of thing happened from time to time. "Are there extraordinary circumstances?"

"About as extraordinary as things get around this town."

The skirts, shawls, and even the turquoise jewelry continued to swirl.

"We have met before," the therapist said. "You're..."

"I'm Zoey Riddle's grandmo—" Zirconia coughed. She never could say that word in reference to herself. "My last name is Riddle. You know my family. You treated Archer Caine, Zoey's father."

"The genie. Yes." She took in a breath and blew it out through closed lips, making a horsey sound. "I don't usually see people without proper notice, but perhaps we could sit and talk for a while."

Zirconia got to her feet, cheering internally. It was always satisfying to achieve a goal, even for something as pointless as seeing a therapist.

"Unofficially," Tallulah added. "We would just be talking, and I won't charge you for today."

"Like friends," Zirconia said.

"Like friends," Tallulah agreed with a sly wink. "But just for one day. After today, you'll pay my full fee," another wink, "so I can afford to buy more skirts and jewelry."

"It's a lovely outfit," Zirconia said. "You dress beautifully."

Tallulah blew out air again in the horsey sound.

"We don't lie in therapy," she said.

She gestured for Zirconia to enter the adjoining room, which was even more orange than the waiting room. That room had a window, and the natural light made the space glow like a level ten light-casting biohazard.

Tallulah said, "Enter, and tell only the truth."

"In that case, your magazines are old, your reception sign is terrible, and I detest the color of your walls. Who is your decorator? Peter, Peter, Pumpkin Eater?"

"Very good," Tallulah said with a horsey, big-toothed grin. "That's a good start."

CHAPTER 48

Breakthrough Wednesday

Zirconia woke up on the sofabed and continued to lie there, very still, staring up at the stains on the ceiling. The ceiling in the hotel suite wasn't bad, compared to the ceiling at Tallulah Swiftwater's office. That ceiling was green, and had flypaper hanging in the corner.

She'd been staring at the dead horse flies on the flypaper during a recent session—number ninety-nine for her, number one for the therapist—when she'd come to a big decision.

The breakthrough was all thanks to the therapist's gentle prodding for her to keep moving forward in her life.

Tallulah had said, "The worst thing you can do is not make a decision, because that is a decision by default. It's the decision to sit passively, and let the days repeat."

Tallulah had assumed they were talking about a metaphorical loop. Zirconia had told her several times about the time bubble, but the memory hadn't stuck.

But a breakthrough was still a breakthrough.

Today would be different from all the other Wednesdays.

Today, the vampire was going to track down Rhys Quarry, her quantum entanglement, and make him end whatever mischief he was doing.

Today was the day.

It was too bad Xavier wouldn't be going with her.

Oh, well. It served him right for being such a petulant child.

He was being such a petulant child, in fact, that he hadn't seen her once since their fight on the grassy hill.

She'd expected him to try again to get himself turned into a vampire, but apparently he was a quitter.

She'd actually planned to give him exactly what he wanted, if only to satisfy his curiosity. He would turn back to his regular human form again the next day, anyway.

Probably.

She didn't know for sure that the powers wouldn't survive the day along with his memories. She couldn't have known because she had never tested it. She hadn't been in a time loop since becoming a vampire.

Would it be so bad if Xavier became a vampire? Then she wouldn't be so alone. She'd have someone else—

Her sister cut into her quiet thoughts.

"I know you're awake," said Zinnia as she brewed her tea. "I heard your creaky, old eyelids open like a couple of rusty barn doors."

Zirconia jumped out of bed, and changed from her pajamas to her clothes with vampire speed. She shoved the mattress back into the sofa with equal haste.

"Careful," Zinnia said. "You could have sandwiched Boa in there. You know she likes to nap inside the couch hollow." She stirred her tea. "You ought to take the cot. It would be safer. You're always saying—"

"Have whatever you want. I'm leaving."

Zinnia blinked. "Leaving?"

"I'm getting on the plane this afternoon with Zara. I need to talk to her father about something very important."

Rhys Quarry was currently living in the same city that Zara was flying to for her interview. It might have seemed like a coincidence to someone naive, but Zirconia knew it was no coincidence. Rhys was the one behind Zara's foolish idea to pick up and move again, only eighteen months after having moved across the country the first time.

“You're going to see Rhys?” Zinnia got that same dreamy look she always did whenever the topic of Rhys Quarry came up. Even now, decades later, and knocked up with another man's bear cub, she still had her girlish crush on the man.

Poor Zinnia. She only ever wanted what she couldn't have. Didn't she know that the secret to happiness was wanting what you already had?

That was something Zirconia had learned from her therapist. Tallulah Stillwater looked like just another dippy middle-aged ding-dong with a magical thinking delusion, but she was actually quite competent.

“He's not interested in you,” Zirconia said. “He never was. Pull your head out of your childish fantasies, and wake up. Ethan Fung is a fine man. He's never going to make you feel like you're a teenager with a crush because you're not a teenager. Get your head on straight and let that man marry you.”

Zinnia's face contorted through multiple emotions.

Psychic blasts of indignant phrases flitted from her mind in incoherent bursts.

She opened her mouth and closed it.

Then the air went clear.

She was speechless, from her mouth to her mind. She had achieved a blank state. She was ready for change magic to come rushing into the void.

Zinnia Riddle was a big believer in change magic. Her birthday came on the heels of the start of the new year, at the point when other people were already giving up on their New Year's Resolutions. Zinnia believed the time around her birthday could be a catalyst for transformation, and yet she never really changed that much.

She was pregnant now, but she was still the same old Zinnia, stubbornly clutching to the past. The other witches in the coven had to cast extra protective wards to ensure they wouldn't be visited by another buttfaced Pain-Body Cacodemon.

“Good,” Zirconia said to her sister's blank face. “I've given you something to think about. It's time to make some changes. I'm still going to get the house, but you might not be invited to live with us.”

Zinnia regained some use of her mouth. “Wha-what house?”

“I'll tell you after I get a few things settled. While we're on the subject of things you should do, throw out your eye cream. It's not doing you any favors.”

“Bu-but the lanolin comes from the sebaceous glands of Woolly Prairie Diggers.”

“Exactly. Have you seen a Woolly Prairie Digger?”

Zinnia frowned. “Do you really think I should marry Ethan?”

“Everyone does. Literally every single person. My therapist says it's so obvious, it's painful.”

“Since when do you have a therapist?”

“You don't know everything about me,” Zirconia said with a lofty air.

The cat jumped onto the counter and knocked over the stack of paperbacks. “Ham?”

Ham? That was a simple enough request.

Tallulah had talked to Zirconia about the benefits of giving in to other people's simple requests. It didn't mean you had to cave on the big things, but it created harmony in relationships.

Zirconia went to the suite's fridge, pulled out a package of deli meat, and gave all of it to the cat.

Boa meowed, “Ham, ham, ham!” She kept talking while eating, so it sounded like she was saying, “Ham, ma-ham, mmm, ham, mah ham.”

The budgie shrieked, “Find me, find me!”

“Okay, Marzipants,” Zirconia said. “You hide, and I'll find you.”

The green bird flitted down the short hallway.

Zirconia found him easily. He was perched on the handle for the bathroom.

Marzipants squawked happily then jumped onto her shoulder. "I found you," he said contentedly. "You found me, and I found you."

He hadn't found anyone, but like most talking budgies, he could only repeat the phrases he'd heard.

Zirconia knocked on the bathroom door.

"Zolanda?" She called her granddaughter by her full name at times. "Zolanda, I don't care what you're doing in there, but I would like a hug before I leave for the day."

The door whipped open.

Zoey Riddle and her best friend stood fully clothed in the small bathroom. Both girls hid their hands behind their backs. It didn't take a grandmother's wisdom to know they were up to something they shouldn't have been doing. They should have been restoring the witch's hair to a natural color, or removing some of her black eye makeup, not making things worse.

"You'd better not be doing beauty magic," Zirconia said.

The girls shook their heads but didn't volunteer any alternative explanation for their guilty expressions.

"Those spells always backfire," Zirconia said. "And besides, you're both perfectly lovely in your natural states."

She patted her granddaughter on the head, and then the other one. Her bleached-white hair felt as bad as it looked. Her name was Andie, or Abaleen, and she was worried about her body, like most girls her age.

"Don't worry, dear," Zirconia said to the teen witch. "You'll grow into those big flipper feet of yours. I can smell your HGH levels, and you're heading into a growth spurt. You're going to be nice and tall within a year. You'll still have flipper feet, but for a good reason."

The teens exchanged a look, then the girl with the bleached hair and dark eyeliner burst into happy tears. Black makeup streaked down her pale cheeks like the tendrils of Black Startwists that formed witchbane.

Zoey said, "Thanks, Gigi." She said it earnestly, and meant it. Zoey had not inherited the full dose of her mother's poisonous sarcasm.

The teen witch also said, "Thanks, Gigi," and hugged Zirconia.

It wasn't much of a hug because she still had her hands behind her back and there wasn't a lot of room in the doorway, but it gave Zirconia confidence that she could be more than an irritating know-it-all to her family.

She left the girls to their business—it was almost certainly a forbidden beauty spell, judging by the scent of the magical ingredients—and closed the bathroom door.

Zirconia made the very short trip back to Zinnia, who was still in the small kitchenette. Zinnia talked to someone on the phone while resting her round belly on the countertop.

She said into her phone, "I'm calling in sick to work." Pause. "No, no, I'm fine. It's something else. Are you free today?"

Zirconia swiveled her ears to catch the sound of the person on the other end of the call.

It was the Chief of Police, Ethan Young. He said he was a busy man, but always had time for her. They would see each other that Wednesday.

Well done, me, Zirconia thought smugly.

She left her sister to the conversation, and went to another closed interior door, the one for the bedroom.

Zara was on the other side. Zara and her grief.

Zirconia raised her hand to knock on the door but stopped herself.

This particular approach rarely went well. Going directly into Zara's private space always put her in defensive mode.

It was always better if Zara came to her.

Marzipants chirped happily on her shoulder. "I found you, you found me," he said happily.

She took him back to his cage and set him on top, where he liked to perch. He turned to the window and let out another happy cry, as though he'd just realized the sky was blue, and that blue was his favorite color.

Zirconia was starting to understand why people kept animal pets.

There was just one more thing she had to do. It was for the cohesion of the day's events. Not for her own pleasure. Not at all.

Zirconia waved to get her sister's attention.

Zinnia put her finger over her phone's microphone. "What?"

"Wear something else when you go out. That dress makes you look fat, and old, and sallow."

Zinnia's jaw dropped.

Mission accomplished.

CHAPTER 49

Zirconia waited for her daughter to come to her.

She waited in the hotel lobby, sitting on the couch.

It was the same couch she'd used to kill Xavier during a particularly gruesome play session. She stroked the throw pillows, feeling nostalgic.

She wondered how he was doing, with his vacuum cleaner experiments and his futile attempts at making his ex-girlfriend love him. Poor Xavier really needed guidance. It was his loss that he'd soured their relationship with his petulant, childish demands.

Zirconia leaned back and closed her eyes. The darkness was such a relief.

She heard the redheaded storm coming before she saw it.

Right on time, trouble stomped into the lobby wearing a pair of pointy-toed, mismatched boots.

Zara was, as usual, crackling with magical fury.

"What did you do to Aunt Zinnia?"

"I made her angry on purpose, for my own reasons that I'm afraid I can't disclose."

Zara's body, which had been arching like a sail full of strong tailwind, relaxed.

"You... what?"

"I insulted her intentionally. To be perfectly honest, most of the time I insult her it is intentional. But this morning, it was for a very good reason. There's a magical event going on right now. It's nothing to worry about, but you need to trust..."

Zara wasn't paying attention.

At the mention of a *magical event*, she'd immediately started casting spells.

It was just like her to play detective at the drop of a hat.

Zirconia waited while Zara cast a series of threat-detection spells and other assessments.

Zara's face lit up. She'd found something.

“I knew it,” Zara said triumphantly. “There are people sleeping where they shouldn't be sleeping.”

She went to the janitor's closet and opened it to reveal the Darnells, blissfully in their slumber. Zirconia was making some changes that day, but she did plan to keep getting the house.

Zara did a quick wave of magic into the closet, and woke up the Darnells.

They got to their feet, exchanging confused looks.

“There's been a gas leak,” Zara said to them. “Take your suitcases, and go to your rooms.”

Debbie said, “We were checking out.” She grabbed her husband's hand and said, “What's happening?”

“Continue checking out,” Zara said. “Leave quickly, and don't talk to this lady.” She pointed at her mother. “Don't even look her in the eyes. There's something very wrong with her, and it's not safe for you here.”

The Darnells grabbed their suitcases and left quickly.

Zirconia said with a sniff, “So much for our dream house. I'll have to stash them somewhere better on my next try.”

“Leave those people alone,” Zara said angrily.

“I was helping them,” Zirconia said, which was technically true. “They were going to earn a huge commission on the sale of a house. I'm not all bad.”

“Oh.” Zara's anger ebbed. “You help people now?”

“Of course I do. And I'd like to help you, too.”

“Like you helped me tidy up my closet, back when I had a house?”

“You didn't need all those corsets and costumes. You had a pair of clown shoes at the back corner. Actual clown shoes. You could have given them to Adella for her flipper feet.”

Zara shook her head. "You mean Ambrosia. I heard you talking to her about her feet. Did you mean what you said, about her growing into them?"

"Yes. As soon as time rolls forward, she'll grow. She'll grow, Zinnia will have her baby, you'll move beyond your grief and get over Bentley, and I'll get—"

"I don't want to," Zara said.

"You have to."

"No. It's not going to change, but that's okay. I can live like this."

"That's not true. You're trying to run from it," Zirconia said. "I know about your job interview, and your apartment."

"You do, huh?" Zara nodded. "Who told you? Was it Ribbons? You two are like the bookends on a shelf full of bad stories."

Zirconia let her daughter think the wyvern was the one who'd tipped her off, even though he hadn't been around that Wednesday. He and Junior were on another continent, touring an active volcano.

Zara said, "I'm leaving, and you can't talk me out of it."

Well, that wasn't true at all.

Zirconia knew that, with the right circumstances, she could talk Zara into just about anything. One Wednesday, the two had jumped out of an airplane in a tandem parachute with Xavier right behind them. That had been a wonderful day, ending with a picnic on the beach. They'd all been so happy until Zara kicked over some children's sandcastle like a human tornado, and then sank to her knees in the wreckage to cry about Bentley.

Zirconia spoke the truth. "I won't try to talk you out of anything today. All I want is to go with you to your interview."

"It's too late. I've got a flight out this afternoon. The plane is sold out. I was going to add Zoey, but it was too full."

"I already have my ticket. Should I give it to Zolanda, or do you consent to having me on that flight?"

Zara's face bunched up. She didn't like the second option, but wasn't selfish enough to request the first.

Zirconia said, "Is there anything else I can say or do that would make you happy about having me along?"

Zara looked down at her mismatched boots. Her eyebrows went up and down. She was having an active debate with herself inside her head.

Zirconia picked up a few psychic whiffs, as only a mother could. There was something that sounded like, *Zara is a good witch, Zara does this, Zara doesn't do that.*

Zara looked up at her mother with an oddly triumphant expression.

"I'm onto you," Zara said. "This is about my father. I'm planning to see him tonight after I fly in."

"Oh, you're seeing Rhys tonight?"

Zirconia played it cool, even though she'd known for many, many Wednesdays exactly what the two had planned.

"I am," Zara said. "He's taking me to a friend's restaurant for dinner."

"How lucky for you. We all know your father can be a difficult man to find."

"He's the one who got me the job interview," Zara said.

"I'll have to thank him when I see him tonight. Do you think his friend will allow one more seat at the table?"

Zara suddenly whipped her hand back, and cast a spell straight at her mother's face.

It felt to Zirconia like a wave of cold ocean water.

It was cold, and liquid. And wet. Really wet. It *was* ocean water, and it was in her mouth.

She sputtered and spat out the salty brine.

"What was that for?"

Zara smiled. "You have to forgive me, Mother, but I had to do it. You're behaving so strangely, and had to check that you were really you."

"With a spell?"

"You know me. I'm always casting spells first, asking questions later." She shrugged one shoulder. "I'm not very good at restraint. Isn't that what you're always saying?"

Zirconia spat out more salty water.

If she had to do this part of the day again, she'd have to remember to duck that spell.

Little did she know, she would not get the opportunity.

CHAPTER 50

The Flight

Zirconia and her witch daughter walked down the cramped aisle of the little plane.

Wisteria was a small town, with a modest airport that mostly saw small planes for local domestic flights.

"You can have the window seat," Zara said. "I'll be sleeping."

"How can you possibly be tired? All you do is sleep. And, while we're on the subject, I don't think the eye cream you've been borrowing from Aunt Zinnia is doing you any favors."

Zara glared at her mother.

That was it. All the goodwill Zirconia had earned that morning burned up.

Zirconia made a mental note to not mention the eye cream on their flight. She would instead give her daughter a compliment, such as that her eye bags weren't too bad, all things considered.

Little did she know, she would not get the chance.

Zara pushed in front of her mother and took the window seat herself.

Zirconia took the aisle. The little plane had only two seats per side. There was, tragically, no First Class or Business section. Everyone sat together, like they were at a state fair jamboree.

Zirconia settled in, and flagged down a woman in a red vest.

"Champagne, please," she said.

Red Vest walked right past their row and took a seat at the back. She wasn't a flight attendant.

Zirconia made a mental note for her next try, which she believed would come around soon enough. The days were starting to whip by now, starting and restarting as rapidly as the breaths of oxygen she drew.

Zara craned her neck to look out the window. She elbowed her mother. "Is that Xavier Batista out there on the tarmac?"

"Who?"

"The dark-haired kid you keep calling Zander."

Zirconia pressed her cheek against her daughter's so she could peer out of the small porthole of a window.

Sure enough, the young man was out there. He looked the same as he always did.

She was so relieved. There was a part of her that had started to believe he was dead—truly dead.

Zara said, "I wonder what he's doing. Oh. He's getting on this flight. That will be nice. I haven't seen him in ages. We can catch up."

Zirconia detected an enthusiasm in her daughter's voice that was never directed at her mother.

Jealousy flared like a green monster. She was actually jealous of Xavier Batista. What a strange Wednesday this was turning out to be.

Zirconia said, "If you're such a big fan, maybe I should switch seats with someone so he can sit next to you."

Zara's eyebrows rose in more enthusiasm. "Would you do that? Thanks, Mom."

Thanks, Mom. The words might have felt good, had the situation been different.

Xavier walked up to their row and stopped. He did a not-so-subtle double take. He wasn't the best actor.

"Zara!" He did another, even more fake double-take when he met Zirconia's eyes. "Ms. Riddle! What a surprise. I didn't know you two were going to be on this flight."

We don't lie in therapy, Zirconia heard in her therapist's voice. *Lying is a barrier, not a boundary.*

Zara nudged her mother to get moving.

"Xavier, you can sit here," Zara said. "My mother wanted a different seat anyway. Sit! I want to hear all about what's going on with you. How's Liza?"

Zirconia got to her feet, aided by a shove from her daughter, and relinquished her seat to the interloper.

The two time loopers locked eyes as he slid past her.

Through gritted teeth that threatened to turn into fangs, she said, "What a coincidence that we're all on the same flight. Tell me, Zachary Bartholomew, what business do you have in the city?"

"Probably the same business you have, Ms. Riddle."

"Which is what, exactly?"

"Looking up an old acquaintance to chat about physics."

"That's awfully specific. How odd that you would think I was doing the same thing. Tell me something, is this your first time on this flight?"

"My word as my bond, this is my first time on this plane."

Zirconia nodded.

Fair enough.

The young man had been keeping tabs on her. She should have been doing the same thing instead of wasting all her time at a therapist's office.

She took a seat in the spot he should have been in, way back near the washroom, and settled in.

The man next to her was recording a video of himself on his phone. He kept saying, "I'll be back," in an Austrian accent and laughing.

I'll be back, indeed.

That was the theme on that Wednesday.

Xavier was back, and they were finally on their way to see Rhys.

Was this it?

Were they about to break free?

CHAPTER 51

Zirconia fell asleep on the plane, and woke disoriented.

It was strange to not wake up on the sofabed in the hotel suite, to wake up next to a man, and not her sister making tea.

Her seatmate, an athletic fellow with short, wavy hair, slept with his forehead against the rounded plane window.

Zirconia yawned and stretched like a jungle cat in her seat.

Xavier Batista made his way down the aisle and stopped beside her.

He said, "I fell asleep. Probably an hour. Were you asleep, too?"

There was no animosity in his voice. The bad blood between them was on hold for now. This plane had no Business Class, but it was, for the time loopers, a business trip.

"I did have a little cat nap," she said.

"We were both sleeping at the same time," he said.

"Everyone gets sleepy on planes."

He looked pointedly at the collection of miniature bottles on her tray. "Sure. And some people black out, too."

"I barely touched those." And it was true. She'd touched them just enough to pour them into her pink grapefruit juice.

He grinned and asked, "Don't you want to know how I knew you were on this flight?"

"No. But clearly you want to tell me, so go ahead."

His grin didn't falter. "I hired Boomer to tail you."

She was genuinely surprised. "That woman is better than I thought. I had no idea she was tailing me. How many days?"

His grin fell right off. “Okay, I just started hiring her today. I would have done it ages ago if I actually cared what you were doing before today.”

Her fingertips tingled. “Why today?”

“I dunno. This morning when I woke up, things felt... different.”

A jolt of electricity shot up Zirconia's spine. Her cool blood pumped at maximum vampire speed.

She said, “Different, how?”

Xavier glanced around at their fellow passengers. He didn't want to speak about it if others could hear.

If Zirconia hadn't renounced her witch powers all those years ago, she might have cast a sound bubble. Instead, she waved her hand and made everyone in the seats around them fall asleep.

She gestured for Xavier to explain himself.

“It's hard to explain,” he said. “All the other days feel like they were a dream, like they didn't actually happen, and now today is the day that's real.”

“Today does feel different,” Zirconia said. “I thought it was because I had a real breakthrough at my therapy session yesterday.”

“Therapy?”

“I've been seeing Tallulah Stillwater at ten o'clock every day. I took Jason's appointment.”

Xavier jerked his head back. “I've been seeing her at two o'clock. I traded with Pam.”

“Oh, you shouldn't have done that. Pam has a serious disorder. She needs her slot.”

Xavier snorted. “What about Jason? He's got real problems.”

Zirconia sighed. “We're both terrible, selfish people. We've got a lot of work to do.”

“Speak for yourself,” Xavier said. “I'm not terrible, and I'm not selfish.”

“Then you're not a person, because everyone is a little bit terrible and selfish.”

Xavier looked down at his feet. He mumbled, “It's true. I only want to be a hero because I think it will make me feel whole.”

“And that's fine,” Zirconia said. “Tallulah explained it all to me. There's virtually no difference between a good person who wants to do the right thing and someone who doesn't, but makes the conscious choice to do the right thing because it generally works out in their favor. Virtually no difference, in the end.”

Nodding, Xavier said, “Tallulah is an amazing therapist.”

“Did you sleep with her?”

“No!”

He looked away.

Zirconia said, “Are we keeping secrets from each other now?”

He lowered his voice. “There was one day I didn't take the appointment, and I bumped into her at a grocery store. I definitely could have, but I didn't.” He wrinkled his nose. “It wouldn't have been right.”

“How many other women did you *bump into* at the grocery store?”

“I'm not like that.” His light-green eyes blazed at her. “What about you? Did you figure out a way to hook up with Nick?”

“Yes.”

“Really?”

“It's been a lot of Wednesdays.”

“Two thousand and seven,” Xavier said. “I've been counting.”

“That can't be right. That's... over five years.”

“It's pretty accurate, give or take a couple days. I had to remember in my head.”

Another shiver rippled through her body. She usually experienced no discomfort from cold, but these jolts were getting to her.

"Xavier, I've never been stuck in one of these for that long," she said. "What if...?"

"Don't think that way," he said bravely, with that cute, stupid Xavier bravery of his.

Oh, how she'd missed her friend all these days. Why did she always get into scuffles with people and drive them away? Besides all the reasons Tallulah Swiftwater had told her. There had to be something that was unique to Zirconia. She couldn't have been bungling up her life in the exact same mundane manner that regular women did, with hurt feelings and a lack of forgiveness.

Xavier kept going with his pep talk. "We're going to see your ex, and we're going to fix this whole quantum entanglement thing." He pointed down the aisle behind her. "Right after I use the bathroom."

"Oh, Xavier. Didn't you go before you got on the plane?"

"No, because I didn't have you there to remind me."

Both smiled, remembering all the times he'd wet his pants on their skydiving jumps.

She'd missed this. Having someone who shared so many of her happy memories.

He took two steps down the aisle and stopped.

The plane was shaking.

They made eye contact.

Turbulence?

The plane shook again, more strongly.

People around them started waking up from their light glamours, making confused noises.

Someone at the front of the plane screamed.

Then everything tilted.

Xavier left the ground, flew over her head, and crashed into the row behind her.

For a brief instant, Zirconia felt genuine joy for her friend. Xavier had acquired the magical ability to fly.

Her brain immediately corrected the cognitive error.

Xavier wasn't flying.

The plane was falling.

They were about to crash.

It took another ten minutes of absolute bedlam, but, sure enough, it happened.

They all crashed and died.

CHAPTER 52

Wednesday

Zirconia woke from sleep disoriented.

It was bright, she was reclining in a seat, and a man was sleeping next to her.

She was on the airplane.

She sat forward with a gasp, knocking the tiny empty gin and vodka bottles to the floor.

Her seatmate was still asleep.

They hadn't crashed.

Had it all been a dream?

Xavier came running toward her down the aisle, staggering wildly as he tripped on the braces for the plane's seats.

He said, "Tell me you woke up back home, in your bed."

She wanted to tell him, but she couldn't. She had not woken up at home. She'd woken up right there, on the airplane.

She didn't have to say it. Xavier could see the horror on her face.

"We screwed up," he said.

"*We* screwed up?"

"We both fell asleep at the same time. It rebooted us to here, instead of where it was supposed to."

"I don't think it works like that."

He pressed his hands to his ears as though the sound of her voice was causing him physical distress. She could make her voice do that, but she didn't think she had.

Then he threw his hands outward and yelled, "You don't know how it works! You don't know anything! You've wasted it all! You've wasted your whole life!"

She jerked her head back. “This is projection,” she said, quoting Tallulah. “You're projecting your own insecurities onto me.”

“You don't know what you're supposed to know, and now we're all going to crash!”

All around them, heads popped up over seats. The other passengers could hear everything. Zirconia hadn't charmed them to sleep on this Wednesday. This probably-very-short-and-ending-in-fiery-disaster Wednesday.

People murmured to each other in confusion, then one woman said to Xavier, “Why are you saying that? Are you a terrorist?”

“No,” he said. “I'm a good person. I could be a hero, if I had the chance.”

The woman said to her seatmate, “He's a terrorist.”

More voices joined in, agreeing that Xavier had to be a terrorist. The more he insisted he wasn't, and that he only knew the plane was going to crash because he had special powers, the more certain the other passengers were.

Within a minute, a trio of men from the nearby seats put together a team and subdued Xavier. They tied him up with shoelaces donated by other passengers.

The trio's victory didn't last long, though, because the plane crashed.

And they all died.

Zirconia died trying to shake the last few drops of vodka from a miniature bottle into her mouth.

CHAPTER 53

Part Four

A Few Short Wednesdays Later

The plane kept crashing because the pilot kept dying at the controls.

Once the time loopers had discovered the problem, fixing it should have been easy enough.

Death wasn't necessarily death, if the right supernaturals were around.

Three people huddled over the body of the pilot: Xavier Batista, Zirconia Riddle, and Zara Riddle.

They were alone in the cockpit.

Zara, being a witch with excellent healing powers, was trying to revive the pilot.

Zirconia had tried to revive the man with a few drops of her blood, but no matter how quickly she ran up to the cockpit when she woke from her nap, she could never get to him in time.

Zara, who didn't know about the time loop but did understand their lives were all in danger, was working hard to save the pilot. She had one hand on his shoulder and one on the top of his head. Her eyes were closed. She was deep in a trance of concentration.

"She's in too deep," Xavier said.

"My daughter can handle herself."

"No. She can't. She needs us."

"Riddle women are tougher than we look."

"We've gotta pull her out," he insisted. "Look at her color, how it's draining out of her face. Look at her shirt. Her vest. The color's actually draining out of her clothes. That's not good."

Zirconia snapped back, "I'm cool-blooded, not blind."

"Do something," he said. "She's turning gray."

"Give her another minute."

"We don't have a minute. I can read the street signs out the plane's front window."

Zirconia wasted a full second actually turning her head and looking out the plane's window.

There were no visible street signs. They were still well above the town they were about to crash into.

Xavier was wasting precious time with his inane comments. Apparently he had spent some of his time alone working on his comedy routine. She was not a fan.

Xavier tapped on Zara's shoulder. "Hello in there. Zara? It's okay. You can't save him. Pull out and we'll try something else."

Zara didn't acknowledge him. She kept holding onto the dead pilot, pouring her life into him.

But there was no *him* there. Only death.

She kept pouring herself into death.

"Stop," Zirconia said. "Zarabella, stop."

But Zarabella didn't stop. She had turned the color of ash, and now she was turning *into* ash. Particles of her lifted, floating into the air. First her hair, its lush red hue now nearly white. Her eyelashes fell like snow. Her gray clothing disintegrated, showing bare shoulders that turned from pink to ash as well.

Zirconia had to grab her daughter by the wrists and pry her hands off the dead pilot.

The color instantly returned.

Zara's hazel eyes flashed like amber fire as she glared at her mother.

Zara growled, "Why did you stop me?"

"He's too far gone," Zirconia said. "He must have died shortly after takeoff, while the plane was still on a program."

Xavier chimed in, "It's called autopilot."

Zara yanked her hands from her mother's grip, and once more grabbed hold of the pilot. Her color ebbed away again, faster this time.

Zirconia said, “As your mother, I command you to stop.”

That didn't do any good.

Zara was too determined.

Not to revive the pilot.

They both knew it was too late for him.

Zara was determined to follow his spirit out of that world and on to the next one.

Zirconia circled around and grabbed her daughter from behind.

They were about to crash—there would be no survivors—and they would all be resurrected in their seats once more, so it hardly mattered if Zara died a few seconds earlier. It hardly mattered, except for to her mother, who couldn't bear to watch.

Zirconia hugged her daughter from behind and pulled her back from death, back from darkness, back from oblivion, back from never waking up again.

Zirconia pulled her back from the brink.

The *brink.*

She'd never thought about that word until today.

People just said it.

The brink of death.

Brink was a funny word, not used much except for steep cliffs and death.

But when you were near it, when you were staring into it, watching your daughter float away into it, the word brink wasn't that funny.

The plane crashed, and Zirconia died with the ringing sound of her daughter's outrage in her ears.

CHAPTER 54

Many Plane Crashes Later

"Easy now," Zirconia said.

"Stop micromanaging me," Xavier said.

The time loopers were both in the cockpit of the plane. Xavier sat in the pilot's chair at the controls, and Zirconia stood behind him, watching his nervous hands as he flicked switches on the control panel.

The pilot was slumped on the floor behind them, dead.

There truly was no way to save the man. He'd been deceased for at least thirty minutes before the time loopers woke up from their naps.

If they could have woken up at their usual time, back home in their beds, they could have prevented all of this.

But the rules of the game had changed, and the loop began on the plane. On the plane with a dead pilot.

The man couldn't be helped by Zara's healing magic, or Zirconia's blood magic, or any combination of the medical supplies on board the plane.

On previous loops, they had canvassed the flight for other magical assets. They'd turned up a couple of mages, but they might as well have been Nothing People for all the help their skills provided.

The duo had given up on saving the pilot, and focused their efforts in a more productive direction: flying the plane themselves.

They had a few problems, though.

Firstly, there was nobody around to teach them how to fly the plane, and no communication with the outside world—the stretch of airspace they were in was weirdly dead.

Secondly, they didn't have very much time between waking and crashing. Far less than an hour, closer to ten minutes. And a lot of those precious minutes were wasted getting from their seats into the locked cockpit.

They streamlined it by having Xavier make an announcement that he was an off-duty pilot and there was nothing to be concerned about, but he did get tackled for being a suspected terrorist during the early runs.

It wasn't going well.

Each time Zirconia woke in her seat, she wished she would open her eyes to the hotel suite.

She longed for the hotel suite, with the creaky bed, the stained ceiling, the noisy pets. Even Zinnia insulting her. She wished with all of her dark, heavy heart that she might wake up there again.

If she could only do it all over, she would get it right. She would live—really live—in each moment. She would be present. She would be serene, and kind, and good. She would never complain about anything ever again because she'd be so grateful to not be trapped in this... this awful cycle of crashing over and over.

This...

This *Hell*.

Xavier said, "I got the landing gear down." He sounded so pleased with himself. Was he having fun? Was this like a video game to him?

She cuffed him on the back of the head. "We're in a nose dive, you fool. Why are you wasting time with landing gear?"

"Everything adds up," he said. "Did you hear that?"

There was a rumbling sound.

"We just dumped fuel," he said proudly. Another rumble. "And that would be the luggage."

"What?"

He turned to her, grinning. "Sorry about your bags. You'll have to buy yourself a new toothbrush after we land."

She would have told him not to waste time joking around, but it was too late for that. It was too late for anything.

She could read the street signs of the town they were about to land on.

They crashed and died.

CHAPTER 55

Another Wednesday, Another Flying Lesson

In spite of their bickering, the two time loopers were learning how to fly the small plane.

The previous day, they'd kept it aloft an additional forty seconds... before flying into the side of a mountain.

As their inevitable crash destiny grew closer, they discussed their circumstances.

Zirconia said, "Maybe we did lose our place in time because we were both asleep at the same time."

"Duh," he said.

"I'll give you that, even though I don't buy it. It still doesn't explain why we're crashing."

"Duh," he said again. "We're crashing because we don't know how to fly this thing."

"But this plane wasn't crashing before," Zirconia said. "Zara was on this flight many times. I may have my blind spots, but it would not have escaped my notice that my daughter died in a plane crash. They do notify the families."

"Mm hmm," Xavier said. "Why's that yellow light flashing?"

"Therefore, the plane is crashing because something changed due to the two of us being on the plane."

"Never mind about that. Check under the seat again. Maybe there is a manual."

"Xavier, it's crashing because of us. The two of us being here is causing—already caused the pilot to die. It must have been me. My vampire energy. Or, as you call it, my*emotional vampire* energy."

Xavier didn't say anything.

"You think it was me," she said.

"No," he said. "Don't be so hard on yourself. You didn't do this."

"But you can't know that it wasn't me. The plane never crashed before I got on it."

"It wasn't you," he said with a snarky tone. "The world doesn't revolve around you, Zirconia."

She didn't have to take that. "I'm going back to my seat. You can crash this plane on your own for a while."

"Wait."

She waited.

Xavier leaned forward in his pilot's chair to take off his lightweight summer jacket.

Under the jacket, he wore someone else's uniformed shirt. Zirconia knew it wasn't his own because she'd never seen him in something that required ironing.

"I took someone else's seat," he said, patting a brass name tag above his lapel.

He was wearing a pilot's uniform.

She had never noticed.

"This guy was off duty, heading home," Xavier said. "He wasn't scheduled to fly this plane, but he was on it, so when the pilot died, he must have stepped right in."

All the anger and frustration Zirconia had been feeling reached a boiling point.

"This is all your fault," she said. "If you'd let me get on the plane by myself, this guy would be here, and we'd be landing safely. I'd be able to fix everything with Rhys. Now we'll never get there." She threw her hands in the air. "Thanks a lot. Thanks for making my life a living Hell."

As the plane screamed through the last thousand feet of sky toward a mountain, Xavier growled, "You can stay back there in your seat from now on. I don't need you—"

They crashed and died.

CHAPTER 56

Another Bumpy Flight

Zirconia sat in Xavier's seat, which had been her seat, and nudged her daughter awake.

Zara's eyes flew open in alarm. "Bentley!"

"Shh." Zirconia touched her daughter's arm. "It's okay. You're here with me."

Zara turned to her, confused. "Where is he, Mom?"

"I don't know."

Zara's eyes glistened. "But he promised. He promised to protect us."

"He did what he could."

Zara turned away from her mother, and looked out of the rounded window.

"He'll be back," she said. "He always comes back."

Zirconia patted her daughter's shoulder.

The only sound over the plane's engines and air circulation was an excited Hurrah from the cockpit.

Xavier must have figured out another piece of the puzzle. Good for him. He probably would have learned it faster if she had been up there with him, but some people had to learn things the hard way.

"I can feel him with me," Zara said, still with her head turned away, hiding her face. "But then sometimes I can feel that he's gone, and it's just as strong a feeling. It's like a shadow that comes between me and the sun." The witch shivered. "I'm so cold. It's so cold in the world without him."

"Zara, he wouldn't want you to suffer like this."

Zara's head whipped around so she could face her mother. Her hazel eyes were like burning amber again.

"Don't," she said coldly. "Don't tell me all those things that people say. Everyone wants to say something to me.

All day long. They've all got something they're so desperate to say. Like *time heals all wounds*, and *there's a plan for everything*, and *one day I'll move on*. Why do people have to say those stupid things? I wish everyone would just go away and shut up and let us be."

"Us?"

"Me and..." Her expression went blank. The plane shook. She glanced up at the flashing fasten-seatbelts signs. "Is there... is there something wrong with this plane?"

From the cockpit, Xavier yelled out, "Boo-yeah! How'd you like them apples?"

Zara looked deep into her mother's eyes. "What's happening? Is this a dream?" Her brow was beading with sweat.

Zirconia used the sleeve of her shirt to wipe her daughter's forehead.

"Shh," the vampire said. "This is all a dream. Close your eyes and go back to sleep."

"We're crashing," Zara said with detached curiosity. "This plane is crashing."

She said it loud enough to set off a panic in the rows around them.

"Yes," Zirconia said. "The plane is crashing."

"We won't survive."

Zirconia shrugged. "You never know. Why don't you go back to sleep?"

Zara closed her eyes, and leaned back in her seat. The expression on her face was serene, pure surrender.

From the cockpit, Xavier could be heard yelling, "Hang on, hang on, I got it! I got it!"

Then, "I don't got it."

CHAPTER 57

Touchdown

Zara slept fitfully in the seat next to her mother.

The vampire had glamoured her to sleep as soon as she'd woken in her own row to restart the sequence.

She'd pushed out the magic from a distance, so she wouldn't have to watch her daughter surrender. And also so she wouldn't have to receive the angry glare she'd get the instant Zara figured out her mother was breaking their rules.

Zirconia had already put every single one of the passengers on the plane to sleep. Xavier's whole hero operation ran more smoothly that way.

He was up ahead, doing his part now.

She yelled encouragement toward the cockpit, "You can do it!"

"Captain Jiminy Whoozat could use a little help," he yelled back.

Xavier had taken to calling himself by the fake pilot name he'd adopted on a previous cycle. He was disassociating from the stress. She hoped it wouldn't be permanent.

"You've got it this time, Jiminy," she yelled up. "You don't need me."

"I know that, but Captain Whoozat's got something really cool to say after he sticks the landing, and it's not cool when you have to yell it."

Zirconia kissed her sleeping daughter on the cheek, and went up to the cockpit.

Xavier looked like a competent pilot, sitting in the pilot's chair, wearing a pilot's uniform.

Zirconia didn't want to make him overconfident, so she said, "That uniform is two sizes too large. You look like a child playing dress up on career day."

"And you look like the world's oldest stewardess."

"We call ourselves flight attendants now."

"But not when you started, am I right?" He held up his fist triumphantly.

Zirconia reluctantly gave him a fist bump.

"Captain, either your sense of humor is improving or I'm losing my mind."

"Jiminy Whoozat has an excellent sense of humor," Xavier said. "He went to clown college. At Yale. It's very exclusive and secret."

She looked out the front window at a view she'd never seen before.

The mountain was passing *by* them instead of *through* them.

"Well?" Xavier turned to her, grinning. "We're going to make it to our destination ahead of schedule. I'm going to land this plane, and we're going to find your ex, and we're going to move on from this thing."

"What if it doesn't work? What if it's not him?"

"Not a problem," Xavier said. "The way I see it, we've got a plane now. We're in a much better position than we were before. With this thing, we can go anywhere." He tapped a digital display. "I didn't even dump fuel this time. We've got a decent range."

"You really are something," she said.

"Captain Jiminy Whoozat did it all with no magic. No powers."

Zirconia bit her tongue. No magic? He'd died and been resurrected so many times. What was that if not a power? He'd been studying at the Immortals Academy of Flight, where no mistake was deadly.

They were flying smoothly now.

He released the manual controls, and shook out his hands.

He nodded to the passenger area and asked, "How's our girl doing?"

"Sleeping."

"If you'd told her what was happening, we might have gotten to this point a lot faster, you know."

"I know."

"Why didn't you want to wake her up?"

Now it was time for Zirconia to reveal her own secret.

"I told her a hundred times," she said wearily. "She didn't believe me. She didn't believe her own mother."

"You should have let me take a crack at it."

"You were busy learning to fly, Captain."

"She didn't believe her own mother? That's gotta hurt. I'm sorry, Z."

He'd started calling her Z, pronounced Zee—not Zed the way Ribbons said it—a while back.

She called him B, short for Batista. The letter X for Xavier didn't roll off the tongue.

They would have to put an end to the familiarity once time restarted.

Zirconia said, "Zara swore she believed me, that she'd heard about time loops from her aunt, but then she reset the next wakeup just the same." Zirconia didn't say it, but she blamed Bentley. His memory and the loss of him was all her daughter could think of when she woke, and it wiped away anything else.

"Maybe it was because she didn't nap when we did. For all she knew, she woke up in the hotel bed this morning. Maybe that's why."

"Maybe," Zirconia agreed.

"Maybe it's for the best."

"Maybe it is, B." She ruffled his hair the way she would if he were her son. In that moment, he was her son. This version of him had been born and raised within their cozy loop of two.

He didn't pull away. If anything, he leaned into her touch and moaned a little with pleasure.

Zirconia yanked her hand away.

The young man needed to get out of the loop and back to pursuing girls his age.

"Xavier, do you ever wish you hadn't woken up?"

"Nah."

"Promise me something. If you ever wake up in one of these again, and I haven't, don't tell me."

"Okay," he said.

Okay? Just like that?

He said, "I'll only wake you up if I get really desperate."

"And don't you dare come to me on the first of April, or any other day, and tell me there's a time loop when there isn't."

"What?" He laughed. "I never thought of that."

"Here's why you're not going to do it. If you come to me with a prank, the first thing I'm going to do is pick up the nearest blunt instrument and club you to death with it. If it's a prank, you'll be dead forever."

He gave her a wide-eyed look, and then they both burst out laughing.

Their sense of humor had been co-evolving.

They made it safely to their destination.

For the first time ever.

Captain Jiminy Whoozat landed the plane like a real, professional pilot—more or less—and they laughed once more in relief.

He was so happy, he forgot to say the cool line he'd been saving up for the occasion.

CHAPTER 58

Grounded

The airport was large, but the plane was small, so it was the type of flight where the passengers were let out directly on the tarmac.

After a little fuss with the mechanism for the door and the stairs, the time loopers got the plane open, and revived the slumbering passengers to deboard.

It was late afternoon, and the summer sun perched proudly above the city, glinting off the office towers. The air was surprisingly humid compared to the seaside town from which they'd left, and downright moist compared to the recycled airplane air. Zirconia noticed the tips of her hair frizz immediately. She didn't like this city. It was trying to steal Zara away from her, plus it was terrible for her hair.

Xavier was the last to leave the plane.

An instant after setting foot on the warm, black asphalt, Xavier dropped to his knees and kissed the ground.

The passengers definitely noticed their pilot was kissing the ground. Heads turned, and people murmured the usual suspicions that the young man might be up to something nefarious.

Zirconia said loudly, "Captain Jiminy Whoozat, you're such a joker! Don't be silly. It was a perfect flight, as usual." She explained to everyone watching, "This is one of our little comedy routines. At Leapfrog Air, we get you there, and we always care... about putting a smile on your face."

The passengers smiled, and continued toward the airport. Leapfrog Air was known for its extra-salty pretzels and quirky safety presentations.

Zirconia's former seat mate, the athletic mage who had powers for detecting nests of insects within building structures, patted Xavier on the back.

The man said, "There couldn't have been that much turbulence. I slept right through it."

Xavier replied, "I know, Gene. I'm just grateful to be alive. It's a beautiful day." He pointed a finger gun at the man. "Have a great time at your exterminator convention."

Gene's memories of the flight were quite vague, having been scrambled by Zirconia's magic, so he didn't notice that, for a stranger, the captain sure knew a lot about him.

Gene pointed a finger gun right back. "I sure will. We always have fun with the kids who can't read, and sneak in because they think it's a Terminator convention. You should hear my Arnold Schwarzenegger impression." He turned serious and said in an Austrian accent, "I'll be back."

"Good one," Xavier said. He'd stopped kissing the ground, and gave Gene a complicated handshake as the two carried on toward the airport building.

Zara took hold of her mother's elbow and said in a soft voice, "Something odd is happening. What have you done now, Mother?"

They were back to *Mother* again. So much for Mom.

Well, you could replay the day thousands of times and never would get it perfect. Such was life.

"I'll tell you everything tomorrow," Zirconia said.

Zara rubbed her temples. "I've got a splitting headache. I'm going to blow this job interview."

"You'll be fine. Take what's left of that eye cream Aunt Zinnia gave you, and eat it."

Zara gave her mother a sidelong look.

"Trust me," Zirconia said. "It won't do anything for your headache, but at least you'll stop spreading it on your eyes, where it isn't doing you any favors."

Zara rolled her eyes at her mother, and then picked up speed so she could walk ahead on her own.

Zirconia smiled to herself. She was a good mother. When Zara was annoyed at her, with her negative emotions focused on that task, at least she wasn't worrying about her interview or pining over Bentley.

Xavier circled back to Zirconia, skipping the whole way.

"Now what?" He bobbed up and down urgently. "Now what?"

"We go see a man about our quantum entanglement. Why are you bouncing around like a Hairy Spider Snatcher with a new yo-yo?"

"I have to go to the bathroom. Number one. I've been holding it for, oh, about a year."

"Why didn't you just relieve yourself?"

"And waste precious time? The washrooms were all the way at the back."

"Given our situation, you could have simply gone anywhere."

"Ew." He wrinkled his nose then ran ahead, straight for the washrooms.

Zirconia caught up to her daughter in the airport's food court, which held a cornucopia of smells. After a year of recycled airplane air, the scents of frying meats and carbohydrates were an assault on Zirconia's refined palate.

Few people on the planet had a palate as refined as Zirconia Cristata Riddle's. She had used her time loops, and the hospitality of her wealthy friends, to taste every kind of food imaginable, including the poisonous ones. Even at the age of twenty, her skills at wine tasting exceeded that of the world's top sommeliers.

Did having such refined taste make it difficult to enjoy the pedestrian wines on offer in small town restaurants? Yes. But only the first few sips.

Zirconia found her witch daughter at the counter of a place that sold giant cinnamon buns. Zara was looking up at the menu board.

"You should get one," Zirconia said.

"I can't eat a whole one," Zara said.

"You and I both know that's not true."

"Do you want to split one with me?"

Zirconia hesitated. She did not eat food that came from a *court* unless actual royalty were involved.

But she remembered the promise she'd made on the plane, the promise she made about how she'd live her life if she ever got off the Hellish plane. She would be in the moment. She would seize the day, taste the low-quality cinnamon buns, etcetera.

"I'd love to," she said to her daughter.

They ordered a giant cinnamon thing—it was more of a family-sized cake than a bun—to share.

They dined on what passed for chairs and a table in the food court.

The dough was surprisingly flaky, and the icing had the tang of real cream cheese. It wasn't good, but a year without eating anything at all had made Zirconia appreciate even lowly fare.

They were fork-battling over the last non-soggy pieces when a shifty-eyed shifter approached in an ill-fitting suit.

Zara jumped up, arms outstretched. "Dad!"

Dad? Zirconia was *Mother*, but he got to be *Dad*?

Zirconia felt the all-too-familiar emotional dagger stab her chest. Would any amount of therapy ever give her the armor to protect her soft and tender feelings?

She rose from the plastic stump with her usual poise, clenched her jaw against the humiliation, and air-kissed Rhys Quarry in greeting.

Here we are, she thought. *I know what you've been up to.*

His eyes revealed nothing.

CHAPTER 59

The four of them—Rhys Quarry, Zirconia Riddle, Zara Riddle, and Xavier Batista—walked through the airport to the tube that would take them to the parkade.

Nobody gave them a second look. They were just another family, like so many other four-person groups.

Rhys kept yawning. "I got here early and had a nap in my car. I'm not quite awake yet. Any chance you Wisterians brought me some of that purple coffee your friend Maisy Nix brews?"

"Next time," Zara said. "I'll bring you a suitcase full of beans when Zoey and I move here."

"That's what I like to hear," her father said.

They walked through the tube to the parkade.

Rhys Quarry led the way, and Xavier trotted up front to be next to him.

Xavier gushed about how fun it must be to shift into fox form at will.

"It's not all it's cracked up to be," Rhys said. "Sometimes my clothes get turned around. It can be very uncomfortable."

"I'm still just a Nothing Person," Xavier said sheepishly. "Even though I can land a plane."

The two Riddles were right behind them as they wove their way through the busy parkade. Zara was quiet. Zirconia's stomach groaned noisily in protest of the enormous cinnamon bun.

"That's not what I like to hear," Rhys said to Xavier. "Don't let anyone tell you you're a Nothing Person. You have to focus on your abilities. Every person is unique. Every person can do something that nobody else can."

Zara piped up, "Speaking of which, why were you in the cockpit, Xavier? And why do you keep calling yourself Captain Jiminy Whoozat?"

"Long story," he said with a glance back at his vampire partner in crime.

Zirconia decided not to string it out.

"The pilot died, and he had to fly the plane," she said. "It was a whole thing."

Zara shot her mother an angry look. "That's why you put me to sleep. Why did you do that?" She stopped walking. "Did you eat the pilot? Mother!"

Rhys laughed. "You and your appetite," he said with an eyebrow waggle.

"It was nothing like that," Zirconia said. "Never mind. It's nothing any of you need to be concerned about."

Rhys gave her a look that said *we'll discuss this later.*

Zara also gave her a look that said *we'll discuss this later*, but it was more of a threat than a promise.

Xavier gave her a look that said *have we seriously already moved on from the breaking news that I just landed that plane? What does a guy have to do to get some respect in this family?*

They located the car on the third level, climbed in, and left the busy airport.

Zirconia was grateful to be sitting in a vehicle that wasn't airborne and heading for a mountain.

* * *

They took a brief tour of the city before delivering Zara to the building where she had the job interview.

"I won't be long," Zara said. "They'll probably kick me out after I blow the first question."

"Don't say that," her father said reassuringly. "You can handle anything. You'll make your mother and me proud."

"I'll try."

They all got out of the vehicle and stood on the sidewalk to wish Zara luck.

"Knock 'em dead," Rhys said as he hugged his daughter. "Not all the way dead, but enough to let 'em know you're the one."

"Thanks, Dad," she said.

Dad. It stabbed Zirconia's heart, right in the tender patch at the center.

They all wished Zara luck, then got back in the car.

It was a comfortable drive.

The spacious sedan felt like a stretch limousine after the confines of the small plane.

Rhys drove, and Zirconia took over the passenger seat after they'd dropped off Zara.

Xavier fidgeted in the back seat, eager to get back to peppering Rhys with questions about the vehicle. He was obsessed with the vintage sedan. Where did Rhys get it? Did it really run on free-floating carbon from the atmosphere? How fast could he accelerate on the open highway?

Zirconia settled in her spacious, comfortable seat and let the two men talk about cars.

She was in no hurry to get to the business at hand, the quantum entanglement.

If they didn't get to the bottom of it today, she would try again, starting from waking up on the plane. Then Captain Jiminy Whoozat could stick the landing, and say the catchy quip he'd thought up. They would get the day perfect before it ended.

Rhys played tour guide, pointing to the sights whizzing by outside their windows.

"They'll turn this whole swamp into luxury townhomes," Rhys was saying.

Xavier said, "What about the water?"

"They'll drain it, son."

"But the water will come back with the first flash flood. Water always comes back."

Rhys rubbed his smooth-shaved chin, keeping his eyes on the road. "Not really my department, son."

"It's my department," Xavier said. "I've taken over permitting for rain gutters, drainage and floodplain management."

"Oh? That sounds important."

"It does?"

Rhys chuckled. "You sound like an ambitious young man in search of a new opportunity. I'd like to introduce you to some people."

"I can fly planes. As I mentioned earlier."

"You're a pilot? Is that why you're wearing that shirt? It's a bit large on you."

"I'm not really a pilot. I know how to land, but not how to take off."

"Do you want to be a pilot?"

"I dunno." He didn't sound excited about learning how to take off.

"How old are you, son?"

"I just turned twenty-six, sir."

"Call me Dad," Rhys said. "Zirconia loves it when people call me Dad." He shot a knowing look over at the vampire.

She pretended to have not heard him.

Xavier said, "I couldn't do that, Mr. Quarry."

"Then at least call me Rhys. Mr. Quarry's my dad's name."

"Okay, Rhys. I appreciate your help and everything, but you should know I'm a Nothing Person. My options are extremely limited."

"Oh, I hardly think you would be assisting a powerful vampire on her mission if you weren't without skills. I can tell by your smell and vitality that she's not using you as one of her blood bags, so, tell me, what is the deal with you two?"

Zirconia felt Xavier looking at her. He wanted her to be the one to broach the topic of quantum entanglement.

Fair enough. It was about time.

She cleared her throat and said to the roomy car's driver, "Rhys, it's time for us to put a stop to this endless cycle, and get on with our lives."

"Are you asking me to give up on our daughter? Because I can't do that, Zed." Rhys called her the letter Z, but pronounced Zed, the way Ribbons said it, not Zee the way Xavier said it.

Zirconia put the clues together. He was doing the time loop to manipulate Zara. It was so obvious.

She said, "What's your end goal with Zara?"

"To get her out of Wisteria," he said. "Isn't it obvious?"

Indeed, it was.

"You can't win," she said, lifting her chin defiantly. "You can rewind this day a million times, but you will not prevail. The bond between mother and daughter is too strong."

He snorted. "My daughter and I would be much closer if *your* awful family hadn't kept me from her all those years."

"So this is retribution? Revenge? On me? I'll have you know that had nothing to do with me. It was my elders. I had no choice."

He took his eyes off the road and shot her a dark look with his shifty eyes. "You had a choice."

She looked away. The swamp at the side of the road looked very wet, not suitable for development. Not that it would stop anyone.

Rhys made his voice lighter and addressed Xavier, in the back seat. "Did you know the Riddle family only allowed me to see my daughter one day a year?"

Xavier said, "Uh, I'm not sure I need to be here for this conversation."

"They said it was for Zara's benefit, but I know it was payback for... my failure to deliver the goods I'd been hired to provide. By which I mean a suitable mate for Zed."

Zirconia murmured, "Don't call me that."

He carried on as though her voice was part of the song playing on the car's stereo. This was why a woman needed to use her vampire powers to be heard.

"Zed was supposed to marry someone of great power," Rhys explained. "Her offspring would be the beneficiaries." He took on a campfire story tone. "You see, the magic in the Riddle family was starting to peter out. The great river of magic had begun to meander and pool in pockets. It was becoming swampland." He waved at the swamp beyond the car windows. "They were once a powerful clan. Not as Riddles, but by other names you'd probably recognize, such as—"

"Don't," Zirconia said. She shot some glamour into her voice so that he would hear her over the stereo and his own mind.

"You get the picture," Rhys said with a chuckle. "I was hired to refresh the bloodline. To drain the swamp and turn it back into a mighty river."

Xavier, who was growing more uncomfortable and releasing acrid sweat, said, "You know, you can just pull over here and let me out."

"But Zed had other ideas," Rhys said. "And she knew my weaknesses as well as any enemy."

The door handles in the back rattled. Xavier had tried and failed to open the door.

Zirconia said to Rhys, "Stop it, Q. The boy doesn't have to hear all our dirty laundry."

"Q." Rhys smiled as he tapped his hands on the steering wheel in time with the music. "I haven't heard that in a while." He shot her a flirtatious, dangerous look. "Zed, you started calling me that a week before you tricked me into your bed."

She couldn't believe his wording. Xavier, who was like a son to her, was going to get the wrong idea.

"I didn't trick you," she said.

"It's true," he said softly. "You didn't trick me at all."

He glanced over, affection in his eyes. His attractive features became more handsome.

Zirconia said, "Interesting how the story changes depending on when it's being told."

His voice deep and gritty, he said, "Our story is always evolving." He waggled his rust-colored eyebrows.

The vampire's usually cool blood went up two degrees.

"Oh, Q." She tried to look away but couldn't. He could be so charming, even as he aged. "You're just a shifter, but you do know how to make me feel wanted. You're a talented con artist."

"It's not a con," he said huskily. "I always wanted you for myself. From the instant we met."

The vampire's internal temperature went up another two degrees.

"Stop it," she said.

Xavier cleared his throat in the backseat. "Yeah, I'm still here. You can pull over anywhere and let me out." He tried the locked door handle more forcefully.

"You're even more lovely than you were that day," Rhys said.

"That was a long time ago. You don't remember it."

"You wore blue," he said. "A blue dress with a big, tacky, pink sash."

She gasped. "I loved that dress!"

The vampire's temperature was now warm enough for perspiration, if she'd wanted to perspire.

"You looked like a children's birthday cake."

"It was couture, from a French designer."

"A French designer who loved birthday cakes. And you wore golden earrings that cast a warm glow in the hollows of your cheeks."

"I can't believe you remember that."

"I remember everything, Zed."

"Stop talking about this, Q." She tried to get more comfortable in the passenger seat but didn't know what to do with her legs. They were in the way. So were her arms.

"Maybe I *should* pull the car over," he said.

From the back seat, Xavier said, "Yes!"

They were driving along a quiet road. Rhys turned the car onto a dirt road that led them to a lake.

It was a park, the kind of place that was full of families on the weekend, but it was a weekday, so they were the only ones there.

Q put the car in park, and reached for Zed.

She met him halfway.

He smelled as good as she remembered. It had been a long time since she'd kissed anyone, much less her old lover. The chemistry of his genetics was undeniable. They were a perfect match. More perfect of a match than even Debbie and Darren Darnell.

As they embraced, and lost themselves to each other, they barely heard Xavier kick out the back window to escape.

CHAPTER 60

Wednesday - Up in the Air Again

Zirconia woke from sleep in a different place—and time—from where she'd fallen asleep the night before.

The man sleeping next to her wasn't Rhys Quarry. It was Gene, the exterminator with the Terminator impression.

She was back on the plane again.

Xavier came galloping down the aisle toward her.

"I want a full explanation," he said, but he kept going, all the way to the plane's bathrooms. "I'm taking a leak this time," he yelled back before disappearing into the little room.

Zirconia used his bathroom break to raid the air attendant's cart for more little bottles.

The other passengers watched the black-haired vampire with interest as she tipped back the alcohol. A few phones rose above the seats, their cameras pointed at her. People murmured with excitement about middle-aged women behaving badly.

Zirconia used to hate that term—middle-aged—but after being referred to as an "older woman" a few times, or even downright old, as in "that old lady," it didn't seem so bad. The absolute worst was waiters who called her "young lady." She'd fed from waiters for much less serious crimes.

Zara, who wasn't ever sleeping at this part of the day, stood from her seat to see what the commotion was all about.

She saw her mother tipping back a bottle and said, "Good grief, Mother! Must you?"

Xavier returned from the bathroom looking only partly relieved.

He said, "That didn't help as much as I thought it would." He glanced around. "Why is everyone awake?"

Before she could answer the first question, he asked, "Why are we back here?"

"I couldn't get Rhys to stop the loop," she said.

"Why? What's he trying to do, and why's it taking so long?"

She didn't want to tell him.

Xavier frowned. "Why?"

She still didn't want to tell him.

"It's because you didn't ask him to stop it," Xavier correctly guessed.

She shrugged.

"Okay," he said. "But what did he say when you told him about the whole quantum entanglement thing? That we both know all about it?"

She still didn't want to tell him.

This moment, *the morning after*, had seemed so distant the night before.

She'd hoped that Rhys would decide on his own to stop things.

Had he not achieved his goals? How could his day get any more perfect than ending with her in his arms?

As she'd fallen asleep the night before, she'd believed the day wouldn't come around this way again.

But it had. What did that mean? Had winning her back never been part of his plan?

Xavier shook his head. "You didn't even tell him." He didn't have psychic powers, but he knew her quite well by now.

The plane shook as it hit a patch of turbulence. The pilot had been dead for nearly thirty minutes. They would crash soon.

Xavier didn't identify him as a pilot, or run to the cockpit.

He stood in front of his mentor, shaking his head in disappointment as though he was the mentor.

Zirconia finally said, "I was waiting for the right time."

"You mean a time when you didn't have your tongues inside each other's mouths? Yeah. I can see how that would have been difficult."

She stood up straighter. "That never happened."

"I was there. I saw it with my own... oh. Oh!" He shook his finger at her. "You wanted a do-over! You did this to us! We're going to crash in a ball of fire, with every one of these innocent people screaming in horror, because you wanted a do-over!"

The passengers around them definitely heard that.

A panic ensued.

One of the men stood and said, "That guy's a terrorist! He's trying to do something to this plane!"

Xavier said back, "Stop jumping to conclusions because of the color of my skin. I'm half Mexican, one eighth Puerto Rican, and I'm trying to save all of you."

Another man rose and said, "Save us from what? From our Western decadence?"

Then the usual trio got up and tackled Xavier.

He'd developed his fighting skills over the time loops, and he almost fought his way free of the flight's heroes, but not quite.

Zirconia quickly put her daughter to sleep to spare her the screaming.

The vampire walked up to the front, punched in the access code, and entered the cockpit. She closed the door behind her, shoved the dead pilot from the chair, and took a seat. She couldn't fly the plane and didn't bother trying.

It was nice to have somewhere quiet to think.

As the plane plummeted toward the ground, she wondered about two things.

One, how long might it take her to learn how to fly this thing?

Two, if today had been tomorrow, would Rhys have been calling her for another date?

CHAPTER 61

The Very Next Wednesday

Xavier successfully landed the plane.

"That was perfect," Zirconia said, clapping for him. "Now say it."

He frowned. He'd been very quiet during that day's flight.

"Go on," she said. "Say the line. I know you want to."

"No," he said. "You don't deserve it."

"Don't be like that. I told you I was sorry I didn't talk to Rhys."

He tilted his head to the side. "Did you? Funny. I don't remember you saying you were sorry."

"Well, I did."

"Nope. You never say you're sorry."

"That's ridiculous. I apologize all the time. I'm constantly apologizing. I'm sorry my efforts to communicate with you always fall on deaf ears." She pointed to the air, as though her words were floating there, like in a comic book panel. "See? I just did it."

He scowled as he got up from the pilot's seat, and headed back to deboard.

Opening the door and extending the stairs was easier that time. There was nothing that didn't get easier with practice—even dying.

They exited in the same manner they had after the one previous successful landing.

Zirconia didn't like the tension between them. It would be bad luck for the mission.

As they stood on the tarmac, she leaned in and said to Xavier, "Remember that time we hit a marsh, and some of us survived the crash, and I had to mercy-kill a dozen passengers? That was hilarious."

His eyes widened. “What?”

“Oh, never mind. You didn't make it that far.” She waved a hand. “It really was hilarious, but you had to be there.”

He stared at her, still wide-eyed.

“Technically you were there,” she said. “Your head, anyway.”

“Just go. Go have your cinnamon bun with Zara. We'll do this one the same way, but after we drop off Zara, I'll take the front seat.”

Then he stomped off in the direction of the airport's bathrooms.

She called out after him, “You already went on the plane.”

He called back, “Not all of it,” and carried on.

Zirconia sat with her daughter once again, and shared another—or the same—cinnamon bun.

The sweet pastry didn't taste nearly as delicious as it had the first time. That was the problem with life's brightest moments. They were never quite as good the second time around. But that didn't stop people from trying.

They were finishing their last bites when a handsome shifter with lush eyebrows and thick hair approached.

Zirconia saw now that Rhys Quarry's ill-fitting suit—too loose in the shoulders and too tight on the calves—was effective at camouflaging what was a strong, athletic body.

Rhys knew what he was doing. He dressed so that people underestimated him, and so that he didn't outshine the other players involved in his various deals.

Even so, if she were in charge of dressing him, she would throw out the terrible suits, and take him to a decent tailor. No business deal could be worth walking around with creases in the wrong places. His trousers actually had pleats. Pleats.

Zara jumped up from her plastic stump seat, arms outstretched. “Dad!”

Zirconia's heart rose in her chest as she made eye contact with the man.

He gazed at her with absolute surprise, as though he hadn't known very well that she would be there.

And perhaps he was legitimately surprised. The last couple of Wednesdays hadn't all been exactly the same for him. The previous Wednesday, he'd ended the day learning that his daughter had died in a plane crash.

He was a good actor, but she could see small signs of grief and relief as he hugged his daughter tighter than ever.

She rose from the plastic stump, and air-kissed Rhys Quarry in greeting.

He leaned in several seconds longer than he had the previous time.

As he pulled back, there was a glint in his eyes. Oh, he knew what he was doing.

“Hello, Q,” she said.

His bushy eyebrows waggled. “Hello, Zed.”

Zara rolled her eyes at both of them, and cleaned up their table.

“Here we are again,” Zirconia said to the man she believed she was entangled with on a quantum level.

“Here we are again,” Rhys Quarry said to the woman that, from his perspective, he had not seen in several months.

Rhys really was genuinely surprised to find Zirconia traveling with his daughter, for Rhys was *not* a time looper—a fact that the actual time loopers would find out shortly.

CHAPTER 62

The Same Wednesday

Zirconia and Xavier hadn't learned the bad news yet.

They stood by on the sidewalk while Rhys Quarry said, “Good luck with your interview,” and hugged Zara.

“Thanks, Dad,” she said. Then she said to her mother, “I hope the two of you can enjoy some sightseeing without getting in trouble.”

Xavier raised his hand. “Am I invisible? Is that my power?”

Zara corrected herself. “I hope *the three of you* have a nice afternoon. You can tell me all about it at dinner.”

Rhys said, “Get going, young lady. You've got this one in the bag, but you'd best not be late.”

“Your father is right,” Zirconia said. “Overconfidence is unattractive.”

Zara said flatly, “Right. Because my biggest obstacle is overconfidence.” She left for her interview.

When the door to the building opened, the scent of books wafted out, causing Zirconia's stomach to turn. The cinnamon bun wasn't sitting well at all.

The three headed back to the car.

Zirconia leaned over to sniff Rhys to clear the bad feeling in her stomach.

It worked. He smelled incredible. She wished she was twenty years younger—and fully human—so they could make another baby together. She wondered if there was something Dr. Ankh could do to revive that part of her. With modern medicine, anything was possible. But just because she could, that didn't mean she should.

They reached the big sedan.

A finger poked her in the back, behind her lifted heart.

It was Xavier. "Nope," he said. "Not this time. You get in the back seat."

She already had the passenger side door open. From where she stood, the back seat looked like a cheap coffin. She didn't want to get in there. She wanted to ride up front with Q.

"Shotgun," he said loudly. "I called shotgun. I get the front."

On the other side of the car, Rhys watched them with amusement.

"Don't be ridiculous," Zirconia said. "I'll ride up front."

"Then I'll stay here. I'll get a drink in that pub."

"You're overreacting," she said. "This is just like that time you thought Boomer was a double agent working for the DWM."

"No. This is just like the time I had to walk around a swampy lake with my hands over my ears to block out the animal noises. Also known as the day before yesterday."

She couldn't refute what had happened.

He made a triumphant sound as slipped his slim body past hers, into the car.

She closed his door harder than necessary.

Zirconia settled into the coffin-like back seat while the two men sat up front and talked about cars.

Rhys played tour guide, sticking to his previous script word for word. He had an excellent memory.

"They'll turn this whole swamp into luxury townhomes," Rhys was saying.

Xavier said, "They can try. They'll drain it, but the water will come back."

Rhys rubbed his chin. "That's an astute observation, son."

"Can you get me a job? I want to work with you, sir."

"How old are you, son?"

"I just turned twenty-six, sir."

"Call me Dad," Rhys said. "Zirconia loves it when people call me Dad." He shot a knowing look into the back seat through the rearview mirror. "Isn't that right, Zed?"

"It's just the three of us here," Zirconia said. "Stop pretending you don't know we did all this two days ago."

"Time is funny," he said. "It does go faster as you get older."

"We know about the time loop," Xavier said. "She knew first, and she told me, and I woke up, too."

"Time loop?" Rhys put on the turn signal and pulled the car over to the side of the street.

He parked in a loading zone.

His face flushed pink as he asked in a hushed tone, "Is the genie back?"

Xavier turned around in his seat and gave Zirconia a worried look. A little too worried. He was hamming it up.

Zirconia said, "Q, your sheets are black."

He gave her an exaggerated look of surprise. "What's happening?"

"We're in a time loop," she said.

"Right now? Today?" Rhys pointed his thumb at Xavier. "Does the kid know?"

"He's been awake for most of it," she said. "I woke him."

"But why him?" The shifter's expressive features showed extreme confusion. "I can understand you coming to me, but why him?"

"I'm right here," Xavier grumbled.

The roomy sedan was quiet while the three sized each other up.

Then Xavier said, "Mr. Quarry, Sir, we're here to get you to stop it. If you need help with something, like a big mission, we'll help. But you have to let this loop end. You can't hold the whole world hostage."

"Me?" Rhys looked like he'd eaten a lemon. "I can't stop a time loop. I can't even fully participate in the deal.

I'm going to wake up tomorrow on my black sheets and have no idea what's ahead of me beyond picking my daughter up at the airport." He jerked his head back. "Does Zara know?"

Zirconia shook her head.

Rhys pulled out his phone and checked the time. "I'm flattered that you came to me, but if I'm going to make some calls, I should get to it."

Xavier glared at Zirconia. "You were wrong. He's not the quantum entanglement."

"Of course I'm not," Rhys said matter-of-factly. "Only a genie can create a time loop. Everyone knows that."

Xavier continued to glare at Zirconia, his green eyes dark with suspicion. "Everyone knows that?"

"It's all theoretical," Zirconia said. "Nobody really knows anything."

Xavier threw his hands in the air. "You don't know anything! Why are we even here?"

Zirconia felt very small and insignificant. "I thought... I thought... maybe...."

"You don't know anything," Xavier said again, angrier. "I wish I hadn't talked to you that day at City Hall. I should have dropped off the Form 100CX, and left."

Zirconia felt something in her stomach. It wasn't the cinnamon bun anymore, but she felt bad. Like she'd done something wrong, but long ago, and there was no way to fix it. She wished she had some little bottles with her. They always helped with that feeling. Well, maybe not always but sometimes.

Xavier was still having his meltdown.

He closed his eyes and clenched his fists next to his face. "I wish I could wake up tomorrow morning, back in my bed, and not know about any of this. I wish, I wish, I wish." He peeked out of one eye. "Isn't that how you make a deal with genies? You make wishes, right?"

The conversation blurred as the vampire retreated into her bad feelings.

Rhys said something about wishes and genies, and how fairy tales had some truth but not all of it.

Xavier asked more questions, and the two talked about what might be happening.

Zirconia felt as small as a mouse in a mousetrap.

How could she have been so foolish that day in the library?

She'd been so certain about her entanglement with Rhys. She'd wanted it to be true.

Quantum entanglement would explain why she thought about him so often, and why she always cared about what he was doing in spite of how hard she tried not to care.

Rhys got out his phone, and made some calls to set up meetings with the powerful players in that city.

He relayed the details to Zirconia in the back seat, but she barely heard him.

She was settling in for a good, deep sulk.

It was the appropriate reaction to reaching a dead end.

She remembered something she'd wisely stashed in her purse on the recent flight.

She pulled a mini bottle from her purse, and tipped it back.

CHAPTER 63

The Next Wednesday

They woke up on the plane again.

Xavier landed the plane while Zirconia filled her purse with bottles.

The Riddles ate the same cinnamon bun, then went on the same drive to drop Zara at her interview.

Before Rhys could drive them away from the building, on the second leg of the tour, they told him the news.

Rhys was astonished. For real. “Time loop?” He looked around wildly, and asked, “Is the genie back?”

“Not that we know of,” Xavier said.

“You're joking,” Rhys said. “This is a big joke.”

Zirconia said, “Q, we're in a time loop. This is our third time seeing you, and the second time telling you. Your sheets are black. The first person you'll want to call is your buddy who fixes horse races, but he won't answer the phone because he owes you two large.”

The fox shifter's expressive face went through seven stages of emotions, then he calmly cursed.

Xavier said, “You didn't feel different this morning? Like you knew something was different?”

Rhys shook his head, then suddenly looked jubilant.

Zirconia's heart rose. Did he have the answer?

He gave her a sly, knowing look. “How do you know my sheets are black?”

“Oh, Q.” She leaned forward from the back seat to pinch his cheek. “You're adorable, but it's never going to happen.”

“But it did happen,” Rhys said.

Xavier said with an eye roll, “It happened. Trust me. It happened.”

Rhys beamed with happiness.

"Don't waste our time," Zirconia said to Xavier. "Now he's distracted. He'll be no good to us."

Rhys waggled his eyebrows. "I'll be good to you, Zed. I promise."

She giggled. She couldn't help herself.

After the letdown of discovering Rhys wasn't her quantum entanglement after all, she needed something bright and warm to hold her in the land of the living.

Rhys said, "There's a hotel up ahead."

Zirconia clapped her hands together.

"No," Xavier said, horrified.

"We can use the business center," Rhys said.

"Oh," Xavier said.

"It's not a five-star, but it will do in a pinch." Rhys reached an arm over the seat to squeeze Zirconia's knee. "Zed, you always did like a good pinch."

She giggled again.

Xavier slunk in the passenger seat, his hand over his eyes.

"This is not happening," he said. "I wish I could wake up at home. I wish I could wake up at home."

CHAPTER 64

Many Wednesdays Later

No matter how many times the time loopers told Zara's fox shifter father about the time loop, he continued to be surprised about it every single time.

But at least he was sharp, and able to move forward quickly. He was even sharper than Boomer had been, needing only a brief review of the calls and meetings he'd made the previous days. He quickly moved on to new avenues of research with his many high-powered contacts.

That Wednesday, the three sat in the business center at the first hotel he'd recommended. They'd tried other hotels, and even the library, but this business center was the best of the bunch.

They'd picked up from where they'd left off the previous cycle. Rhys was finally talking to the fellow who fixed horse races.

Zirconia listened to the phone conversation while lying on the business center's sofa with her arms crossed over her chest. It wasn't a vampire thing, or a therapy thing, just a comfortable way to rest.

She stared up at the outdated light fixtures and cracked ceiling.

This hotel was a far cry from a five star. She missed the Cerulean Lagoon.

At least the hotel back in Wisteria employed lively workers, such as the entertaining boy who guarded the lounge. How adorable had he been, trying to stand up to her, a powerful vampire? And when she'd put her hand in his mouth to pinch his tongue? Priceless! What fun that had been.

She wished she could do it again, but the hotel staff at this new place was far too accommodating and grateful for their business.

She also missed her granddaughter and sister.

At that moment, Zinnia was back in Wisteria, doing something with Ethan Fung. Or so Zirconia assumed. Zinnia wasn't picking up her phone, and was never in her office when Zirconia called to check in.

When Zirconia called the Permits Department, the other office drones told her how strange it was that both Zinnia and Xavier hadn't shown up that day. Might there be an emergency going on that they could jump into and muddle up even worse?

Xavier was being stubborn, and wouldn't talk to his coworkers to put their minds at ease.

"Let them miss me," he'd said grumpily.

Xavier did not have a positive attitude toward the time loop lately.

Probably because their research into genies was getting them nowhere.

"That's another dead end," Rhys announced as he set down his phone. "They're all dead ends." He pushed a pile of scribbled notes into the center of the faux-marble table.

Xavier got up from his chair.

Zirconia knew by the slope of Xavier's brow that he was too disappointed to discuss it.

This was the third time they'd reached the same dead end with Rhys's contacts.

Xavier went over to the ping pong table—the space had a fancy, high-end ping pong table, and was more like a recreation room than a business center.

Xavier picked up the plastic ball and swatted it hard. He played a loud game of ping pong against the flip-up back board.

Rhys watched, mesmerized, as Xavier effortlessly smacked the plastic ball again and again.

"He's really good at ping pong," Rhys said. "How many times have we been here?"

Zirconia said, "You don't want to know."

Rhys rubbed his eyes. "You're right. I don't. I prefer having each day be new and exciting." He blinked at her, refreshed. "Speaking of which... since we've exhausted all my contacts..."

"Not today," she said.

He did a double take. "What? You mean... we?"

"Sometimes," she said.

He leaned forward and whispered, "How is it?"

She shrugged.

He threw his arms out in a triumphant Y. "I've still got it."

She said, "How can you be so happy? We're stuck in this loop, doing the same thing over and over."

"You have to see it from my perspective. It's a pretty good day for me." He fanned out the papers then shuffled them into a neat stack again. "I'm just glad you keep getting on that plane to come see me."

"Oh, we don't have any choice in the matter."

He squinted. "What now?"

"We don't have any choice," she said. "We both fell asleep on the flight, which reset everything, so now every time we wake up, we're on the plane already."

His rubbery features pulled into a central knot, like the bottom of a balloon.

"When I wake up from my nap in my car," he said.

"It doesn't matter when you wake up," she said. "You're not part of it."

He narrowed his eyes, looking foxy.

Zirconia said, "The loop resets for the two of us because Xavier and I napped at the same time."

"That's not how it works," he said. "If the loop reset to a different time, that means—"

"What?"

"It means *something*," he said.

"Let me know when you figure it out," she said with a weary sigh. "I'd like to see you solve this one. You can't even wake yourself up."

He said patiently, "If the loop reset to a different time, it was because the genie changed the spell. Don't you get it?"

Xavier came over, sweating from the exertion of his ping pong game. "Get what? What's going on? Do we have a lead on a genie?"

Do we have a lead on a genie?

Do we?

A genie?

A jolt of electricity shot down Zirconia's spine, as though she'd been struck with lightning—she was familiar with the sensation. She abruptly stood, knocking over her chair.

Rhys also stood, albeit not with vampire speed.

Zirconia covered her open mouth with one hand to quiet the very loud gasp she was having.

It wasn't dignified to gasp like that, showing everyone the inside of your mouth, but she couldn't stop the gasp.

Zirconia had just realized who was behind the time loop.

CHAPTER 65

Secrets Revealed

Zirconia knew who was behind the time loop.

Of course, she'd "known" once before, and that hadn't worked out, so there was some doubt from the other parties.

Rhys sat with his elbows on the faux-marble table and his chin resting on his hands.

Xavier paced the business center room, still sweating from his ping pong game.

Zirconia explained everything.

Or tried to, anyway.

"Wait," Xavier said, wiping the ping pong sweat from his brow. "The loop only reset itself because we both fell asleep at the same time on the plane."

"No," she said, trying not to growl with impatience. "It didn't."

"But it did," he said. "We only got on the plane one time." He paced the room. "One time. Then we were waking on the plane, because we both fell asleep that one time."

"No," she said again. "You assumed that was why the loop changed the starting position, and I let you convince me. You made a bad assumption."

He crossed his arms. "So, this is all my fault."

"In a manner of speaking, yes. But I forgive you. It was a novice mistake, and you're so far below novice that it was inevitable."

His arms remained crossed as he paced back and forth. "When we get out of this, I never want to see you, or anyone in your family, ever again."

She didn't take it personally. He was going loopy from the repetition and didn't mean it.

Rhys didn't say anything. It was still the first day for him, so everything was novel, including the time loopers' relationship dynamic.

"I'm done with all of this," Xavier said.

She replied airily, "If you're not interested in the solution, I'll wrap this up on my own."

Rhys raised his hand. "Take me. I'm handy. I've got a cooler of champagne in the trunk of the car. Do you know about that?"

She tilted her head. "Champagne?" She didn't know about that.

He beamed. "It's good to know I can still surprise you, Zed."

Xavier said, "Never mind about the champagne. Do you really know what's going on?"

Rhys said, "Isn't it obvious? Zed and I have a quantum entanglement. Nature cannot be denied. The woman wants me, and the universe itself will bend to bring us together."

They ignored him. He'd been making that joke more days than not.

Xavier sat at the table. "I'm sorry I was grumpy. What's your new theory?"

"A genie caused the time loop," Zirconia said.

Xavier tilted his head back and groaned.

"And I found the genie," Zirconia said. "I know who it is."

That got everyone's attention.

"It's Zoey," she said. "She's half genie, from her father's side."

The two men stared at her.

Then Rhys said, "Well, that's obvious. I could have told you that. Everyone knows Zozo is half genie."

"But you didn't know it was her," she said. "I figured it out."

He reached for his pile of notes and started leafing through them.

Xavier said, "But how? Why? When?"

"Today, obviously," she said.

Xavier pointed at Zirconia and made monkey noises. "You did something different on our last day in Wisteria. You did something to Zoey, and it changed when she started the time loop."

"I didn't *do* something," she said. "But I did knock on the bathroom door and interrupted her and her friend. The one with the makeup. No wonder they looked so guilty. They weren't doing beauty spells. They were turning back time."

Xavier said, "But why?"

"Oh," said Rhys. "Oh, no." He looked at Zirconia, his foxy gold-green eyes more serious than ever. "Oh, no," he said again.

She nodded. That had to be it.

Xavier said, "What's going on? Why were they doing time stuff?"

"It's so obvious now," Rhys said.

Zirconia kept nodding.

Xavier threw his hands up. "Am I supposed to guess? Fine. Is it so they could make a bunch of money winning the lottery? That's what I would do."

Rhys said, "She was doing it for her mother."

"For Zara," Zirconia said.

Xavier shivered as though a ghost had entered the room.

"Oh," he said quietly. "Okay."

None of them said his name.

All three were on the same page, though.

Zoey didn't mean to rewind time by a single day. She'd been trying to wind it back half a year, so she could redo that fateful night.

The night of the tornado.

The night Bentley died to save her life.

Zoey had been trying to wind back time so she could save Bentley.

CHAPTER 66

At Dinner That Evening

"Pass the bread rolls," Rhys said.

The four of them, Zirconia, Rhys, Zara, and Xavier, were celebrating.

Zara thought they were celebrating her successful job interview, and they were, but there was something much bigger being celebrated by the other three.

The time loopers and their accomplice were hopeful about the resolution of the time loop.

They couldn't have made it back to Wisteria in time to see Zoey Riddle in person, but they'd been able to reach her by phone.

Zoey had confessed to casting a time spell with her friend, the little witch, but swore it hadn't worked at all, except to give both of the girls terrible pimples.

But she promised to try really hard to remember, and when she woke up the next morning, she wouldn't cast it again.

Being part genie, and thus immune to certain aspects of time manipulation, they all had high confidence she would be woken up.

And that was that.

"The bread rolls," Rhys repeated. "Please and thank you."

Zara passed her father the basket of fragrant bread and butter, then pushed her chair back and rose.

"Excuse me for a few minutes," Zara said. "I'm going to step outside for some fresh air. You three can use the time to keep talking about whatever secret shenanigans you have going on."

"There are no shenanigans," Zirconia said to her daughter.

"It doesn't have to be a secret," Rhys said to his daughter.

Rhys gave Zirconia a flirtatious, knowing look. He hadn't kissed her during that Wednesday, but he was acting as though he had.

With a sigh, Xavier said, "My opinion doesn't matter. As usual."

Zara raised her hands. "I don't even want to know." She backed away and left.

Rhys took some bread before passing the basket to Xavier.

Xavier shook the remainder of the rolls onto his plate. "You know what never gets old? Bread. Especially this stuff. I've never had bread like this."

"The chef is a yeast mage," Rhys said. "You should hear all his jokes about bacteria. Here's one: Do you know why we should appreciate bacteria? It's the only culture some people have." He slapped his knee.

Nobody laughed.

Xavier pulled his phone from his pocket.

"Another text from Zoey," he reported to the table. "She's testing me. I think she believed you."

"Of course she believed me," Zirconia said. "Even over the phone. We have a bond."

Rhys buttered his bread. "It's fascinating that all these absurd shenanigans are about to come to an end, and all it took was a quick phone call to Zozo. It's about bloody time."

Xavier said, "What are you complaining about? This is the only version of the day you know."

Rhys shrugged. "I do have an imagination. I can imagine how exhausting it must be to repeat the same day over and over." He shot a flirtatious look over to Zirconia. "Even with such good company."

"It hasn't been too bad," Zirconia said, flirting right back. "The end was better than the middle."

"Shh," Xavier said. "Don't distract me. I gotta do something."

He flagged down a waiter, got a pen, wrote something on a napkin, and handed it to Zoey's grandfather.

Rhys held up the napkin that read, *Yes, Zozo, we are trapped in a time loop.*

Xavier snapped a photo, and sent it to Zoey.

None of them had told Zara about the loop. She likely wouldn't remember anyway, but they could tell her about it after time had resumed its normal path. She could discipline her daughter and the other witch if she wanted to.

"That should do it," Xavier said, taking a big breath high in his chest as he put away his phone. "Now we just have to wait until tomorrow morning, when she wakes up and doesn't cast the spell."

The table was quiet.

Xavier asked, "Will tomorrow be Thursday, or will there be one more Wednesday?"

Both looked to Rhys for the answer.

He said, "Why are you looking at me? You're the experts. I only found out today."

Xavier said, "Well?"

"I don't know," Zirconia said. "I've never found the genie before, and I've never known it was ending until it just ended. We'll find out when we wake up."

Xavier started sweating visibly. He ran the back of his hand over his brow.

"I'd better land that plane right the last time," he said. "If we crash, and it's the last chance..."

"Don't be morbid," Zirconia said. "And don't talk like that, or you're going to curse us."

Rhys raised a finger. "Actually, it's overconfidence that curses most deals. A little trepidation is not a problem."

The time loopers exchanged worried looks.

Rhys puffed his cheeks and blew out air noisily. Then he refilled their wine glasses.

"Either way, I won't know what happened," he said. "Ah, blissful ignorance."

Zirconia said, "You'll know *something* happened when you get the news that your daughter and I both perished in a plane crash."

"And me," Xavier said. "The crazy terrorist who must have busted into the cockpit, killed the pilot, and then flew the plane into a mountain." He slid down in his seat and put his face in his hands. "My parents are going to be so disappointed."

Zirconia saw the opportunity to give the young man some motherly guidance. She would do what his own mother would do, if she'd been there.

"Sit up straight," the vampire commanded. "Pull yourself together, and rest up so you don't crash the plane tomorrow like an idiot Nothing Person."

He did sit up, and he did stop sniveling.

Rhys raised his wine glass. "I know you can do it, son. A toast to our hero, Xavier Batista. Definitely not a terrorist."

Xavier put on a brave face, but his hand was shaking as he raised his glass.

The celebratory air had disappeared.

After a few minutes, Zara returned, looking serene.

"I talked to the bus boys about living around here," she said. "They hate it. They say it's boring, and absolutely nothing ever happens." Tears started to fall from her eyes. "I can't believe it's happening. I'm moving here. It's going to be... so... perfect." The tears turned into sobs.

It took Zirconia a minute to process what was happening. She'd been so focused on stopping the time loop that she'd nearly forgotten about Zara's foolish plans to run away from her grief.

"It *will* be perfect," Rhys said. "I love it here, and you will, too."

Zirconia snapped at him, “She's not moving here. I won't allow it.”

Zara stopped crying to say, “Mother!”

Zirconia ignored her daughter and glared at the conniving shifter who was trying to tear apart the family.

Rhys didn't back down. “This town is perfectly boring, and you'll love it.” His eyes twinkled as he turned to Zirconia. “You should move here, too, Zed. I've got plenty of room at my house... as you have already seen.” He waggled his eyebrows.

“I could move here,” Xavier said, even though nobody had asked him.

Zara dried her eyes. “That would be nice,” she said. “Xavier, you could be my first friend here. It sounds like you'd fit right in.”

Xavier flinched.

Zirconia knew him well enough to feel what he was feeling, just by observing his facial expressions. It was a curious sensation, feeling what someone else was feeling. She'd never spent as much time with any other living person who wasn't a blood family member as she had with Xavier. Her memories of each day weren't the only changes that had been handwritten to her brain.

He was feeling something, and she was feeling it with him, and it was this:

He'd fit right in? To a boring town where nothing ever happened? Because he was just a Nothing Person who might not be able to land a plane tomorrow, and kill them all?

Whoever said words didn't hurt obviously didn't have Zara Riddle in their life. She was always saying the parts that were supposed to be left unspoken. Poor Xavier.

Zirconia would work on Zara's manners.

Tomorrow.

Assuming it ever came.

CHAPTER 67

Wednesday

Zirconia woke up on the plane again.

Xavier raced down the aisle toward her.

"This is it," he said. "No more dress rehearsal." He waved at the exterminator dozing next to her. "Do the sleep thing, and meet me in the cockpit."

The vampire began putting everyone to sleep in waves.

"You don't need me up there," she said calmly. "You can do it yourself."

"We're in this thing together," he said. "We're a team."

"You don't need me," she said again, growing irritated. Why were they wasting precious seconds? This small talk was even more pointless than him using the bathroom.

"Nobody *needs* you," he said. "Nobody needs anybody in this world. We can all do everything ourselves, or we can die trying. That's our right. But it's a lonely life, doing everything in a bubble. I'm not doing that anymore. Now get up, stop feeling sorry for yourself about being old, and help me land this plane, or I *will* crash it into a mountain."

There were gasps from the people who hadn't yet been put to sleep.

Zirconia stood. His speech had been as effective as it had been surprising. But she shouldn't have been so surprised. Xavier was a person, too, with his own internal struggles. He'd had just as much time to change as she had during this time loop.

Both of them had grown so much. Would they be able to integrate with regular people once this whole thing—

People were screaming. A trio of heroes were preparing their attack.

The vampire knocked out the other passengers, including Zara, and followed Xavier to the front.

Once Xavier had control of the plane, she said, "I'm not old."

"You're lucky to be old," he said, his jaw muscles flexing as he stared straight ahead at the mountain top. "My mom isn't my real mom. She's my stepmom."

Zirconia hadn't known about Xavier losing his mother. In all their time together, she hadn't thought to ask.

How old had he been when he'd lost her?

It didn't matter. There was no good age to lose a parent.

She didn't say anything to disrupt the young man's concentration. He really was a very capable pilot now. His first mother would have been proud. Zirconia, his third mother, was proud.

He dodged the mountain easily.

Then it was smooth sailing.

And an even smoother landing.

Better even than any of the previous successful landings.

Once the plane stopped moving, Zirconia waited in the cockpit for Xavier to say his line. The corny catchphrase he'd been planning to say, in the spirit of all action-adventure movies.

In a soft whisper, he said, "Thank you, Mom."

CHAPTER 68

At Dinner That Evening

"Pass the bread rolls," Rhys said.

The four of them, Zirconia, Rhys, Zara, and Xavier, were celebrating again.

Zara had been to her job interview, the same as the previous times.

It would be, Zirconia and Xavier hoped, the last time.

Rhys didn't know about the time loop. They hadn't told him.

"Bread rolls, please and thank you," Rhys said.

Zara passed her father the basket of bread and butter, then excused herself to get some fresh air. They were moving on the same timeline, so she would talk to the bus boys again, and come back excited about moving to that city. Zirconia would deal with that tomorrow.

Rhys bit into another bread roll with an appreciative moan.

Then he said, "Do you know why we should appreciate bacteria? It's the only culture some people have." He slapped his knee.

Xavier pulled his phone from his pocket.

"Another text from Zoey," he reported to Zirconia. "She's..." He frowned. "Uh-oh. That's not good."

Rhys, who was only concerned as a grandfather, said, "What's going on with my Zozo?"

Zirconia waited for Xavier to explain the problem. He handed her the phone instead.

"I can't read this," she said. "The writing is all blurry."

"Here," said Rhys as he pulled a pair of glasses from his suit jacket.

"I don't need reading glasses." She put them on anyway. The writing on the phone changed so it looked normal.

Rhys chuckled knowingly.

"Stop it," she said to him. "This restaurant is too dim. Your friend keeps the lights down to hide the stains on the carpet."

She read the text.

She couldn't believe what she was reading.

She took the glasses off, put them on again, and read the text two more times.

Zoey had sent the following message to Xavier: *We added more power to the spell this morning. If it works, you won't even know I did it. Don't tell Gigi.*

Zirconia shook the phone as she yanked off the reading glasses.

She said to Xavier, "What does this mean?"

"It means she woke up today, and instead of canceling the spell, she added more power."

Rhys said, "What spell? Zozo can do spells?"

"Not without her accomplice, Amber," Zirconia growled.

"Ambrosia," Xavier said.

Rhys said, "I like Ambrosia. Sweet kid. A little misguided and lovesick, like most of them at that age. What are the girls up to?"

Xavier said, "They're messing around with time."

"Time?" Rhys puzzled over the concept for the first time, which it was for him. "Oh. Because our Zozo is half genie?" He furrowed his brow. "She has access to powers much stronger than the rest of us, you know. If she wasn't such a good kid, she could get herself into trouble." He refilled his wine glass and casually added, "She could even create a time loop, if she wanted to."

Xavier struck the table with both palms. "No way you just came up with that." He pointed at Rhys. "You're faking. You know. You've been faking the whole time."

Rhys blinked rapidly. "Oh, no," he said. "Are we..." He leaned forward. "Are we in a time loop right now?"

Xavier hit the table again. "No way! You're faking it!" He gave Zirconia a wild-eyed look. "He's faking it! He's been awake the whole time."

"Of course he has," she said.

Rhys said, "You knew?"

"I knew the whole time," she said, which wasn't even close to true. She'd only guessed just now, when Xavier had made his accusation.

But it was true. Rhys had been faking it. He'd been waking up every day from his nap in his car, then entering the airport to pick up his daughter, all the while knowing exactly what was going on.

And he'd played stupid because... she couldn't imagine why.

It wouldn't be until much later that she would realize why. He'd played stupid so that he could be with her for their first reunion, over and over.

In that moment in the restaurant, though, Zirconia didn't care that Rhys had been faking.

It was hard to care about such a trivial thing.

It was hard to even sit still, with her usually-cool blood turning to fire.

She grabbed the phone, and pressed the button to call Zoey.

The call went to voicemail.

She commandeered the phones of the other diners around them, and kept calling. First Zoey, then Ambrosia, then both of them, at the same time, from different phones.

Neither of the girls would pick up.

"What's going on?" Rhys asked. "What was in that text message? I didn't see it."

Zirconia handed him the phone so he could read it himself.

"This doesn't sound like my Zozo," he said. "She wouldn't put others at risk, now, would she?"

Xavier said, "She is a teenager."

"That's no excuse," Rhys said. "Let me talk to her."

He tried calling his granddaughter, but he couldn't get through, either.

So, this was it.

The proverbial monkey wrench in the gears.

Zolanda Daizy Cazzaudra Riddle, the half-genie, and her witch friend were going to keep casting the time reversal spell.

They wouldn't pick up the phone and risk being talked out of it.

And Zirconia couldn't choke any sense into either of them because they were two time zones away.

CHAPTER 69

Will It Ever Not Be... Wednesday?

Zirconia woke on the plane as usual, and put the other passengers to sleep.

She joined Xavier, who was waiting in the cockpit, having discovered a shortcut in the timeline.

"Captain," she said.

"Co-captain," he said.

They took their positions.

The sun moved from one side of the window to the other.

"U-turn completed," the young man said.

"Some fine flying you're doing today, Captain."

"Your turn," he said, and he left to use the bathroom while Zirconia flew the plane.

It was peaceful up there, above the clouds.

She could see why the bird shifters were so smug about flying.

Zirconia had been able to fly once, too, before she'd renounced her witch powers. She'd been able to, but she'd rarely done it. Straddling a broomstick had been too vulgar, not to mention dangerous.

She did have some regrets. Now that all of the witches had been grounded, she'd never have a chance to fly on anything other than a plane.

Time was such a sneaky thing, closing the doors on opportunities without saying a word.

And you walked down the hallway of life so many times, you got used to it growing dimmer and dimmer as the doors all closed.

You could let it happen, let time have its way with you, or you could start kicking down doors.

You could show time who was the boss.

Xavier returned. "Good work, Co-captain. Would you like to take her down this time?"

"Next time," she said, giving up the seat.

Xavier plopped down at the controls. "This is the last one," he said.

"Is that so?"

"I feel more confident this time. My mind isn't buzzing with thoughts and plans. It's blank up there. Like everything's loaded into muscle memory, and I just have to do it, like a computer program."

Zirconia quietly considered what he'd said. They had been through this routine so many times. She had lost count of the days. They would wake on the plane, turn it around, and land back in Wisteria. It was the only way to get back in time before the day ended.

Then the two would track down the two girls, who were always hiding themselves in new locations, and... try to knock some sense into their teen heads. They'd started with conversations, verbal persuasion only, but that hadn't worked. Zoey and her misguided little witch friend would promise not to cast the spell again, then they would cast it the very next day. They had little to lose, because if it worked the way they wanted to, and rolled time back more than a single day, nobody would know they'd done it.

The key to getting them to stop would be to raise the stakes.

On recent loops, Zirconia had really been upping the stakes, in her own special way. With her fangs. It wasn't pleasant for the teen witch who would suffer the most while her shocked friend watched in horror, but Zirconia had to do it, for the sake of her granddaughter.

"We can do it," Xavier said, even more confidently. "But you have to really let Ambrosia have it this time. No holding back."

"If you say so." Zirconia rubbed her hands together.

A small part of her looked forward to this part of the routine. It provided an excellent opportunity to punish one of the parties responsible for this mess.

They landed the plane, not at the airport that had been their destination, but back at the Wisteria airport. Hence the U-turn.

They did the usual glamours on the ground crew and air traffic controller, then set out to locate Zoey and Ambrosia.

The girls had found a new hiding spot that time, deep in an old tomb.

The tomb was pleasantly dark and comforting. If Zirconia didn't have such pressing business to attend to, she might have slowed down to enjoy passing through the stone entrance and descending into the cool, quiet earth.

The underground was underrated by most people. Everyone thought the peak of a mountain was the place to be for stillness and quiet, but there was more peace below... as long as you didn't go too deep.

Zirconia was leading the way when she sensed something, and paused.

Xavier said, "What is it?"

"There's a doorway here. Hidden by a glamour. This wall isn't solid stone. It must lead to the Wilds," she said.

"The tunnels? You think they're in there again?" He shuddered. The last time the girls had taken refuge in the Wilds, they'd both been killed, and not by a vampire who would have made it quick.

Zirconia sniffed the air and found the scent again. She was relieved the girls had not found the access to the Wilds, and all the menaces that awaited down there.

They located the two teen girls in an interior chamber. The witch had cast some spells to obfuscate their presence, but her spells had been rushed. Even a brand-new vampire could have sniffed through the sloppy spellwork.

Zoey Riddle was reading an old book with a lantern. She looked up in surprise when her grandmother and Xavier entered the chamber.

"Gigi," she said, dropping her book and jumping to her feet. "Don't!"

But Zirconia wasn't taking orders from her granddaughter.

The vampire pushed aside the redheaded half-genie, and grabbed the young witch with the bleached hair.

Ambrosia screamed with the terror of someone who knew exactly what was about to happen.

Xavier, who was right on Zirconia's heels, said, "Remember what we talked about."

She did. *Let her have it.*

Zirconia plunged her fangs into the girl, not using any magic to numb the pain she was causing.

It was a pleasure to punish Ambrosia, for she was juicy. Like a good sparkling wine. But with blood.

The vampire was so focused on her task she almost didn't hear her granddaughter's words.

"Truce," Zoey Riddle was saying. "Stop, Gigi! We didn't cast the spell today!"

She was hysterical now, bawling noisily, red-cheeked and runny-nosed.

"Don't hurt Ambrosia," Zoey cried. "I swear we didn't do it. My word is my bond, strike me dead by lightning, we didn't cast a single spell today. It's over."

Zirconia delicately extricated her fangs from Ambrosia. The little witch slumped to the ground of the tomb, a couple pounds lighter than when she'd entered.

Xavier checked the witch's pulse. After a tense moment, he gave everyone the thumbs up.

"I knew it," Xavier said triumphantly. "I knew it was over. Today felt different. Everything felt *right*."

The door to the tomb opened again, and Zara came in.

She was holding her head, unsteady on her feet, and confused.

She had fallen asleep on a plane flight to another town, and woken up back in Wisteria. She'd gone looking for her daughter immediately, as usual, and found her inside a dark crypt she'd last been to while tracking a dognapper.

What Zara saw was a confusing sight: her daughter crying her eyes out, Ambrosia crumpled on the ground clutching her bleeding neck, and Zara's vampire mother standing over here. And Xavier, for some reason.

"What's going on here?" Zara asked. "Mother?" She did a double take. "Xavier? What's going on?"

She passed by the real victims—Xavier and Zirconia—and focused on the young witch as she gasped in horror. "Ambrosia, you're bleeding!" She crouched, and began healing the girl's skin.

Zoey cried out, "Mom," and ran over to Zara. She buried her face in her mother's side. She continued to sob, "Mom, I tried. I tried so hard."

Xavier and Zirconia stepped back and let the scene play out as though they were at a very strange community theater production.

Zara finished healing Ambrosia, and turned her focus to her daughter. "Zoey, what's wrong? What are you talking about?" She looked around. "The last thing I remember, I was on a plane. What's happening?"

Zoey sobbed, "I tried to get Bentley back, but I couldn't do it. I'm not strong enough. I'm so sorry."

Zara held her daughter to her chest and rocked her. "Shh," she said. "Shh."

Xavier whispered to Zirconia, "Your granddaughter and her accomplice might be faking. We don't have any proof they didn't cast the spell."

Ambrosia heard them. "You do have proof," she croaked.

She got up and approached the other time loopers, trembling as she did.

She had her hands outstretched, offering something in her palm.

It was a magical creature, the likes of which Zirconia had never seen before. The creature wriggled on the teen witch's palm. It stood on six furry legs and roared—or coughed—a puff of colored smoke.

Zirconia recognized the creature from an old book of magic. It was a timewyrm.

Zirconia reached out to touch it. The creature recoiled, rolled into a ball, and rolled off Ambrosia's hand.

Then it continued rolling, by magic, until it disappeared into a crack in the stone wall of the tomb.

Ambrosia didn't try to retrieve it.

Timewyrms were thought to be extinct, as far as Zirconia knew. One of them, even a tiny baby one that was little more than a grub, would certainly have been hard to come by. That must have been why it had taken half a year for the girls to find one for casting the spell.

"Your ingredient is gone," Zirconia said.

"We were going to sacrifice it for the spell," Ambrosia said. "Except we didn't. Zoey told me we already cast the spell. She said we did it yesterday, and it didn't work." She shivered. "I'm so confused. I don't remember, but she swears it happened. And she said... you killed me? I didn't believe her until..."

Xavier said, "She killed you, all right. So many times. So many places. Always in front of Zoey."

Ambrosia's lips trembled. "Why?"

"To call Zoey's bluff," Xavier said. "We raised the stakes. She could turn back time, but there would always be an additional sacrifice. You."

Ambrosia shivered and looked over at her best friend—the one who'd allowed her to be sacrificed multiple times up until this recent one.

Zoey was still hugging her mother.

Zara was saying, "He's gone, and we have to move on. We can't keep reliving that day. There's nothing we can do about it."

Zirconia caught her daughter's eye, and they stared at each other.

Images and sounds and emotions blasted between them in a psychic cascade.

Zara's eyes revealed something. A haunting darkness that was parting like curtains.

For an instant, it seemed to the vampire that her daughter knew everything. That she remembered. All those plane crashes. And then every cinnamon bun at the airport. The job interviews. The family dinners, and all her father's corny jokes about bacteria. All those good times.

But then Zara's eyes changed, and Zirconia realized that Zara didn't know, after all.

She didn't know they'd been in a time loop, and hadn't seen her father that day, let alone hear his jokes.

It was something else in her eyes.

It was a resolution to move on from grieving Bentley.

She had to move on, for her daughter, and for the sake of all the people who were still there.

CHAPTER 70

Sunday Morning

(Not Wednesday)

The Riddle family's hotel suite at the Cerulean Lagoon was quiet.

Zoey was off with Ambrosia somewhere.

Strangely, the two girls had been avoiding Zirconia. It probably had something to do with Ambrosia's memory of being bitten once by the vampire, and Zoey's memories of her friend being tortured and bitten dozens of times.

The two girls shouldn't have held that against Zirconia, who was only doing what needed to be done, like any caring grandmother would. She was, after all, the matriarch of the family. That meant something.

Zinnia was also absent. She'd learned about the loop on the following day, when it was too late for her to be caught in it, and yet, she'd still been resentful of her big sister. "Why didn't you tell me?" Zinnia had said. "You should have woken me up instead of torturing the girls the way you did."

There was no winning with Zinnia.

Zirconia checked the refrigerator. It was empty, except for a bottle of wine.

She took out the bottle, and a glass.

Marzipants chirped, "Find me, find me!"

Boa swished around Zirconia's ankles, falling forward on her fluffy face then rolling onto her back where she lay with her murder mittens in the air, tempting the vampire with her fluffy belly.

Zirconia put the bottle back in the fridge, pulled out a fresh package of deli ham, and fed the entire thing to the cat.

Then she played hide and seek with the budgie.

Once the pets were played out, she went into the suite's only bedroom to check on her daughter.

Zara was sitting on the bed, holding a different boot in each hand, staring into the room's closet as though it was a stage for a very small play.

"Take them both," Zirconia said.

Zara kept staring at the nearly-empty closet. "I don't know if I should."

"Zarabella, don't procrastinate. Sitting there being indecisive isn't helping anyone."

"How long was I in the loop?"

"It doesn't matter. You don't remember any of it, so it didn't happen."

"Zoey remembers."

"The days that weren't real will fade away."

"But she remembers. For her, the days were real. Every one of them. Every single time I left without even telling her where I was going, or what I had planned for both of us."

Zirconia didn't say anything. She'd learned about the power of occasionally listening, thanks to her therapist, Tallulah Swiftwater, whom she'd technically never seen for a single appointment.

Zirconia sat and listened, like Tallulah did.

"She's years ahead of me," Zara said. "For her, he's been gone for years now."

"It doesn't really work like that," Zirconia said. "The days run together and fold in on themselves, more like daydreams than reality. It must be a coping mechanism, a failsafe to keep us from going insane."

Zara murmured, "Something... something about you being insane."

"Was that... was that your attempt at a joke? At your mother's expense?"

Zara shrugged.

Zirconia continued to sit on the bed next to her daughter. Both stared at the closet.

Zara said, "I can be sad anywhere."

Zirconia nodded.

"Which means I can be happy anywhere," Zara said.

Zirconia couldn't dispute that logic.

"I can't leave this town," she said.

"You can."

"That's right. I can. But I don't want to. If I'm going to be sad, I'd rather be sad around here. I'd rather see Frank and Kathy every day. Sometimes when I'm at work, I'm not sad at all."

"You do love your job at the bookstore."

Zara sighed.

"I'll come visit, wherever you are," Zirconia said.

Zara turned to her mother. "What?"

"I'm leaving," Zirconia said.

"But you can't. What about the house? Your dream house?"

"You let my real estate agents out of the janitor's closet, and I didn't get the house."

Zara frowned. "Is that what that was about?" It had happened on their last run through Wednesday morning before the flight, so she did have a memory of it.

"They were a nice couple," Zirconia said. "True soul mates."

"I don't think Bentley was my soul mate," Zara said. Then she looked down quickly. "That was a terrible thing to say. I'm so sorry. I take it back."

"It wasn't terrible," Zirconia said. "You're coping."

Zara looked up at her mother, her eyes shining. "If you're gone, who's going to look after Zinnia when the baby comes?"

"She can look after herself. As can you." Zirconia kissed her daughter's forehead. "We Riddle women are tougher than we look."

"Where are you going?"

“There are some old friends I'd like to see again, before time closes the door.”

Zara looked down at the mismatched boots that were still in her hands.

“I'll need a regular place to live if I'm staying here,” she said. “This is no good for Zoey.”

“I know just the place. I'll give you the name of the businessman you can buy it from.”

“No. Not the house that looks like a box taking a dump.”

“I beg your pardon?”

Zara smirked. Her old spirit—what she had left of her tattered soul—was coming back after all.

“I'd better get to the library,” Zara said. “Before they give my job away.”

She pulled on the boots.

Zirconia said, “Those don't match. They're not a true pair.”

“They're close enough,” Zara said, and she rushed out.

Now the suite was empty except for Zirconia and the pets, who were both sleeping off their ham-eating festival.

It was so quiet.

Zirconia went to the fridge and took out the bottle of wine. It was already open, with a temporary stopper to slow the oxidation. It was going to spoil—a great excuse to pop it open.

Zirconia took out the stopper.

A delicious scent whirled up, like a Tuscan vineyard in late summer. Wine wasn't as good as fresh blood, but it was a close second.

Zirconia went to the sink, and poured it all out.

CHAPTER 71

Epilogue

Zirconia leaned back on the teak recliner next to the shimmering swimming pool.

The weather in that part of the world was usually too sunny for her that time of the year, but with her new vampire-friendly sunglasses, it was just right. Everything was just right. But something would probably irritate her in the next day or two, and she would move on to a new place, which was just fine. Travel was only travel if you weren't still for too long.

Zirconia had plenty of funds for traveling, thanks to some very lucky trades she'd made in a single day on the stock market. She did lose an awful lot of her fortune the very next day, but there was still enough for two people to tour the world for at least a year.

One of the mansion's many attendants appeared with a tray and two glasses of sparkling water. The refreshing beverages were flavored with lemon wedges and cucumber slices.

The two travelers lounging by the pool took their drinks.

After the attendant left, Zirconia turned to her travel buddy.

"Here's to finding a grand, old mansion with a brand-new pool," she said.

Her travel buddy, Xavier Batista, clinked his glass to hers.

"Here's to skydiving tomorrow," he said.

"Is it already your turn to pick?"

"Come on. We looked at tiles all morning," he said. "And upholstery samples, too."

"Okay, okay. We'll do your thing tomorrow. Skydiving it is."

The two settled back and enjoyed their afternoon.

Zirconia giggled to herself as Xavier flirted with all the female employees at the resort. He'd had a lot of time to improve his game, and he was as bad as ever.

But that was okay. He was young, and had plenty of time to learn and grow ahead of him.

Compared to him, Zirconia Cristata Riddle didn't have nearly as much time, but she was going to make the most of it.

They would live life fully while it lasted, and worry about tomorrow when it came around.

* * *

The sun was setting after a perfect, unique day.

Zirconia was in her room getting ready for dinner when she got the sudden urge to check her phone.

She picked it up.

There were no notifications.

Then it buzzed in her hand.

She answered, "Hello, Zara."

Zara said breathlessly, "Mother, it's happening."

Zirconia jerked to attention. "What's happening? Did Zoey and Applesauce get another timewyrm? I'll strangle her with my bare—"

"Not that," Zara said. "Zinnia's having the baby."

Zirconia went to the room's window, and looked out over the pool. Xavier was taking a cannonball off the diving board.

Zirconia said to her daughter, "I can be on the first flight in the morning."

"You don't need to," Zara said. "We can handle it. I just called because... Aunt Zinnia would want you to know. I guess she's nervous, and thinks you have some wisdom to pass on. Pretty crazy, huh?"

"She'll be fine," Zirconia said. "Give the baby a blessing for me."

There was a long pause, and then Zara said, “Thank you.”

“For what? I haven't even sent a gift. I've been looking around the baby shops, but what do you get the baby who's going to have everything?”

“Yeah,” Zara said. “I know what you mean.”

There was another long pause, and then Zirconia said something she'd been meaning to say for a long time.

She said, “I'm sorry.”

“Hang on. There's something wrong with the line,” Zara said. “It sounded like you said you were sorry.”

“It must be a technical glitch,” Zirconia said, then, “Talk to you again soon, darling.”

“Mom?”

“Yes, Zarabella?”

“Thank you.”

For a full list of books in this series and other titles by Angela Pepper, visit

www.angelapepper.com

Printed in Great Britain
by Amazon